T0065231

PAWNS, QUEENS, KINGS

...THE ENDGAME

BARRY BRYNJULSON

authorHOUSE®

AuthorHouse™
1663 Liberty Drive
Bloomington, IN 47403
www.authorhouse.com
Phone: 833-262-8899

Published by AuthorHouse 02/07/2023

ISBN: 978-1-7283-7796-4 (sc)
ISBN: 978-1-7283-7795-7 (e)

Library of Congress Control Number: 2023901042

Print information available on the last page.

For Joan, who deserved a much better ending, and for all seniors who struggle to find purpose, esteem, and human connections near the end.

CHAPTER ONE

THE FIRST

He stopped in front of the door to room 212 holding his six-string in one hand, and looked down the hall in both directions. No one. Harris had made it this far without being seen, although he had an excuse, a fabricated explanation at the ready, should he encounter anyone.

At 9:45 PM, it was usually quiet in the halls at The Ridge Senior Living, save for the sound of the occasional loud TV. He had made this walk up a flight of stairs and down the hall to the front of Miranda Wheeler's door last night at this hour to test the route, and went undetected. While relieved to see no one this night, he was not surprised.

Turning the door knob quietly, it was unlocked as she indicated it would be. As he entered her tiny apartment and closed the door softly, he whispered, "Miranda? It's me." The recessed light under the microwave in the kitchenette was the only source of light in the four small rooms.

"I'm in here," she said with her 78-year voice that did its best to sound calm and hide an excitement she hadn't felt in too long.

"Hi," Harris said as he poked his head through the open door of her bedroom and could barely make out the figure of his friend lying on her side under the covers.

"Hi," she replied. "There's a chair next to my bureau. Can you see it?"

"Yes." Harris made his way to the wicker chair. It made the sound that only wicker does when he sat and pulled the guitar strap over his head. After several seconds of quiet, he began plucking an instrumental, something he called *Morning*... a tune he had composed years earlier. It was melodious and sweet, and despite the title, something that suited the quiet calmness of the hour. The fingering he used was uncommon, something someone from his past had shown him. Harris, while excited too, plucked the strings gently, fitting the song and the occasion.

After a few minutes, the song wound down to the slowest, faintest notes. When finished, the night was as quiet as it could be. He listened for her breathing, wondering if she had dozed off. He realized she hadn't when she asked meekly, "Can you do Bojangles?"

Without saying a word, he slid the capo onto the neck of the guitar and up two frets. Strumming a G chord twice, he could tell the capo was on correctly, the guitar was still tuned to his liking, and was reminded how to start the song. *"I knew a man, Bojangles, and he danced for you…in worn out shoes."* He sang with tenderness, his eyes closed. Though his palms were moist and his heart raced, his voice stayed true. He gained confidence with each completed verse.

After the song, she said nothing. He listened again, unsure of what her breathing meant. He played another instrumental that he thought might be relaxing and appropriate. Earlier in the day he wondered about the number of songs he should play during these visits. This was new territory, and he was uncertain. He decided three was about right. Part way through the third number, he knew it would be the last for this, his first tuck-in performance.

When finished, he stood from the chair as quietly as possible, and, as he moved past the foot of her bed toward the door, he said, "Sleep well Miranda."

"Thank you," she said in a contented voice. "The dollar is on the counter."

Harris took the money off the grey faux-granite counter next to the white refrigerator, and stepped through the door into an empty hallway. He too felt content but slept unevenly that night, the first of many in his new venture.

CHAPTER TWO

FOUR MONTHS EARLIER

"What's going on? How's the food?" he asked while scanning the roundtable of five who were part way through their lunch.

Four of the five people seated at the table looked up at him. A man in a wheelchair did not, but kept spooning the chicken rice soup in front of him. The three ladies at the table looked at Harris, smiled, and said some version of, "It's good."

The fifth person at the table, a burly man, chimed in with a drawl, "It'll probably keep you from starving."

"Oh, come now Rex, it's not that bad," said Sandy the high-heeled, redheaded Sales Director mainly to the man she was giving the tour.

"It's the only decision I'll have to make today… enchiladas or mac and cheese. I reckon I made the right one," Rex replied a little louder and slower than most people spoke.

"We have two seatings for lunch, Mr. Archibald: 11:30 and 12:30."

"Are you new here?" asked Diana from the table. She was wearing four sports team hats on her head for some reason.

"Mr. Archibald is considering The Ridge. I'm showing him around," said Sandy. "We're all going to show our best side, aren't we, for Mr. Archibald?"

"It's Harris, actually."

"Well Harris, I've been told my back side is my best side," Diana said smiling at him before glancing around the table. The others smiled, nodded, or laughed softly having heard remarks like this from Diana before.

Harris chuckled nervously, somewhat uncertain how to respond but definitely concerned about a future that might include unfiltered flirtations from octogenarian women. He shifted his eyes to Sandy.

"With that, Mr. Archibald, I think we need to keep moving," suggested Sandy who extended her right arm to indicate the direction they would be headed. "Enjoy your lunches," she said to those at the table while taking her first steps away from it.

Nudging 70 with a full head of grey-flecked wavy brown hair, still a touch over six feet on a medium frame that he owed more to metabolism than exercise or diet, and with lines that creased his kind face, Harris Archibald was going to be the youngest and most mobile male at The Ridge if he decided to sign on. He couldn't know yet, but Diana flirted with most every male she encountered. His inability to respond to her playfulness was due both to being out of practice as well as having never been very good at it. Though she didn't come right out and say it, Diana may have found him ruggedly handsome, for that could apply. But Harris didn't think of himself in that way. He had never been told that by a female in his life and he had learned to live most of the last two decades without female affirmations.

After leaving the dining area and heading down a hall, Sandy showed him the common living area. Harris remembered the white baby grand piano, the groupings of upholstered moss green, beige, and brown chairs and sofas from his previous visit. There was also the white painted brick fire place with large, never-lit candles instead of logs, and the small table with a chess set on it. The latter had caught his attention only because he'd once played a lot of chess, but hadn't in years. He wondered momentarily, but doubted that he would find a playing partner in a place like The Ridge. Sandy went on with her well-worn spiel, "We have all kinds in here. It runs the spectrum physically and socially. Some like to be left to themselves even though we have a wide range of activities every day. At the very least, they get to the dining room two or three times a day for their food and a little socializing. How about I show you a couple of apartments that we have available? You'll see there's no stove or oven in the kitchenette. There is a microwave. There's no real cooking in the apartments."

"I remember the kitchenettes from my last visit. How many residents currently?" Harris asked.

"It's just short of 100 currently, with two married couples. It's almost 65 to 35, women to men. I have no doubt you'd be very popular here, Mr. Archibald," she added while erroneously assuming this notion was important to Harris.

Harris only nodded slightly. Being around others was a secondary factor in his decision to look at senior communities, but romance was not. Having observed many females with walkers, canes, or four hats, as well as all being more aged than himself, did nothing to alter his thinking.

~

Three weeks later, after Harris Archibald had signed the papers with Sandy, and after a rudimentary screening and health assessment, he moved into The Ridge. The Ridge was a nicely furnished senior living complex with 100 one-bedroom apartments and 20 studios. There were 22 vacant rooms before Harris arrived, a number that alarmed the local administration and its corporate headquarters enough to float a half-off special to Harris and others as incentive to sign immediately.

The Ridge did not provide lifetime medical care as some of the newer senior facilities did in the area, nor did it provide memory care. It did, however, gladly take any one over 60 years of age in reasonably good health who was willing to pay the monthly fare. The Ridge residents could choose from a menu of other services for an additional fee, including medicine management, bathing, dressing, wound care, incontinence, and wheelchair or other physical assistance as needed. Weekly housekeeping was provided along with three adequate, semi-nutritious meals a day. For many residents, The Ridge was their last address. But Rex was correct…it was not because anyone starved to death.

After getting oriented for a couple of days and setting up his apartment, Harris found himself at the Friday 3:00 PM Happy Hour. Tiny glasses of inexpensive white and red wine were served while listening to live entertainment that was brought in every week for exactly one somewhat happy hour for the residents. Harris' assigned "buddy", Armando, had told him they needed to attend this event. "It sets up my whole weekend," he told Harris.

When Harris opened his apartment door at 2:55 to see Armando in a red, pink, and white plaid jacket, beige slacks, as well as white and orange saddle shoes, he was stunned. When the smell of Old Spice followed Armando's movements, Harris said, "You didn't tell me I had to dress up for this thing."

"Hey, the ladies like it. Just watch."

Harris and Armando strolled toward the main lobby which opened into The Ridge's common living room. Chairs had been taken from the dining room and arranged in rows next to sofas facing the piano. Harris and his buddy sat in the third row, with Armando taking the end seat. Harris had walked behind him from the hall to the living area and noticed him strutting peacock-like, smiling and waving to the other residents who had arrived before them. Of the 40 or so seated residents, nearly 30 were women. Some were nicely dressed for the occasion, others wore their daily attire, including Diana with her four hats.

The afternoon's entertainment was provided by Frederica, who sang show tunes accompanied by recorded music played through one small Bose speaker. When she opened with *Bali-Ha'i* from South Pacific, the quality of the music and Frederica's voice surprised Harris. Both were better than he'd expected. What also surprised him was when Armando stood early in the song next to his chair and begin moving his arms and hips a little with some semblance of rhythm. Harris watched Armando as he kept inching forward to the edge of the first row, apparently both to be more noticed and to scan the faces of the ladies. Harris watched as some smiled, while others leaned into a neighbor, said something, and shook their heads. Many women resisted looking in his direction, appearing to care less what Armando was up to, or deciding to avoid eye contact.

Harris wasn't sure what to make of all this, but sat back to observe and enjoy this new experience. He helped himself to a glass of red wine the staff brought around on trays. When Frederica was into her second number, *Some Enchanted Evening*, Armando took the back of the wheelchair situated at one end of the first row with a woman in it whom Harris had not yet met, and began to roll her around in front of everyone in dancing motions. Armando did his best Fred Astaire leg movements, while moving the woman and her wheelchair back and forth, punctuated with little turns and wheelies. These antics no one could ignore. Clapping and laughter came from some of the those seated. Frederica, momentarily stumbled with the lyrics, apparently not having seen Armando in action before. Harris laughed throughout the dancing wheelchair performance, but only a week later discovered that the wheelchair dance was a regular Happy Hour occurrence.

During the next 50 minutes, Harris sat back and took it all in. His initial thoughts alternated between *this is friggin' bizarre* and *how charming*. While it was much too early to make an assessment about his decision to move into The Ridge, he was already vacillating between *what have I done* and seeing possibilities for fun and uncomplicated companionship. Looking around the room, Harris, at 69 years old, realized he was the youngest at The Ridge. Outside of Armando, who seemed just a couple years older than himself, everyone else was deep into their 70's, if not 80's or 90's.

Before that thought could slide him into a funk, Harris' wandering mind was jarred back to the present during *All That Jazz*. Frederica was well into her set and had loosened up. Clearly, she enjoyed performing and loved her selected tunes. During this number, with top hat she pranced in front of the onlookers while singing. At one point during the song, she started snapping her fingers while singing and dancing. At the other end of the front row was another wheelchaired female whom Harris did not know either. Frederica, playing to the crowd, went toward that woman snapping and prancing and singing for everything she was worth. The wheelchair-bound woman sat stoically watching this performance not clapping, nor singing along, nor smiling approval. Suddenly, during a brief non-vocal musical bridge, the seated woman blurted out, "Stop snapping!" Frederica, in this case, never missed a beat, turned and kept high-stepping toward the other end of the row. Harris howled as did a few others who witnessed it. For Harris it triggered something else. He knew right then that this place was going to be different than any other portion of his life. At this very moment there seemed to be some possibilities for, if not happiness, at least contentment. He was good with that.

When Frederica ended her set with *Whatever Lola Wants*, and thanked the group for their nice response and participation, she apparently misinterpreted the kind closing applause as an encore call. She said, "Okay, if you insist. But just one more." Before she finished the final note of *Cabaret*, Harris and some others were standing just to make certain the music would truly end.

Armando and Harris walked back down the wide burgundy and oatmeal colored carpeted hall toward Harris' room. "I didn't expect it to be like that. The entertainment was pretty stinking okay if you ask me, including you!" said Harris.

"Ahh, the ladies don't know what their missing," replied Armando apparently alluding to the fact that he, once again, was headed back without a woman at his side.

"You'll get 'em next time," Harris said to his buddy. Armando just looked at him in silence. "Hey, you want to come by after dinner and watch the Dubs?" he added. "They start about 6:30; playing in Phoenix."

At 6:23 Harris picked up some loose garments that he'd strewn over the arms and backs of chairs in the living room. He tossed them onto the floor of his bedroom closet. He also grabbed a near-empty bag of Cheetos and brushed its crumbs off the glass coffee table into his hand before carrying both to the garbage bag under the sink.

Armando knocked at 6:30 although he had no idea that the Dubs referred to the Warriors or that the game was basketball. He, like most residents of The Ridge, struggled with the long nights. He longed for companionship, preferably female, but this new guy Harris was friendly enough. At this point in his life, he'd become a staunch *yes* person, never turning down an invitation.

"Grab a seat," beckoned Harris, motioning toward the two, beige, faux-leather Barcaloungers on opposite ends of a light blue loveseat, all of which nicely filled the small living room. "Want a beer? A glass of wine?" Harris asked while opening the small refrigerator door.

"Whatever you're having."

Harris grabbed two Heinekens. "Beer goes better with ball games. You follow the Dubs much?"

"Not too much," Armando said while sliding into one of the chairs and seeing that the athletes warming up on the large flat screen were playing basketball.

The men watched the game together, one keenly interested in the game's outcome, the other in just being there. Small talk was not yet easy for the two men. They got into their second beers midway through the second quarter. Harris appreciated the company too, even though Armando knew little of the strategy of the game or its players. When half-time came, Harris muted the sound, turned to Armando, and asked, "So, tell me…how long you been here?"

"Ten months."

"Where'd you live before?"

Armando took a long swig from the bottle before saying, "I lived in a parish house about 20 miles from here."

Harris looked at Armando trying to process what he had heard. "What do you mean?" asked Harris in a tone that expressed real interest with a dose of confusion.

Armando knew Harris was questioning his reference to the parish house more than the mileage, and answered, "I've been a parish priest for 42 years."

"Wow, good for you," said Harris shifting his weight in his chair and rubbing both of his thighs with his hands while buying some time.

"Priests rarely get wealthy, unless they inherit," Armando added. "I don't have much money. They offered me a good deal here. With the three meals and no taxes, insurance or utility costs, I think I can make this place work indefinitely. I hope so anyhow."

"Half off?" asked Harris curious about the deal Father Armando got.

"Yes."

"Good. Me too," Harris confided. "I haven't been really good with my money. I needed something like this," Harris revealed before falling silent. Armando was quiet too, uncertain where to take the conversation.

"Does most everybody here know you were a priest?"

"I'm still a priest. I can still say Mass, and preside over weddings. I just don't belong to a parish or have weekly obligations. I'm just retired. And *yes* to your question. I imagine the word has spread here that I am a priest."

"I'm sorry to be so dumb about this," said Harris. "I didn't know priests retired and were just left to fend for themselves. I thought they put you in some priest home or monastery or something."

"No. They do that with some orders of nuns; not priests usually. We have to manage for ourselves. We get paid a small salary as priests. Usually, we're given food and lodging while we belong to a parish. We're able to put a little into an IRA. We also get Social Security. Some dioceses provide a retirement supplement at age 70 or 75."

"I guess I never gave it much thought beyond that the rich Catholic Church must certainly take care of its own."

"Common misconception. We take a vow of poverty, and we never lose sight of that."

Harris drank from his bottle then asked, "Should I call you Father?"

"I wish you wouldn't."

"How about Mondo'? Anybody ever call you Mondo?" asked Harris while thinking it sounded nothing like a priest's name.

"Not since my youth. I kinda liked it then. I'm good with that."

"Alright Mondo," Harris said grabbing the remote and unmuting the TV as the second half got underway. "Let's see if the Dubs can put these Suns away."

Harris and Mondo checked out the activity whiteboard every day and went to many events together including blackjack, bingo, indoor putting and evening movies. They passed on chair-yoga and town hall meetings.

Bingo was funny at the start for Harris with most numbers needing to be verbally repeated for the hard of hearing. But with each game taking three times longer than it should, Harris told Mondo, "I can't do that anymore."

When Mondo finished last in the weekly putting contest on the bumpy eight-foot artificial turf strip and received significant ribbing from some other participants, he told Harris, "I think that's my last putting contest."

Harris and Mondo got together for Warrior games on TV, and for Sunday football. Mondo learned some strategy of each sport and began to have favorite players, often choosing someone on the second string to root for.

The televised games and The Ridge activities took only small portions of slow-moving days. Harris lapsed back to his routine prior to The Ridge when he watched too much crappy tv and read. He'd gone through phases when he read only non-fiction. *Seabiscuit*, *The Boys in the Boat*, a story about golf called *The Match* were among his favorites. For years he settled on different themes. One year he read six books on sports psychology hoping to discover some insights that might help his poor golf game, while another year he read five books on near-death experiences, curious about the light at the end of the tunnel so many people who had had near-death experiences claimed to have seen or travelled part way through. He now read mostly fiction.

Reading more than television helped him pass the time, and had helped him endure his semi-solitary existence of the past few years.

One evening for dinner Harris and Mondo sat at a round table with Miranda, Diana, and Rose. He noticed how slowly most residents ate, with many having an odd way of gently pushing food around their plates with their forks between bites. This meal the conversation did not flow easily. Comments about the news and food, were followed by long silences. While Harris had seen this pattern at meals before, it still made him fidget and say things he normally wouldn't. The more seasoned residents seemed to have grown accustomed to it and did not feel the need to fill the silences.

Finally, Rose Hannigan said that housekeeping had lost a bra of hers the last time they did the laundry.

"How could that happen? It's the second time! Who wants my bras?"

No one had an answer for her questions. More silence. Harris, without having a plan, asked the ladies if anyone liked football?

"My husband used to watch it all the time," Diana said. "I liked the 49ers when they had Joe Montana. He was a cutie."

"They were good," said Harris understating the obvious.

Miranda dabbed the corners of her mouth before speaking. "My husband watched too. He'd want me to sit with him during the games. It seemed like just a lot bodies pushing each other around at first. But then he explained things. Once I learned some of the strategy, I enjoyed it."

"Sounds like your husband was a good guy," suggested Armando.

"He was," she said with a sad smile before looking at her plate.

Harris glanced at Mondo before saying, "Well, the 'Niners are on Monday Night Football right now. Probably started a few minutes ago. If anyone would like to join Mondo and me in 117 to watch any of it, or all of it, you're welcome. We'll supply the beer and wine."

"That sounds like fun," said Diana. "Party in 117. Woo-hoo."

As dinner ended and three of them began to move toward apartment 117, Diana leaned into a couple of tables who were still eating. "We going to watch football in 117 now, if you want to join us. Party in 117."

Miranda had been non-committal about watching the game. The suddenness of the invite caught her off-guard. She had always been one who liked written calendars and planning things out well in advance. In three and a half years at The Ridge, her calendar had few entries save for an occasional doctor or hair appointment, or a rare scheduled visit from a friend. While other women at The Ridge were aggressive and knocked on men's doors, she was not and had not. The days moved slowly, but Miranda was comfortable in her own skin and enjoyed her own company. Three times a day to mingle in the dining room was enough socializing for her. There had been a time when she longed for more, some human connection, but those days were gone. But Harris and Armando seemed kind. Armando was a priest after all. This evening's football and wine invite did make her pause. She headed to her room to freshen up and think about it. Clearly Diana would be there, so Miranda would not be alone with two men. While this all seemed innocent enough, she was always wary of men's intentions.

Her husband had been kind, she thought wistfully while powdering her nose and checking her hair. It had only been stupid football, but she had often thought back fondly to Sundays with Ken on the couch. He was always so intent on the game on the screen. He talked himself through the moment; "Fourth and eight. Hold the Browns here and with a minute 57 left, we can run out the clock."

Miranda remembered chiming in with something like, "Doesn't the other team have three timeouts?" only to hear Ken say, "They're down to one. We could run just run out the clock." How he kept track of timeouts while everything else was going on was beyond her.

She waited awhile after acknowledging to herself that her hair looked nice, still unsure if this was a good idea. She turned on the television to make certain the 49ers were truly playing. They were. She could stay in her own apartment and pour herself a glass of white wine, like she did most nights…and flip channels or read. She liked red wine better, but early in her marriage she'd heard that red wine-stained teeth, so she settled for decades of white.

She had taken care of her entire self all her life, not just her teeth. She had been a beauty in high school. She had thought about being a cheerleader, but was too shy for that. And besides, cheer practice took time away from homework and chores. She helped her parents around the house and by babysitting neighborhood children throughout her high school years. Any babysitting money went straight into the family money jar, along with whatever her recently departed brother could earn from mowing lawns. Mom even put in her earnings from odd housekeeping jobs.

Her dad had held onto an appliance sales job all through Miranda's high school years, something important to her and her mom. Prior to high school, the family had moved twice in the middle of the night because they couldn't make rent after Dad lost jobs.

Ken had swept her off her feet at Pepperdine University where she had earned a scholarship. They married shortly after Ken passed the bar exam, had their only child, Beverly, and lived a comfortable lifestyle while Ken practiced corporate tax law. Miranda had wanted for nothing before taking the phone call about Ken's massive heart attack at work when he was 64. She wanted nothing now except for Ken to spoon with her in bed, and be with her on the couch Sunday afternoons during football season.

The 49ers were down early this Monday evening to the Seahawks as she stood looking at the TV and weighing her options. After a few minutes more, she grabbed the remote to turn off the game, stood, glanced in the mirror for a final spot-check, and headed out the door. She was satisfied. People often said she looked great for her age. She always thanked them. Sometimes she even agreed with them, though she remembered long ago when *her age* was not part of the compliment. As she had since college, she picked out a different nice outfit each night for the next day. Jeans were almost as rare for her these days as were dresses. Pant suits were her normal fare with blouse and a tailored blazer dependent on the temperature. She used a cane while walking due to a hip replacement gone bad, and tonight would be no different. Inside the elevator she paused while looking at the floor numbers on the inside panel.

Before pushing '1' she shook her head while thinking this was unlike her, and that this might be foolish.

As she approached the door to 117, she could hear Diana's voice shouting, "Go, go, go" followed by a man's voice hollering, "He fumbled! Are you kidding me?"

Miranda stood there in front of the door. It sounded like they were having fun inside, but more than that, she thought, there was some life going on. The Ridge, for all its plusses and the staff's good intentions, lacked spontaneity.

"Anyone ready for another," Harris shouted.

"I am," replied Diana.

"Me too," added Armando.

Miranda stood on the other side of the door for many long seconds before thinking *no, this wasn't her*, and headed back toward her room.

CHAPTER THREE

Harris Archibald was born and raised in the Bay Area of Northern California. Firmly entrenched in the middle of his class academically, Harris was liked well enough to cross cliques at a private Catholic high school. After graduation he headed to San Francisco State primarily because it was inexpensive, nearby, and his grades and family finances left few options.

He lived 18 miles away from the university, on the Oakland side of the Bay, and commuted. Missing out on dorm life, someone suggested to Harris that he join the Gator Club, a sanctioned school spirit club comprised of commuters and campus residents. The Gator Club, now long defunct, was chartered for organizing athletic pep rallies, dances, and social mixers for students, but during Harris' time was more noted for pranks and drinking.

During high school, there was classmate that Harris liked a lot. He and Jennifer went to Junior Prom and Senior Ball together. She asked him to two Sadie Hawkins dances. Jennifer was a high-achieving academic, much more so than Harris. Both were nice looking, and had activities that kept them busy. Harris played Frosh and JV Baseball for three years, never being quite good enough to make it to Varsity. Jennifer participated in cross country and track all four years. Fate had made them biology lab partners and they had other classes together each year. Harris had just enough cute shyness and struggling-student-needing-help appeal for Jennifer. Harris welcomed her academic assistance. To most everyone in their class they seemed like a couple, although they only ate lunch together occasionally. Other students erroneously assumed they called each other most nights and went out often on dates.

The truth was that neither happened. Harris and Jennifer thought about calling every day, but just couldn't. Harris' reason was that he wasn't ready to do the steady-dating routine. Even though he liked her a great deal, he was unsure how to go about it, what to say. Jennifer, on the other hand, didn't phone Harris because in the '60's, in her house, that was not something young ladies did. But she often wished that Harris would. When they did have lunch together, she felt excitement, happiness. Maybe it was only young love, but what else could there be at her age? She never pressed Harris for anything more, short of her parting comment to *stay in touch* whenever they ended their time together.

The Gator Club knew the protected bars in the city, where underage drinkers were served. Harris' faction of the Gator Club would sometimes meet at the *Cozy*

Cove or the *Tender Trap* for a beer or six after school, and usually on Friday and Saturday nights.

During his freshman year at S. F. State, Harris called Jennifer three times to ask her out. She had gone on to UC Davis, 75 miles away from where Harris still lived, so dating needed to fit around holidays or the odd trip home for Jennifer. The first two dates after high school went well, as there was much catching up to do. They still felt a connection. But Harris came away from them even less certain how to make a serious relationship work than he did during high school. The afternoon prior to their third date, Harris got a call from a fellow Gator who explained the plan for the night was to ski down Lombard Street, the most crooked street in the world. Harris never called Jennifer to cancel and didn't show up for the date. Afterward, he felt bad but couldn't get himself to call to apologize.

At their five-year high school reunion, they ran into each other for the first time since Harris' no-show. Part way through the event Jennifer cornered him, wanting to know what happened, and how come he hadn't even called. Harris said, "I don't know. I'm sorry." Both statements were true.

Jennifer looked him squarely in the eyes with her chin up and shoulders back, flummoxed that there wasn't more of an explanation or excuse. After three or four seconds of silence, she said calmly but firmly, "I deserve better. Best of luck to you, Harris." Jennifer then spun, placed her wine glass and napkin on a nearby table, and left, never to by seen or heard from again by Harris.

He knew that she was right, but the sting of those two sentences made their mark immediately and stayed with him.

Harris did, however, have a series of female friends he dated during his twenties and thirties, while working at, then running, a small ball-bearing manufacturing company in nearby Hayward. Ball-bearings were not a growth industry, and Harris knew it. But when the aging owner of the business, Darrell, talked of slowing down and selling the business to Harris, Harris listened. Harris knew he lacked options and drive to create more in his life, so Harris and Darrell worked out a mutually beneficial agreement to transfer ownership. Darrell agreed to stay on for a year in a consulting capacity, but died nine months later in the desk chair that he had always worked in.

The ball-bearing business with Harris as sole proprietor and CEO, remained mostly flat over the next several years. He'd lose an account once every so often, and sometimes new business would find him. He knew he should move the business to Nevada, a state with lower rent, labor, and taxes in order to drive cost out his business, but he could never find the time to search for a new location. The thought of a managing a move of that magnitude was overwhelming to Harris and beyond his capabilities.

In a similar sense, the relationships he had with women never evolved. They seemed to get stuck in the early dating phase, never maturing into committed relationships. Harris never knew if it was a flaw within himself for not knowing how to take a relationship from dating to marriage, or if it was just happenstance between himself and the females he encountered, who themselves never seemed intent on leading him to the altar.

Once he turned 37, the quiet nights alone began to bother him. He tired of bars and meeting women that way. Most of his S. F. State and high school friends had married, begun families and were no longer available for ballgames, bike rides, and spontaneous excursions.

Around that time, he met a woman who called on his business. Marjorie was a sales rep for a box manufacturer. She tried to get Harris' business, and was successful after they began dating and had sex. Marjorie, a year older than Harris, was large boned, seemed nice, and unmarried, a status she did have an urge to change. She led Harris through the relationship, insisting on an engagement ring before giving up her apartment and moving in with him. It all seemed a logical evolution to Harris. He liked Marjorie enough to marry her.

The first 18 months of their marriage were fine. Marjorie and Harris balanced work and play, which included an active sex life. Both of them were initially eager to make up for some lost time in the latter regard.

After that early-marriage flurry, things began to change. Marjorie was less and less interested in sex. She no longer offered to wear frilly things, citing self-consciousness with some weight gain. Yes, Harris had noticed it too, but it mattered little to him. When she was mysteriously laid off the following year, she seemed content to be a potato-chip-eating, couch-lying housewife, and Harris became alarmed. She gained 30 pounds her first year of being unemployed, and ten more each of the two years thereafter. No amount of prodding from Harris could get her to the gym or out jogging or change her eating habits. Whether it began with depression or not, Marjorie acted depressed and was depressing to be around.

Harris no longer wanted to be seen with her socially. He suggested counselling. She tried it for a while and was prescribed Zoloft. She quit both after a few months.

Harris stayed married for 11 years to Marjorie. After seeing no willingness to change on her part, he initiated divorce proceedings. Nudging 50, and only wedded to his struggling business, his social circle had shrunk further, and he believed he was destined to lead a life alone.

He bought a guitar and learned to play some with the illusion he would join a band.

By his early 60's, Harris sold the business, getting $975,000 for it. Along with his Roth IRA and a small amount he had inherited after his parents' passing and splitting that estate with his three siblings who had all moved out of state, Harris guessed he could make the money last. He spent the next few years without a job to go to, without hobbies other than reading, playing the guitar before bed, and some poorly-played golf. By this time, he was without female companionship. He ate out seven days and nights a week, usually having a couple of drinks with his dinner before heading home. While eating and drinking alone many nights, he reflected that love had not been kind to him, nor had business, and his retirement was equally unsatisfying. He knew he had played the leading role in the outcome of each. He also began to realize his money would not last many more years at the rate he was going through it. A waitress who had seen too much of Harris in the restaurant he frequented, suggested a senior facility when he turned 68 as a means to control expenses, and to get much needed human interaction. He wondered if a change of scenery would be more positive than negative. He wondered, but like most other things in his life that he wondered about, inertia prevailed.

Nearly a year later, and feeling much too young for a senior community, he did visit a few out of curiosity and for something to do. When he realized that he could get a free meal if he scheduled a tour late morning or late afternoon, he set up a few more. Though meeting the needs for controlling expenses and providing some companionship, albeit more elderly than himself, at $4500-6000 per month for these places, his savings plus Social Security might still not last. With each tour, he explained this and planted the seed that if they ever ran a good special, they should give him a call.

Many months later, The Ridge called and inquired about his status, asking if he had ever moved into a senior facility. Hearing *no*, Sandy, the Sales Director, sprung the 50% off deal to him…if he were able to commit in the next five days. It was then that Harris set up his final tour of The Ridge with her.

CHAPTER FOUR

Harris walked out of his room unshaven and with his long-sleeve corduroy shirt mis-buttoned to swing by the library one morning. He was, by then, in the habit of heading to The Ridge's library around 11:00 six days a week. The mail might have already been placed in the secure mail slots for each resident which were embedded in one of the library walls. At the very least he could read the morning paper. If the mail was not yet there, it would come by the time he finished the sports page, Dear Abby, and tried the Sudoku puzzle. No one else had ever seemed interested in the puzzle, so he filled it out, except for Fridays. Fridays Sudoku's were labeled 'Diabolical' forcing him to guess. He didn't like to guess, but rather relied on deductive reasoning and tactics he had learned from doing the puzzles for years. By the time he had finished collecting his mail and reading the paper, it was time for lunch.

The morning library ritual also allowed him to see the same faces almost every day. A gaggle of women residents gathered in the lobby near the receptionist for part of the late morning. Five or six of them could be seen and heard gossiping or complaining most days. Harris had never seen the women eat together, perhaps that would have been too much and ruined their relationships. Instead, a pattern had developed for them to gather in the lobby at 10:30 or 11:00 and catch up. This day, Rose Hannigan would eventually leave the group and approach the receptionist. "When is housekeeping supposed to do my room?' she asked.

"Thursday is your day, Mrs. Hannigan...every Thursday," the receptionist advised the woman.

"I don't think they've changed my sheets in weeks."

"They do every week, Mrs. Hannigan. Remember we had this conversation last week and the week before, and I checked with housekeeping both times for you?" the receptionist said trying to not sound impatient, but was failing in Harris' mind.

"Well, if you say so," said Mrs. Hannigan to the receptionist before heading back to the circle of ladies to go over it with them. Her friends were far more sympathetic than the receptionist had been, although they had all heard some version of this before from Rose.

One lunch a few weeks after making The Ridge his home, Harris wandered into the dining area by himself. Sometimes he ate by himself, but tried not to. Mondo had advised him, "Stick out your hand and introduce yourself to everyone the first couple of weeks. You may need to repeat your introduction, from one day to the next. Some memories are not so sharp around here."

"Good advice."

"And try to sit at different tables. Some people eat with the same two or three people every meal. Who wants that?"

"Yeah," Harris responded, "who wants that?"

This day, Harris approached the round table that he and Sandy had talked to the day of his tour weeks before. Everyone was there except Rex, Harris thought the fella's name was…the guy who was a little louder than the others, the one who had softly endorsed the food.

As he approached the table, he asked, "Mind if I join you?"

The others looked from side to side before Diana said, "That would be lovely."

Some at the table were eating their first course already, so Harris scanned the menu quickly before giving Esmerelda his order. "Anyone else having the tacos?" he asked to no one in particular.

"I am," said Miranda. "The crew usually does a fine job with Mexican food."

"I'll have the beef tacos," he told Esmerelda. "And a side salad with thousand…and an ice tea."

"Very good sir," she replied.

"So, how's everybody doing today?" Harris asked his table mates with enthusiasm in an attempt to ramp up the energy level.

"I'm doin' great," chimed in Diana first who was wearing her *Spoiled Rotten* cap on the top of three other hats this day.

"Great," said Harris who looked around the table for any other responses. When none came, he added, "Well, I dusted off my guitar and played a bit this morning. First time in a long time."

Miranda asked, "Really, what type of music do you play?"

Harris was beginning to explain his musical tastes and guitar-playing preferences, when the missing Rex approached the table. Rex stopped behind Harris's right shoulder and, in lieu of greeting anybody, said loudly, "Why the hell didn't you save my place?" His eyes scanned the faces of all the members of the table.

The others looked down at the table and said nothing.

"Goddammit, you know this is my seat…every damn lunch. This is where I sit."

"I'm sorry," said Harris while turning red. "I didn't know."

"Well, you know now," the man said looking straight at Harris, but more upset with the others.

Harris sat there awkwardly for a few moments before realizing what he must do. He removed the napkin from his lap, placed it on the table, stood up from his chair, and looked around for other seating. He saw an open two-top along the window wall and began silently moving in that direction. As he took his third step, he turned back to face Rex who was still standing and glaring at the others, and said to Rex, "How was I supposed to know? You don't have to get so mad."

"Well, I am mad, and where I come from if some son-of-a-bitch steals your seat, you're entitled to get mad."

Rex sat down in the chair that Harris had left. Harris turned and continued toward the empty table.

No one at the round table said anything until Rex said, "Don't let anybody do that again, goddammit. Not to my seat."

Silence again. The man in the wheelchair spooned his soup. Diana took a sip of ice tea. Miranda sat stoically, very upright with her hands on her lap. After a few seconds of watching Rex scan his menu like things had returned to normal, she turned to Rex and said, "You should be ashamed of yourself."

"Well, I'm not."

"That was horribly rude just now," she added. "You were very late. We thought maybe you were skipping lunch."

"I never skip lunch. You should know that by now. I was doing my constitutional if you must know," he added huffily.

"What you did to that man was unforgivable," she continued.

Rex put down his menu and turned slightly to face Miranda before raising his voice even more and saying, "Well I don't need your forgiveness. But I *do* expect you to do me the common courtesy of saving my goddammed seat."

The others looked at Miranda, wondering if she would respond. They all knew Rex had a way of shouting people down, of getting in the last word. But they also knew that Miranda had had some history with Rex.

She was quiet for many seconds, hands on her lap still, thinking things through. Rex resumed reading his menu and others returned to their food or beverages thinking this latest incident had ended in typical fashion. It hadn't. Miranda spoke up with conviction, "Well I, quite frankly, am done with your boorish behavior." She took the green cloth napkin off her lap and placed it on the table in front of her as she got up. Leaving her soup, and the others behind, Miranda calmly headed toward Harris' table with the help of her cane. Diana and the man in the wheelchair stopped eating, their heads slowing turning to follow Miranda's movement. Rex kept his eyes on the menu acting like he didn't care.

When she neared the table along the glass wall, she stopped a few feet from it. Harris was looking down at his clasped hands and exhaled deeply, his long, angular face red and agitated. Miranda waited a few moments before saying, "Mind if I join you?"

He was startled by the sound of her voice and jerked his head to look at her. "Yes, certainly… if you want," he said, motioning toward the empty chair with one hand.

Once she placed the cane on the back her chair and settled in, he asked in his more normal cadence, "Are you sure you won't be ostracized by your group?"

"I might be, if I'm lucky," she said as she placed a napkin on her lap. After she scooched her chair in a bit, she added, "I'm tired of his opinions. They're the only ones that count at that table. Everyone else is afraid to speak up to him. You gave me a way out, so thank you."

Harris chuckled feeling better with the sudden turn of events. "No, thank you. Very kind of you to join me after that episode. I'm so fatootsed by this, I don't know what to say."

"You don't have to say anything more. There's a lot of history with that table. Not all of it's good. I've wanted to exit that group for a while. I needed to do it the right way. I did. So, when I say *thank you*, I mean it."

He looked at her for a couple of seconds then surprised himself by saying, "You're welcome. Perhaps I should say I planned out the whole thing to get you to come over to my table," then instantly worried he had said something stupid.

"Very noble of you to rescue me like that," Miranda replied smiling and warming to her first taste of banter in much too long.

Harris laughed lightly, his face softening with her remark, shook his head, and rearranged his silverware. "I just didn't see that coming. Any of it. Seems like there are some things I need to learn about this place." He paused. She smiled and said nothing. "Where's my man Armando?" he added trying to lighten things. "He's supposed to look out for me."

Esmerelda had no trouble rerouting their food and beverages. Before long, Miranda asked again, "So really, what type of music do you play?"

Later that day and throughout a sleep-deprived night, he ruminated on the events of the day. He didn't recall ever being that embarrassed, but the kindness that Miranda had shown him might have been equally rare. Two diametrically opposed events had occurred within three or four minutes of each other. He felt mortified at having gotten up at Rex's badgering, and having had it witnessed by others at the table and nearby. He began having imaginary re-do's of the sequence where he responded differently to Rex. *Maybe you need to get your butt here on time*, or *snooze, you lose* didn't sound good in his mind, so he was glad he didn't blurt out one of those. What could he have done or said differently that would have made him seem like less of a submissive victim? Nothing came to mind, and that did not settle well with him.

He also couldn't stop thinking about the actions of Miranda, and what courage that must have taken to get up and leave that table. It had made an impression on Harris and perhaps others at the table, even if Rex pretended like it didn't matter. He noticed that afternoon and deep into the night that some of his imaginary conversations about events of that day were with Miranda.

Maybe it had been Miranda's interest that nudged him along. Certainly, the fact that he had opened his guitar case that one day, dusted the wood off, tuned the strings, and played a bit were necessary first steps. But the real driver for Harris was the realization that long, slow passages of time needed to be filled at The Ridge, and playing his guitar once or twice a day fit well in this new life of his. The songs that had gone into cold storage, forgotten chord sequences and rearranged words, began to come back into his mind and fingers.

He found that besides stumbling to remember certain songs that he'd once known, he also noticed his voice was thinner. He'd once had a fine singing voice. Nothing world-class or disarming, but a fine voice. Resonant and on pitch all the time, it fit the James Taylor, Elton John, Cat Stevens melancholy music that he often played. The few friends who had heard him in the past, were put to ease as listeners, knowing Harris' voice would stay in tune, never straining to hit a note, cracking, or worse yet, sounding off key.

It was a couple of weeks of playing at The Ridge, just to himself, and with the help of some warm tea, that Harris found his voice again. To him, it sounded whole, good enough to use in front of others should the occasion arise.

Toward the end of those two weeks, Armando knocked on and entered Harris' unlocked front door, that he noticed Harris playing for the first time.

"Oh man, I lost track of time," offered Harris when realizing it was game time for the Warriors.

"I didn't know you played," said Armando.

"Getting back into it. It's been a long time," said Harris.

Armando found a seat, the two men popped open beer cans and settled into the game. At halftime, Armando told him, "I play too…guitar. Maybe I could bring mine down sometime."

"That would be good," Harris replied.

The men watched the second half together, this game ending in a disappointing Warrior loss because of too many turnovers down the stretch. Armando, however, left pleased he had found more common ground with his friend.

~

The next day they saw each other at lunch, and discussed a time to get together. At 2:30 that afternoon, Armando brought his guitar case to Harris's apartment. After showing Harris his instrument and letting Harris strum it, they settled into taking turns playing and singing songs. Each man felt some tightness singing his first song, but after the ice was broken, neither thought anything of doing so after that. Armando liked Spanish and mariachi music, but could play many kinds. Harris discovered Mondo was much stronger on his 12-string *Paracho Elite* than he was on his six-string *Yamaha*. For some time that day, Harris sat back and enjoyed watching his friend play. It was a style that Harris had never sat in on before, and as Mondo played it well, Harris watched with admiration. He also looked at and noticed his friend in ways he had not before...his cherub round face that was missing the deep creases of most of the people their age, and his salt and pepper short-cut hair style that fit his olive complexion well. When the priest felt he had played enough on his own, he suggested it was Harris' turn. It wasn't long before Armando provided some interesting back up to Harris' chording and singing.

At the end of *Mr. Bojangles*, which Harris sang, and Armando's accompaniment sounded particularly good, both men said, "Nice."

"Pretty stinkin' okay," added Harris.

"Not half bad," replied Armando.

As that afternoon's session wound down, the men agreed to get together again with their guitars. They played three times over the next two weeks. Armando taught Harris some fingering he had not seen before, along with some accents. Armando's voice was fine, although higher pitched and younger sounding, having sung parts of Mass for many years. It was, however, not quite as pleasant and pleasing as Harris', but their voices together were strong and satisfying to the ear. The men enjoyed this shared activity, but were reluctant to overdo it.

It was three weeks into their playing together that Mondo showed up one session with a flyer announcing that The Ridge Community Talent Show was scheduled for the following Tuesday afternoon. He showed it to Harris, and said, "What do you think?"

Harris read quickly, looked back at Mondo, smiled and said, "Yeah…I don't know."

"I think we need to jump in," countered Mondo. Soon Harris acquiesced.

They practiced everyday leading up to the competition. They tried different songs, but kept coming back to *Bojangles*. Mondo experimented with different ways to accompany Harris' singing and basic chording, before settling on some accents and a beautiful guitar bridge. Mondo also found ways to softly harmonize with Harris' voice without overshadowing it. By Sunday they had buttoned down their one and only song for Tuesday's event.

"Were you around for last year's talent show?" Harris asked.

"It musta been just before I got here or else they skipped a year."

They found out later that while the talent competition happened most years, it was not held the previous year because The Ridge's Activities Coordinator had quit just before it. When the new person came on, she said they'd shoot for this year.

The Tuesday morning of the contest Harris was surprised by his excitement, and also more than a bit anxious. *This is such a tiny thing* he thought. *How good could the competition be?*

There were eight acts signed up including three pianists, a juggler, one violinist, and three guitarists. It appeared that Harris and Mondo were the only duo. The defending champion always went last. Sylvia, a pianist, who had won the last two events, pointed out that tradition to Patricia, the events coordinator who was leading her first talent contest. Harris and Mondo were scheduled for third from last.

The turnout was much larger than most Friday Happy Hours, 70-80 residents, including the performers, were present for the event. Additionally, some staff members stood in the back or along the walls.

One by one the acts were introduced. As they got closer to being called, Harris felt more tense, and Mondo felt more excited. This was Mondo's time to shine, he thought, and take another step in shedding the priestly image that had hounded him since his arrival at The Ridge. As they sat watching the first four performers, Harris was struck by the talent at The Ridge. The juggler had a couple of missteps, and while no bowling balls or fire sticks were used, it was clear had he'd real talent in his earlier life. The violinist was occasionally screechy, but made her arthritic fingers find the correct positions on the strings and fingerboard. A couple of the pianists were good with only incidental timing and chording issues. Harris' illusions of local glory and stardom, which he had kept to himself, did not diminish. At the very least he knew they would not embarrass themselves.

When it was their turn and Patricia introduced them as Harris and Mondo, they strode in front of the audience. They had decided to stand and perform. All the others had been seated except the juggler. As they strummed some warm-up chords and adjusted their microphones, Mondo leaned into Harris and whispered, "It's not too late to run."

Harris was pleased to realize Mondo had said that just to ease the tension, and replied, "Whenever you're ready, friend." With that, Mondo began plucking simply, and elegantly, and when the time came, Harris entered with, *"I knew a man Bojangles, in worn out shoes…"* the first few words came out as clearly and as on-pitch as he had ever sung them. They knew then, they would be better than fine. Mondo's guitar bridge was perfect for the song, adding to it, making it sound more like a professional performance than one by two retired amateurs. When they finished to rousing applause and a few hoots, Harris put his arm around Mondo's shoulders, and Mondo put his arm around Harris' waist. They each held their guitars by the neck in raised conquest as the strode back to their seats to watch the final two contestants.

When Sylvia played *Clair de Lune* as beautifully as it could be played, they knew why she had won the two previous contests. They were also not surprised when she won her third.

The two men received pats on the back and voiced admiration from many of the residents and staff members after the result had been announced. They congratulated Sylvia and returned to their rooms feeling more alive and better about themselves than they had in a long time.

CHAPTER FIVE

Rex Hornsby Jr. was born and raised in Galveston, Texas. The eldest of four sons, his dad had worked on offshore oil rigs all his working life, and Rex had followed his footsteps. Oil rigging shift work could provide well for a family in Galveston's economy, but equally noteworthy, it was dangerous work and it didn't always lead to a quality family life. 12-hour shifts were one thing, but two or four-week hitches on the rig to which a worker was helicoptered, were a bigger part of the family challenges. Rex Sr. and Rex Jr. had hunting and a thirst for beer and women when they got back on land. Their wives had learned to raise children and run households just fine in their absences. During Junior's teenage years, he and dad did some hunting together, and had bonded in that way, and dad had given his son his first beer at 15. But when Rex Jr. graduated from Ball High School with a 2.13 GPA after majoring in football as a 206-pound offensive lineman, dad got him an interview for a rig job.

Rex Jr. met his first wife in *The Wizzard*, a divey jukebox bar, shortly after he turned 21. They were married 17 months until Rex Jr. came home after a four-week rig stint and discovered that Cindy, his wife, had been keeping company with multiple men she'd met at *The Wizzard*.

Rex met his second and last wife, Rebecka, at the *Galveston Island Wild Texas Shrimp Festival* the year following his divorce. Rebecka was two years older and also single after an unsuccessful marriage. Rex had his eye on her as they went through the gate for the festival. Rex made a point of gathering many strings of beads throughout the day. When he approached her in the late afternoon and handed her a beer without her asking for it, he said, "Looked like you were slipping below the legal limit."

She took the beer and said, "Where'd you get all them beads?"

"Jealous? I bet you know how to get some."

When she raised her sleeveless blouse to reveal a lacy, pink bra, he handed her three strands and thought he had met the ideal woman.

While neither were close to perfect, they were a perfect match as single people, partying hard when Rex was off the rig. When Rebecka became pregnant with their only child, Lauren, Rex proposed. Rex was not a good husband the second time around, nor a great father. But Rebecka was a terrific mother and a lonely wife. Lauren was a good kid and a great student, who majored in Engineering at Texas A&M. Hired as an intern for Chevron in Houston, she landed in San Ramon, California, working at Chevron's headquarters.

Rex bounced from rig to rig over his working life always in search of a dollar more. In doing so he failed to build up much of a pension. Injuries led to an aging body breaking down. When Lauren was finishing up A&M, Rebecka decided she'd had enough of Rex. With her dad on his own and in decline, Lauren found The Ridge Senior Living near her work, and suggested to her dad that he move there so she could check on him easily.

Rex was not the acquiescing type, and after much hemming and hawing, he agreed to check out the place. One knee replacement and two bad hips had left him less than fully mobile. He hadn't hunted in 11 years, been inside a bar in three, and his old buddies and siblings didn't come around much anymore. He had no one besides his daughter. With her being in Northern California and he in Texas, Rex was a little more open to her suggestions than he'd ever let on.

After their tour of The Ridge, Lauren took her father to the *Peasant & Pear* in Danville for dinner and to get his reaction. "So, what did ya think, daddy?"

"Well, I've seen larger hotel rooms than what they call a one-bedroom apartment. And it don't have no kitchen to speak of."

"There's room enough, and they don't want anybody burning down the place by cooking…so they don't have full kitchens. Walking to the dining room three times a day gets you some exercise, and forces you to interact with others."

"I don't need no forcing."

"It seems like a nice place," she added. "I think you should consider it. They did say there were over 60% women there, and you'd be close enough that I could visit every weekend."

"I reckon I would brighten up the miserable lives of several women in there. I suppose I could try it for humanitarian reasons."

"It is just month-to-month, so you could bail at any time if you didn't like it, daddy."

Rex did try it and never bailed. It was hard to say if Rex became popular at The Ridge or just the loudest. He was noticed by all and avoided by some. He steered most meal conversations with his table mates. Most men disliked him and some women did too. But some women were drawn to him. He brought energy and life to The Ridge that most men did not. Miranda was one of the women who was drawn to him…for a while. While not utilizing anywhere near his vocal volume, she often waited until Rex ran out of steam during one of his political diatribes, to counter with something thought provoking and with calm confidence. She enjoyed the discussions, and he did as well.

Rex took to walking the halls of The Ridge most evenings. He liked the exercise, and the routine broke up the long, lonely nights. Also, if there had been anything going on between the residents, he would have noticed, but mostly there wasn't.

Some months after Rex's arrival at The Ridge, the staff took notice of Rex leaving Miranda's room most Saturday evenings after 9:30. Eventually Rose, Miranda's neighbor, saw it too. It was not long afterwards that everyone knew, fueled by Rose's speculation. That was okay by Rex.

CHAPTER SIX

Harris and Mondo continued playing guitar and watching games together. Both also had cars and drove. Not many others at The Ridge did. Mondo drove to say Mass when needed at different parishes in the area. Harris liked to jump in his car and get away. Some days he needed to pick up beer and wine and his prescriptions. Other days, the quiet and routine of The Ridge was more that he could bear which prompted a drive.

Even after forming a friendship with Mondo, he'd take off once or twice a week alone. Walks along the nearby Ironhorse Trail or across the Golden Gate Bridge broke up the day and were different sceneries, but ultimately, he was still alone. Aging and being alone were aspects of life he had resigned himself to, but he still didn't care for them. Occasionally, he asked Mondo to come along. Mondo always agreed.

One Tuesday morning outing, after picking up toilet paper and a prescription, Harris and Mondo crossed paths at their mail slots. Harris said, "How about lunch out today? My treat. You like philly cheesesteaks?"

"I think I do, but it's been a long time. Sounds good, but you don't have to treat."

They got into Harris' 11-year-old green Toyota Camry and headed to one of Harris' favorite lunch spots a couple of miles away. Part way there, when it was quieter than Harris could stand, he turned on the radio. The sports talk show hosts droned on about whether Barry Bonds should be in the Hall of Fame. It was topic that had been run into the ground at least seven years earlier and while Harris had strong beliefs that he should be in the Hall of Fame, he wasn't going to tolerate another second of this tired drivel. He hit the CD button and instantly Bob Seger's *Old Time Rock and Roll* began playing. Some music needed to be played loudly including this song, so Harris turned it up. Within a few seconds he realized the song required more volume but that would be weird with someone else in the car. He also realized that rarely did music sound really good when someone else, especially someone new, was in the car. He turned it down.

"You don't have to turn it down for me," Mondo said.

"Do you even know who that is?" asked Harris.

"Not off the top of my head, but I remember the song…sort of."

"Bob Seger," he replied and turned it back up. Louder than before…to the volume Harris would listen to if he were in the car by himself. They listened to the music until they had parked and *Night Moves* was starting. Harris didn't say anything, but even at his desired volume the music still didn't feel as good as if he were alone.

At lunch, they each ate a large philly cheesesteak with sweet peppers and mushrooms. They shared steak fries. When they had finished, Mondo pushed himself back from the table and said, "Oh man. I don't remember *ever* having one that good before."

On the drive back, Harris took a different route, and hit a couple of red lights. At the second stop light, when the it turned green, Harris didn't move the car forward. He stared straight ahead trance-like. The driver behind Harris tapped his horn twice. Mondo said, "It's green."

Harris pretended not to hear him or the horn, holding his car's position until the light turned yellow. Once it did, the driver behind them laid on his horn. Mondo shouted, "Harris!"

At the last instance of yellow, Harris stepped on the gas and quickly rolled through the intersection laughing, while the driver behind stayed there, reaching out his window with a one-fingered salute.

Mondo was confused by what he just witnessed, but hearing Harris laugh, he realized that Harris just resurrected a prank that'd been done by teenagers since the first stoplight went up.

"What was *that*?" he asked Harris with some anger. More Harris laughter while keeping his eyes on the road.

"What… are you 16?" Mondo asked sounding genuinely disgusted. No response again from Harris, but also no more laughter.

After a few seconds of uncomfortable silence, Mondo went back to it, "No, really, why did you do that?" asked Mondo clearly perplexed and agitated.

Harris shrugged his shoulders and said, "It was funny."

They drove the rest of the way in silence, with Mondo simply saying, "See ya," once they got to The Ridge lobby before heading to their separate rooms. It was several days before they bumped into each other in the hallway and arranged a guitar session. The oddity of the stoplight incident and Harris's view of what was funny were things Mondo never completely lost sight of about his friend.

~

One warm Spring afternoon, Mondo and Harris took their guitars out onto The Ridge's back patio. The patio was equipped with a built-in barbeque, patio furniture, and a gas fire pit. Harris wondered why this space was never used for outdoor feasts or festivities. He made a mental note to bring it up the next time they had a survey or Town Hall Meeting, if he ever went to one. But this day, he and Mondo would use it for playing their guitars.

The walking path around the property, which several residents used daily, wound its way through the patio, so when the men began playing, they did so in view of intermittent passersby. Most kept walking, but just about everyone made a comment to the musicians. "Well, what have we got here?" was one. "I like it," another. "Wow, Simon & Garfunkel," was from a slow-moving man using a walker. Two simply said, "Excuse me fellas."

Diana's room was right off the patio. She noticed the guitarists and came outside, settling herself in a nearby padded chair. At the end of the first song that she'd heard from where she sat, she said, "You guys are *good*."

As the other residents walked by, Diana encouraged them to stop, sit, and watch with her. "It's free entertainment. Where else are you going get this on a beautiful day?" A man named Norm, along with Mrs. Hannigan, and eventually Miranda sat with Diana in the sun. They politely applauded and encouraged the musicians after each number. The men played most everything they had ever done together, and also did solos they had rarely done with each other before.

When Harris did an old, haunting version of Don McLean's *Empty Chairs*, Diana said, "That was wonderful. I'm thinking about hiring you to sing me to sleep at night."

Mondo and Harris laughed, shifting their weight where they sat, and adjusting their guitar straps.

"No really," she continued, not willing to let it go. "Wouldn't that be something, to have them come to your room at night?" she said to the others sitting with her. "I'd pay for that, yes I would." They others smiled or nodded in a non-committal way.

"Can you play Bojangles?" asked Miranda remembering their talent show performance. The musicians did, plus a couple more tunes that afternoon before they all agreed they would set up again some other time on the patio, that there had been enough music and sunshine for one day.

As they stood up with the spectators thanking the musicians, and the musicians thanking the spectators, Diana reiterated. "I'm serious. Think about what you would charge for a little serenade before bed."

"We'll think about it," Mondo replied.

~

Two days later, Mondo was in Harris' room watching the Giants play the Pirates, when, in between innings, he asked Harris, "So what do you think about what Diana said?"

"What part of what Diana said?'

"About playing tunes in her room. You know… serenading."

Harris looked at Mondo with a scrunched-up face like he was crazy, then asked "Are you crazy?"

Mondo looked and Harris and said a little snippily, "No. I think it merits consideration."

"No," Harris countered, "I think it has trouble written all over it, *especially* with Diana."

Mondo did not respond. The next inning started and the men resumed watching the game.

"Wanna a beer or something," asked Harris.

The men drank their beers and watched the Giants win 7-4.

At the end of the game, Mondo stood, took his beer bottle to the trash can under the sink, and said, "Thanks for the brewskie and ball game."

"My pleasure."

"I'll bring the beer next time."

"You don't have to," replied Harris.

"Oh, I do," he said to his friend. "I'm also going to sing to Diana, at night, in her room."

"You don't want to do that," said Harris using his best warning voice.

"Oh, I do on that one too. And I'm charging one dollar for a couple of tunes before bed. I'm calling it Mondo's Tuck-in Service."

"I think you're crazy."

"And this advice is coming from someone who behaved like a sixteen-year-old not too long ago," Mondo said calmly. "I'll let you know how it turns out."

~

Two days later, Mondo walked into breakfast the same time Harris did. Though the men rarely ate meals together and had never had breakfast together before, Mondo followed Harris to the table that Harris picked out. "I'm having me a waffle, sausage, and two eggs on the side," said Mondo with enthusiasm and without looking at the menu.

"Pretty definite and upbeat for this early in the morning, aren't you?" asked Harris.

"And why shouldn't I? It's a beautiful day. I can order whatever I want. Why shouldn't I feel upbeat?"

"Is that so?" said Harris with no early morning pep. "I'm starting to see why we haven't eaten breakfast together before."

"Besides, last night was the first Mondo Tuck-in, and it went *great*!"

"Really?" Harris asked suddenly sounding more alive. "Diana?"

"Yep. Diana, and I promise to only mention that it went great six or seven more times… I think I found my new calling!"

"Oh boy! So, what happened? How many songs did you play?"

After they ordered, and then while they ate, Mondo was more than happy to go over every detail of the first Mondo Tuck-in performance, all 16 minutes of it by his count. He had played three songs, two of them instrumentals. All slow and appropriately relaxing, Mondo explained. She left the door open for him at 9:30. She was in bed. No, there hadn't been any funny stuff. She stayed on her side as if ready for sleep, but never went to sleep. During his second song, he noticed a couple of stuffed animals on her bureau. After the third song, Mondo explained, he got up, grabbed a stuffed kitten, went over to her side of the bed, slid the kitten under her arm, and tucked the covers around her nicely. He told her to sleep well, she replied *nigh', nigh,* and he left.

"Wait. You actually tucked her in?"

"Actually, yes."

"You didn't really put a stuffed animal under her arm?"

"Sure did…the white kitten, as I recall. She seemed to like it."

"And she said *nigh', nigh*'".

"She did."

"Did you plan all this out?" Harris asked genuinely interested.

"Only the songs. The rest came to me."

"Dude…Mondo…you're a natural… but I fear for you. This has trouble etched all over it…and I promise to only mention that six or seven more times."

"Like what?" he asked as he dipped a fork full of waffle into the egg yolk and chewed it.

"Like, she's going want that every night, for starters, that's what!"

"So?"

"So, she's a blabber mouth and she going to tell others."

"Still not seeing a problem here," Mondo replied.

Harris just shook his head and ate his breakfast without asking any more questions about Mondo's first tuck-in.

As Harris predicted, Diana did tell others, hardly needing to embellish any of her experience. She shared it at lunch. Rex scoffed, of course. "What kind of priest would do that for God's sake?"

"He used to be a priest. He's retired now. I asked him to sing to me."

"What kind of woman would ask a priest to her room late at night?" Rex said sounding as disgusted as he could make himself sound.

"Are you jealous, Rex?" asked Mrs. Hannigan, who had taken Miranda's place at Rex's lunch table. "Why I do believe you're jealous, and I think it sounds lovely."

"It was lovely," said Diana. "You should try it," she suggested to Mrs. Hannigan.

Mrs. Hannigan did knock on Mondo's door the next afternoon and booked Mondo for 9:00 that night. "9:30 is reserved for Diana," he mentioned when she initially asked for that time.

Within three days, Mondo had 8:30, 9:00 and 9:30 booked most evenings. Soon he had a wait list. He then decided to go to appointments every 20 minutes…15 of those minutes were with each client, while allowing five minutes to travel between rooms. Starting at 8:40 he was booked most nights with an 8:40, 9:00, 9:20, and 9:40 appointment. After four weeks, he had to break it to his faithful that he needed Sunday and Thursday nights off. Mondo's Tuck-in Service needed some rest!

He apprised Harris of his progress every few days. Late one morning, he showed up at Harris door very excited. "You got a minute?" he asked. And before an answer came, he walked toward one of the barcaloungers, moved a shirt from its cushion, sat down, and kicked aside a pair of Harris' dirty socks from in front of the chair. "My calendar's full," Mondo exclaimed. "It's crazy! Women want me! I can't keep up."

"Do you remember me warning you?" Harris asked.

"I remember you warning me," Mondo replied while smiling.

"And for the record, they want your guitar playing and that little tuck-in thing you apparently do," Harris said instantly regretting throwing cold-water on Mondo's ego parade. "Please tell me you don't really tuck in a kitten or teddy bear with everyone, do you?"

"I play it by ear. Assess the situation, you know. It comes with lots of experience," replied Mondo sounding authoritative.

"Ahh, I see. Mr. Experienced now, are we?"

"You want in on the action? I can send a little your way, if you want?" asked Mondo half seriously and half rubbing it in.

"Naw, I'm good. Thanks anyhow."

"Check this out." Mondo handed him a business card. Harris looked at it.

"*Days End Tuck-in Service*?" read Harris flipping over the card to see an image of a guitar propped up on a bed's headboard.

"Yeah, decided against *Mondo's Tuck-in* just in case you ever join me."

"How considerate. By the way, dude, you're getting the hang of this single stuff in ways I never imagined. Leavin' me in the dust, actually."

"Why thank you." Mondo went over and pulled Harris' landline phone out of its charging cradle. "Look at this. Can you see what my number spells?"

Harris looked at the business card and then at the phone. "488-2546." He pondered it awhile before saying, "Too many possibilities. No idea."

"4-tuck-in. 488-2546 is 4-tuck-in. It was available when I called to check on numbers. Is that amazing or what?"

"Pretty amazing," Harris said less than convincing.

"I tell ya, you oughtta get in on this," replied Mondo before heading out the door.

CHAPTER SEVEN

Harris was in his room one afternoon after Mondo had given him another update on his new enterprise. He was happy for Mondo. He really was. Tuck-ins may not have been exactly what Mondo was looking for, but he seemed really charged up and no longer the geeky, pathetically desperate priest Harris first witnessed. Of course, Harris was happy for him. Mondo was a good guy. He deserved some esteem, some affirmations. It seemed like they were coming in abundance now for Mondo.

Harris, on the other hand, had hit a funk. He had been at The Ridge long enough to have its newness wear off, with routine and boredom taking over. What had he really hoped for, expected? College life part two? Wild card games? Keggers in his room? Mating opportunities with hot 75-year-olds?

None of that had occurred, nor was it likely to with a life relegated to flipping channels and hanging out with Mondo. It wasn't a bad life, he thought. Three squares every day with more calories than he could possibly burn. Someone cleaned his place and did his laundry once a week. Even the tiny, one-bedroom apartment did not bother him. It even seemed like things were going to work out financially, that he wouldn't run out of money. Still, he had hoped for more. Instead, he watched himself revert back to the Harris of the previous two decades…an introvert who didn't have much going on, or, in this mind, have much to offer. Since his divorce he had chosen the tv remote and his chair almost continuously over getting up and trying something new and making something happen. Habits die hard. Changes of scenery only go so far.

Harris would look at his self-advice in the *Notes* part of his phone periodically that reminded him to *be active, get out, be around other people, volunteer, create, play…do something*...and he'd think *that's pretty good, I'm going to do that*. A couple of times he jumped into his car and drove. Once he caught the ferry to San Francisco, walked around, and had a fine time. Another day he played nine holes with a retired couple. He played lousy and it ticked him off. The couple was nice, but they had each other, and that amplified his aloneness. He went back to his apartment that day feeling worse than when he left.

One pleasant spring day he sat in the chair watching the walkers pass by outside with more interest than whatever was on TV. He wanted to get up and go outside, but couldn't summon any ambition until he saw Miranda walking. She held a cane, but was moving well. The two had hardly seen each other since the Rex incident and the guitar playing on the patio, only twice sharing a meal at a table with others. But if anyone seemed grounded and reasonable besides Mondo, it was Miranda. He had felt a connection with her since that Rex table debacle.

Without thinking, he stood up, went out his back door and caught up with her. Simply taking these steps in her direction surprised him and made him nervous. He wasn't sure what he was going to say, but when he asked, "Like some company?" he was certain what her response was going to be.

She stopped and looked at him, processing who had just snuck up behind her and what he had just asked. "Why, yes. That would be nice."

"Looks like you're moving pretty well these days," he offered.

"The warmth helps. I just need to get out more often."

"The couch and the remote are getting too much attention from me too," he replied with a voice that pleased him.

She smiled, but otherwise did not respond. They began moving at Miranda's pace, clockwise around the property's perimeter.

"It is lovely outside today," she said after a few silent steps.

"Nuthin' like a warm Spring day to change an attitude," he replied.

"My Spring resolution is to get more exercise. I figured there were no excuses today with this weather."

"Good for you," he said. "I'm needing some motivation like that. The newness of this place has worn off. The introvert in me is taking over."

"That happens to all of us, I think."

As they walked and talked about small things, he looked at her. He noticed her in ways he hadn't before. For a woman no more than 5'5", she stood tall, erect. There was no slouching, no stoop to Miranda. It made her look confident, even regal. He also wondered why she carried a cane. Her balance seemed fine, nearly as good as his, and she walked at a good pace, although she did seem to favor one side. He asked her, "So why the cane?"

"I had a hip replaced about four years ago. There were complications and they had to do it over again. It was excruciating. It's still not right, and they tell me the other one is going. I'm going to put that replacement off as long as I can."

"Don't blame you," he said. "Sorry to hear that."

"Thank you," she said with kindest of voices while looking at him. "I've learned to sleep on my back. I'm only good for about 20 minutes on either side."

With the day being in the high 70's already, and Miranda wearing a sleeveless blouse, he noticed her physically for the first time. Her arms were pale from not having seen the sun, but with the slightest hint of color, the remnants of her Sicilian heritage. *You have olive oil in your veins,* grandfather Russo used to tell her whenever she tanned easily and never burned as a young girl.

Harris also discreetly noticed her arms were also a little loose, but not with the severe flabbiness that was too prevalent with women at The Ridge. Her hands were slender and unbruised, a younger look to them than what he was seeing in the other women here. Unlike Mondo, he wasn't hoping or expecting to find a mate at this place, this stage of life, but he did notice such things. But what caught his attention most this warm day in her blouse, was her physique. She had curves. He tried not to stare. He had never been a gawker, but Miranda had real curves. He glanced at them more than once when she wasn't looking. Very quickly. It was something he hadn't noticed before when she was wearing sweaters or jackets.

After some silent steps, they reached a wooden bench which faced the nearby creek. "Mind if we sit for a bit?" she asked.

"Of course not," he answered while looking to help her turn and sit, although she needed no help.

"Just lovely."

"Yes, it is."

"I think most of us are introverts, Mr. Archibald. And we live in this extroverted world with so many expectations for us to be bright and charming and clever."

"Clever seems to have emerged as the front-runner recently, from what I can tell," he said settling into the flow of conversation she was setting.

She laughed a little and added, "I think you're right. And I think being clever is a lot to expect at my age."

"I think you can be interesting, of value, without being clever," he offered.

"Well, that's a nice notion, but I'm not sure I'm all that interesting either Mr. Archibald." She looked at him…a hope for some kind response from him dashed through her mind, before realizing he hardly knew her.

After another short pause without him knowing where to take things, she asked, "Do you listen to podcasts, Mr. Archibald?"

"I've just started to," he said, "out of curiosity more than anything. I wasn't sure what they were all about. I'm starting to like them actually."

"Me too! I like them a lot. They're good company at different points in the day. I learn some things I hope might make me more interesting, or at least entertain me."

"It's funny," he added, "our parents grew up listening to the radio for entertainment. These podcasts use our hearing sense only. It's a nice change from all the visual stimulation of our screens."

She looked at him as though he had said something profound before saying, "I think you're right." She grabbed her cane again, leaned forward, and said, "Can we walk again?"

They continued their loop around The Ridge property. When they came back to the point where Harris had joined Miranda, she said, "I think I've had enough for one day. Thank you for joining me."

"I'm glad I did. Maybe we could do it again?" he suggested more than asked.

"Same time tomorrow?"

"I'll look for you and come out when I see you."

"Excellent," she added. "How about you tell me about a podcast you've liked. I'll do the same."

"Homework," he said. "It's been a while. I'm on it."

"Bye."

"See you tomorrow."

Each of them returned to their little apartment feeling much better about life, in general, and the day, in particular.

Harris was especially pleased with himself and the gumption it took to go outside and walk with her. He also noticed that, though he'd only had a few encounters with Miranda, his voice, his cadence was different around her than with any female in a long time. He liked who he was around her and it made him happy to think there would more opportunities to feel that way.

The following morning, Harris sat in his favorite chair flipping channels but paying little attention to the screen or the noise coming from it. Every few seconds he glanced out his glass back door and the window next to it. He was less than certain what time he had first seen Miranda yesterday, and of course, she might not begin her walk at the exact same time this day, so he felt the need to scan.

He'd done his homework the previous evening. He hadn't listened to that many podcasts but there were a couple that had stuck with him. He selected the one that he thought was most appropriate for their next walk, the one he hoped would go over well. He even thought about how he would tell her about it, getting the words straight in his mind without talking too much or over selling it. He brushed his teeth twice, shaved, and combed his hair with his fingers. He reminded himself of the advice he might give Mondo to not try too hard. He even found a different clean shirt. Eventually he saw her. She paused to look toward his window.

"Good morning," he said as soon as he came out the patio door.

"Good morning. I was wondering if this was your place. I'm sorry if I'm a tad late. I've slowed down in front of some other back doors so you wouldn't miss me. I forgot which one was yours."

"I've got the two hanging fuchsias, and a little patio set," he said pointing back toward the wrought iron table and chairs that were on his apartment patio.

"Ahh, I'll remember it now," she said as she resumed walking in the direction they had gone yesterday.

They walked for a while making small talk before Miranda brought up the homework assignment. "Did you come up with a favorite podcast?"

"I think I did. I don't recall the name of the podcast exactly. I think it was a *Fresh Air* segment from a couple of months ago."

"I love *Fresh Air*," Miranda interjected.

"Me too. The one I'm recalling was about childhood logic or something like that. Did you hear that one?"

"It doesn't ring a bell," she said.

"Good. The podcast interviewer," he began, "talked to different adults about the thinking they used in their childhood to make sense of the world. It was just a bunch of different anecdotes."

"Like what?" she asked.

"The one I remember best was about a seven or eight-year girl, I'll call her Jennifer, who was playing with her friend, Maddie. One day, Maddie told Jennifer she knew who the tooth fairy was.

"*Really?* asked Jennifer wide-eyed. *It's my dad*! Maddie replied. Jennifer asked, *How do you know? I saw him,*" Harris said, continuing to play multiple characters in the story.

"That afternoon Jennifer told her mom that she and Maddie knew who the tooth fairy was. *Oh, really*? said the mother trying to remain calm.

"*It's Mr. Henderson, her dad. Maddie saw him one night being the tooth fairy.*"

Miranda smiled with interest while listening to Harris tell the story.

Harris continued, "The mother said, *Oh, well maybe you ought to keep that to yourselves. You know, other children might want to believe something different.*

"So, they did," Harris added. "For years the two girls kept the secret to themselves, never telling anyone else. But over those years, Jennifer was always extremely nervous around Mr. Henderson. He looked like a normal business man going to work in a suit and tie, but she knew at night he was something else…something big. It was years before he could shake that nervousness around Mr. Henderson, even after she was old enough to understand differently."

"That is so cute," said Miranda.

"Of course," said Harris, "Jennifer's parents helped things along by signing the notes under Jennifer's pillow after another fallen-out tooth with *The Tooth Fairy, Mr. Henderson.*"

Realizing he was done, Miranda smiled looking at Harris then said, "That's an absolutely adorable story. I love that." She also loved the way he told it.

"Children's logic," he said. "There were others, but that was the one that stuck with me."

"I'll have to try and find that one. You're pretty certain it was *Fresh Air*?"

"Very certain."

They walked on slowly. After a while, Miranda said, "When I was about five, I had the feeling that someone came into my room late at night and touched me. Not in any perverse way. But I kept my head under the covers not wanting to look and see them. I distinctly remember thinking they had injected me with something what would allow them to follow my every move for the rest of my life. I was five years old! This was way before computers and computer chips, Mr. Archibald. I can't imagine having seen anything on TV at that time which would have triggered it."

"That is pretty strange. You never saw anyone? Maybe it was your mother checking on you in the night?"

"I asked her the next day. She said she hadn't."

"I'd better be careful around you if you've got some alien chip in you."

"Hardee-har-har. I think you're safe. I probably would have a had a follow-up visit sometime over the next 73 years, don't you think?"

"No, really, it's been nice knowing you," Harris said as he turned and pretended to be leaving her.

"So that all it takes for you to bail on me, huh? One little implanted computer chip from 73 years ago? Here I was starting to think you were a nice guy."

When they had finished their lap, Miranda made no signal that she had had enough, and neither did Harris. When it was clear they were going to continue, Harris asked, "So what's your favorite?"

"Well, there are so many I like, but now I'm reluctant to bring up the one I was planning to. If a little implanted computer chip can scare you off, what is *redefining infidelity* going to do?"

"I'm not sure, but you've got my attention."

"I'm not certain I can do it justice. It was fairly complex and might be a bit heavy for our second walk. Certainly not as charming as your story."

"Be not afraid to say what you are not afraid to think," Harris injected. "Someone famous might have said that. I'm just glad we're not talking about the weather."

"Me too. Okay, I'll give it a shot. What I remember is that this psychotherapist, Esther Perel, from Belgium I believe, was being interviewed after she had written a book about *rethinking infidelity*. She was the daughter of Holocaust survivors, and part of the interview was about her parents meeting and what it was like to grow up with them. But then it morphed into infidelity...

something she speaks and writes about. What I remember is how she started by saying *It's never been easier to cheat, and it's never been more difficult to keep it a secret.* She mentioned how most affairs would have died natural deaths before today's technology, but nowadays a phone laying around gets a reckless text, a found email, or a Facebook posting can bring something damning to the other spouse's attention where it is not forgotten."

"Hadn't thought about it in those terms, but yeah," he said showing interest in her topic.

"Then she got into things like *is a non-sexual but intense office relationship an affair?"* she continued. "*What about porn? Is it infidelity when your spouse hasn't wanted anything to do with sex for years and you seek someone else?*"

"Legitimate questions," he suggested while admiring how easily Miranda had taken this conversation to another level.

"I thought so too," she said. "The interview continued by talking about today's expectations for marriage. Today's couples want everything that we used to expect from a traditional marriage in terms of companionship, economic support, family life, and social status. But they also want romance, intimacy, passion, a best friend and trusted confidant, and something called a soul-mate. They expect all these things to last forever, and forever keeps getting longer."

"No wonder so many marriages end in divorce when they realize so much of the marriage comes down to shopping, paying bills, cooking, cleaning, and watching tv together," he said.

She nodded her head slowly three or four times while he finished his thought, then added, "Not to mention dealing with career disappointments, health issues, and those messy extended family complexities."

"I'm kinda glad I'm not on the dating market today," he said. "It seems pretty complicated."

"I think it *is* more complicated nowadays, but the podcast got me thinking about my own marriage, and maybe, sometime, I'll share some of that with you."

"I look forward to that when you're ready to share."

"Were you married long, Mr. Archibald?" she asked assuming that at some point he must have been married.

Harris paused a good while pondering her question, surprised at the turn in the conversation and unsure how much to reveal. "I was married too long."

Miranda looked at him with raised eye-brows wondering if there would be more.

"The woman of my dreams, turned into an overweight sloth who watched tv with me most nights for years…until I couldn't do it anymore."

"Oh my," offered Miranda.

"Details are probably best saved for another time," he said, doubting he would ever share the full story.

She nodded again in small motions, and then stopped walking. They had reached the end of the property where there was a side entrance. "I think I've had enough exercise for one day, Mr. Archibald. I can go in this entrance."

"You want some help to your room?" he asked.

"Thank you, but I think I'll be fine. She stood still and looked at him with a little smile before saying, "Thank you for the walk and talk today. I enjoyed both."

"Is there another homework assignment?" he asked. "Being the moderately perceptive person that I sometimes am, I think I passed the first one."

"Ahh, indeed you did, Mr. Archibald." She looked up at the poplar tree with new growth near them, "How about for tomorrow's walk, we share favorite movies?"

"Sounds like a plan. Same time?"

"Same time," she said smiling and slowly turned to open the side entrance.

The door was heavy. Harris kept it open while she entered the building.

Miranda had difficulty falling asleep that night. Her mind kept replaying their conversation. She could remember almost verbatim his telling of his podcast story about the tooth fairy. The story made her happy, but it really meant something to her that he had selected that particular story, that podcast to share. *And he told it so perfectly.*

She also recalled her words on *Redefining Infidelity*. She liked how she had explained it to him, but had she picked something too bold? What would he think of her for choosing that particular one to share?

She recycled these thoughts several times before drifting off to sleep.

CHAPTER EIGHT

They walked the next day at the same time. Miranda knew to look for the hanging fuchsias and wrought iron patio furniture. She only had to stop and glance a short while behind his apartment before he came out. Harris wore his best Butgachi long-sleeved, baby-blue and gray shirt, and rolled up the cuffs. He left the shirt untucked. Though uncomfortable about wearing it that way, he had noticed younger men always doing so in social situations.

Miranda noticed his shirt which she had never seen before and said, "You look nice."

They walked and talked in a nearly identical manner as the previous day. This day they each shared a few favorite movies. Over the nice spring days that followed, the homework assignments focused on books, restaurants, and places to travel. It was during the walk about their favorite travel destinations that Miranda suggested stopping to sit on the bench they had used during their first walk together.

Upon sitting and commenting about the beautiful day, she asked, "How is your friendship with Mondo coming along?"

"Mondo and I have carved out a nice little friendship. We have music and our ball games."

"He seems like a different man since you arrived," she said.

"It does seem like he's more comfortable in his own skin lately."

"He got rid of that awful plaid sports coat he used to wear every week to happy hour. If you had anything to do with that, thank you," she said with a smile while patting his knee.

"I may have mentioned something to him."

"And changing his name to Mondo…I bet that was your idea too. It was good for him. We don't think of him as a priest so much with a name like that."

"He's a good man. A bit needy and I'm not sure how it's all going to play out for him, but a good man," Harris added.

"He's *very* popular now," Miranda said playfully. "I guess he's been doing the tuck-ins for Diana for a while. Diana is awfully chatty about it all and has gotten others to sign up for it too. Seems like Mondo has a little harem that he cycles between most evenings. He's become a featured topic at dinners lately."

"When he showed me his schedule, I warned him there were likely to be some problems, but he doesn't want to hear any of that now. He's on a bit of a high."

"Good for him," she said as a closing thought on the subject. Miranda stretched out her legs, holding her feet a few inches off the ground for many seconds before putting them back down. "I wonder what he's going to do when a guy asks him for a tuck-in?"

Harris let out a hearty laugh while bending forward from the waist. "That would never happen… would it?" he asked genuinely concerned for Mondo's sake.

"Oh, don't be surprised if it does."

"Really?"

"Really. And don't be surprised if it's Rex. Rex listens to the chatter about Mondo. He likes being the top dog around here, at least in his mind. I could see him stirring things up some way by booking a tuck-in and then making fun of it."

"Oh my," is all Harris could muster.

Miranda turned to face Harris on the bench. "Mr. Archibald, I'm going to ask you something. I want you to feel comfortable saying *no*, if that's what you want."

"That's quite a preface."

"I'm not going to call Mondo for a tuck-in." She paused before continuing, "Both you and Mondo sing and play guitar so well. I was wondering if at some point you might consider singing me a couple of songs right before bed?" She did a closed lips half-smile, as she looked at him more vulnerably than she had looked at anyone in decades.

"Well, be still my heart."

"Like I said, you can say *no*, or you can think about it for a long time, if you want."

"What if I say *yes* right now?" he added.

"That would be fine."

"Under one condition."

"Which is…?" she asked drawing out her last word.

"Mondo asked me to jump in with him on the tuck-ins, but I don't really want to have a big schedule like him. So, if you don't mind keeping our tuck-in just between you and me, I'd appreciate it."

"And Mondo, if you want" she said.

"You and me and Mondo," he clarified. "And could I give him a heads up on your Rex prediction?"

"Sure. Hope I'm wrong, but it can't hurt to be prepared," she added.

He stretched his legs out but kept his feet on the ground. "When do I get started?"

"How about we skip our walk tomorrow and do a singing tuck-in at 9:30 tomorrow night?"

"See you then," he said feeling mixed emotions.

"See you then," she said very happily.

That evening there was no ballgame for Harris and Mondo to watch. He sat in one of his chairs, with the tv and lights off, drinking a beer, while the sun was setting. He again recalled the conversations he and Miranda had had the past few days…their podcast shares, her recollection of possibly being implanted with a chip in her youth…her suggesting a tuck-in and all the other topics. He remembered them word for word. He wondered why she had selected *Redefining Infidelity* among the universe of podcasts to share. Did she mean something by it? Why was he intrigued by what he perceived as boldness on her part to do so? Why did he like his voice and himself better around her? He stayed with these thoughts until it was completely dark in his apartment. Then he turned on a light, pulled his guitar out of its case, and began practicing some songs for the next night.

CHAPTER NINE

Rex ate lunch with the Veterans once a month in the private dining area. It had been a group with a monthly event long before he arrived. He enjoyed the company with the guys, where they could close the door and be a little irreverent and politically incorrect now and then. This day, however, Rex's daughter showed up just as the veterans had been served beverages. A waitress had helped her locate her father. When she entered the room and Rex looked up and saw her, his mouth opened. A look of confusion took over his face.

"Hi, daddy. Am I interrupting something?"

"Oh, hi, honey. What are you doing here? Is today the day we were going to do lunch?"

"I think so. If today's not good, I can come back another time."

"No, no. Fellas this is my lovely daughter, Lauren. I'm going to need to excuse myself because I can't keep track of my busy social calendar." Rex stood up from the table, went over and hugged his daughter who was dressed in a lavender business suit with black heels. "Good to see you, honey," he said softly as he hugged her. "Gents, I'll catch up with you next month. I'm gonna have lunch with the boss."

As they seated themselves at a small table along one wall in the main dining room, Lauren asked "Daddy, who are those men?"

"Oh, that's nothing. It's just a small group of veterans who get together once a month for lunch and to embellish the past."

"Well, I can see how you've fit into that last part, but you weren't in the military."

"Now honey, that don't seem to matter much. A couple of them assumed I was a vet, and I didn't feel like correcting them. They keep inviting me. Must like my company or something."

"Ahh," was all Lauren could offer back. She'd had had a lifetime of partial truths and misconceptions with her father.

Lauren and Rex finished their lunch together as they tried to do once a month or so. "Thanks for coming by dear. I'll try to remember to write down our lunch date next time."

"It all worked out. I'll call you soon. Behave yourself, daddy."

Rex was not much for writing things down. Truth was he didn't have a calendar. He had so little going on outside of The Ridge, he felt it was unnecessary. His daughter kept track of his infrequent doctor appointments besides driving him to and from. When he needed a haircut, he just walked upstairs to the salon. He was secretly glad he'd forgotten about their lunch, or at least pleased Lauren came in and he got to introduce his beautiful daughter to the group. She helped him look good at The Ridge. Also, in some convoluted Rex way of thinking, not bothering with the details of his schedule also helped his *I'm too important to worry about trivial matters* image.

Rex was not an unhappy man. He just thought happiness was overrated, something liberals chased. *Being content* was about all man could hope for, and most days he was content. He prided himself on being a self-made man. Nobody ever gave him anything, was never on welfare, and he tried to stay informed. Not one much for reading, his television was on most of the day, going between the financial news station and FOX News. Between the two, he knew he was getting everything he needed to know about the state of affairs in his country and the world.

Being so well informed, he often shared his insights with his lunch and dinner companions. Just last week he asked his dinner mates if they had seen the controversy and rioting at UC Berkeley a couple of nights before. Some nodded affirmatively, but when no one offered a comment, he said, "They pride themselves on a history of free speech and all, but as soon as someone comes along they don't agree with, they try to stop him from speaking at all."

"But wasn't the speaker a white supremacist?" asked Diana.

"Now there you go. If he was or wasn't, does it make one damn bit of difference? Free speech is free speech. I believe it's guaranteed in the Constitution."

"Yeah, but there are also laws against hate crime and hate speech," she rebutted.

"You can *yeah-but* all you want, but do you want to tear up the United States Constitution and start over?" He paused for effect. "I didn't damn think so."

The group fell quiet, as it often did when Rex punctuated his points by cussing. They resumed eating their salad or spooning their soup in silence, when the man in the wheelchair, Setesh, who rarely spoke, said softly, "I think there is something in there about freedom to protest too."

Rex was quiet for a minute. Arguing with two people at once was rare at meal time, but it was not beyond his capability. He just needed an extra moment to process how protesting fit in the conversation. Finally, in his most calming, patronizing voice said, "You can protest. Go right ahead. They can protest. That is their right. Just don't expect me or anybody else to give up our right to say what we want just 'cause you disagree with it."

"I don't think the people at Berkeley were expecting him to stop his speech," added Diana. "They were probably just calling attention to the fact that giving a white supremacist talk, in this day and age, is wrong."

"Then they don't have to go and listen to the speech if it's not of interest to them. That's all they've got to do. There no need for rioting. It's really quite simple."

"I think you're missing the point," said Setesh.

"I think you all are ruining my damn dinner," said Rex quite disgusted.

Setesh, while looking at his soup bowl, and between spoonfuls, said, "It's about time."

Rex put down his fork and looked straight at the man in the wheelchair. "What kind of name is Setesh, anyhow? Are you even American? What do you know about the Constitution?"

Setesh put down his spoon and looked directly at Rex. The others stopped eating, focusing all their attention now on Setesh.

"Setesh is an Egyptian name, but I am every bit as American as you are. I have been a citizen since my youth, took the same history and civics classes as you, and have paid taxes since I was 16."

"Citizen since your youth, heh? Well, my family has always been American."

"Really? What tribe do you come from?"

Rex leaned forward and glaring said, "Excuse me?"

Setesh looked back at him directly, and with all the feigned kindness he could muster said, "If you are not from a native American tribe, then you and I are not too different after all." He then tipped his bowl to the side and scooped out the last bit of soup.

Rex ate the rest of his meal in silence, as did Setesh. Diane and the others made small talk. Rex was the first one to stand to leave when he had finished but others had not. While he put his crumpled napkin directly on his dinner plate he said, "I hope you all's attitudes improve with a good night's sleep."

The others sat there in silence for a full 15 seconds after he had left before Diane, smiling, said, "Well, that was interesting."

And it was. It had been one of the few times Diana had sparred with Rex, and it was one of the first times Setesh had spoken directly to Rex *ever*, let alone in a confrontational way. Though Rex did get in the last word with his snarky departing comment, his silence after Setesh's remarks was stunning to the group.

The following morning, prior to lunch, Rex called upon Mondo.

CHAPTER TEN

With a regular schedule of women who wanted to be tucked in, business cards, a vanity phone number, and a chatty champion of his cause in Diana, Mondo was set. Not only did he retire his gaudy sports coat and his saddle shoes, but he sat back with Harris during Friday Happy Hour, never standing to dance, rarely scanning the crowd. Sometimes he skipped Happy Hour all together. He was experiencing the wonder of being the pursued rather than the pursuer.

It was a life that couldn't have been more different than his world as a priest. He still said Sunday Mass as a visiting priest when asked, but couldn't remember the last funeral or wedding he had performed. The need to hear confessions had tapered down over the previous decade, people feeling less inclined to confess through a priest than they used to. The only exception to that was right before Easter. Then, most parishes held a community reconciliation night, whereby parishioners were encouraged to confess their sins at least this one time during the year. Father Armando was recruited twice this Spring for that service. He happily went.

Father Armando had long felt that hearing a person's verbal confession was always his greatest responsibility as a priest. Sometimes the most private of things were said in the confessional. Often, sins were verbally delivered cavalierly, without much emotion. Sometimes they were delivered with overt embarrassment and shame. With children, it was often clear they had been coached and were straining to come up with something, anything.

Over time, he began noticing there were patterns by age range. Father estimated he'd heard from children, "*I was mean to my brother or sister*" thousands of times. "*I had impure thoughts*, and *I used bad language*" was common among late teens, twenties, and thirties. Some people in these age groups had felt it necessary to confess solo sex, and others did not. He supposed a lot of the latter had to do with whether the confessor had gone to Catholic schools or not.

It was the people in their 30's, 40's, and 50's that Father listened to the most closely and wondered most about. When someone confessed to stealing property or embezzling a large sum of money, it was not the priest's role to enquire more, but rather only to assume the person was truly sorry and asking forgiveness. But not having stolen a single thing in his life, he couldn't help but wonder how much was embezzled and how they'd gone about it, and whether the person would ultimately get caught. He had never had a person confess murder, but knew of two priests who had. If he had heard someone confess murder, he knew he would abide by the priest's code and not take it any further by trying to remember the voice or do anything that would alert law enforcement. His role was to simply forgive, on God's behalf, the person who had come to confess their sins, and give them a standard penance of Our Father's and Hail Mary's.

Only once had he questioned a person on their remorse and sincerity of confessing. It had been to what sounded like a teenage boy, who had done horrible acts to live cats. The boy seemed too casual, too flippant about confessing these deeds to Father. He asked the boy if he was truly sorry. When the boy said, "Yeah, I guess so," Father told the boy he needed to be remorseful and that he needed to commit to never doing these acts again. When the boy was quiet, Father said, "For your penance 20 Our Father's and 20 Hail Mary's, and I want you to get some counselling from someone who is qualified in such matters. These animals do not deserve what you are doing to them."

It was the only time Father Armando had ever given that many prayers as penance, and the only time he had every suggested counselling during a confession. He often wondered what became of that boy.

He wondered too about the lives of mature men and women who confessed adultery to him. What had become of each of their marriages? Had their spouses found out? Did the adulterers continue their ways with the same partner or move onto others? Most were confessed with genuine shame and sincere regret. He couldn't recall one instance when he felt the man or woman confessing their transgression wasn't committed to changing their ways.

For a priest who had taken a vow of chastity, the mechanics of having an affair seemed more mysterious that the sacrament of confession. How had each affair unfolded? Who had taken the first bold step? What had they said or done that moved it past flirtation or infatuation to the point of no return? How thrilling and scary had it been? How rapidly did it move from A to B to Z? A priest had many quiet evenings. Some of the evenings were spent imagining the sequence of events, and were fodder for his own celibate ruminating.

Only one time did Father Armando behave inappropriately upon hearing a person's confession. A woman, he guessed her to be in her late 30's or early 40's, was doing her first confession in over 11 years. She seemed near tears with her voice soft and nervous while confessing to seven affairs with married men. "Some were brief and some lasted months," she said. "I don't know the exact number of times with each, Father."

Father was quiet for a while. His mind raced from curiosity about her looks, to wondering how these events had unfolded for this woman, to how each had played out for the seven men and their wives. His mind flashed with these and other thoughts including how to respond to this woman who was so ashamed and remorseful. He regretted it the very moment he heard his own voice say, "You must be very good." When she did not respond, he quickly added, "For your penance, three Our Father's and three Hail Mary's. Go in peace. God loves you."

He waited a long time in his confessional that afternoon, long after confession was scheduled to end. He wanted to make certain the church was empty. He had humiliated himself and brought shame to the Catholic Church and priests everywhere. How could he have said that? How could he have been so insensitive? What was he possibly thinking? He confessed this lapse the following week to another priest. He disguised his offense by saying he'd been horribly insensitive to the needs of others. He never did anything like that again in the confessional.

Father Armando had remained celibate all these years. He had struggled with it. There had been instances whereby women, sometimes attractive women, cried on his shoulder. Outside of the confessional, face to face, some women had confided in him too much about their private matters. He learned that intimacy was often not sexual, but was knocking on celibacy's door. He had been tempted, and had come dangerously close multiple times to crossing the line. Sometimes there had been signals from these women, some whom he had known for years, that were confusing to him. Thankfully, he thought, he had never crossed over.

He had missed out on sex with another person, but it was the life he had chosen. After he was ordained at 29 years of age, in those long nights alone he prayed a lot and reminded himself what he received in return for his celibacy. He tried hard to *not* think about what he was missing, what female flesh against his might feel like. He learned that trying hard not to think about it didn't solve the problem.

The seminarians had been counselled about these matters. While their professors and counselors were not entirely dismissive of their carnal needs, their assurances of having a higher calling, and *That is what prayer is for,* were of little help for the lonely priest in his twenties, thirties, and forties with urges. It had been a battle for him, this matter of celibacy. The topic had gone unspoken with friends and other priests, but it had been his biggest life-challenge. The eyes of the church would consider him the victor for having prevailed all these years. Why then, did he feel like he had lost out on something. Why had he often felt like a loser?

CHAPTER ELEVEN

Mondo initially refused Rex's request for a tuck-in that evening. When Rex said, "Well I might have to bring your little shenanigan service to management's attention then," Mondo felt backed into a corner. He fell silent.

"I thought you'd see it my way," said Rex after some time. "I think 9:30 would be about right. Is there anything I'm supposed to wear?" he added just to agitate things.

"I'm booked from 8:30 on."

"Well, that's too bad. 8:00 is much too early. I guess you're going to have to move things around or I'm going to be seeing the General Manager. I'd say it's your move."

Again, Mondo fell silent assessing his options, then said, "I can do 10 o'clock, maybe five minutes after 10."

"That's more like it," said Rex.

"But that falls into my premium time. It'll cost you extra…a dollar a minute."

This time Rex was quiet before saying, "I'll take ten minutes…tonight. You'd better be worth it."

"Leave the door unlocked, and the money on the counter. What's your room number?

"227."

~

"What do I do?" he asked Harris. Mondo had rushed to his best friend's room immediately after finishing the conversation with Rex.

Harris had been planning on chatting with Mondo about the possibility of a guy, maybe even Rex, approaching him for a tuck-in. He assumed he had at least a couple of days to do so. Harris did not think Rex would approach Mondo the very next morning after Miranda had brought it up. Harris was caught off guard by the suddenness of this development and struck by Miranda's foresight. Still at this moment, his friend needed sound advice.

"What if you don't do it?" Harris asked.

"He said he'd go to management, the General Manager, I guess. Says he'd tell all about my shenanigans... the tuck-ins"

"You're really not doing anything illegal or immoral, are you?"

"Neither."

"So, what's the big deal?"

"Management could think tuck-ins were inappropriate and ask me to stop. That is my fear. You know I'm enjoying this. I don't want it to stop."

"So then do Rex. What's he going to do? Get naked and come onto you?"

"Probably not."

"He'll probably tell everybody about it tomorrow. Make fun of it somehow. Can you live with that?"

"I think so. The women I've been doing this for will know what the tuck-ins are like. Rex isn't going to sway them."

"So, there's your answer," Harris said matter-of-factly.

"There's my answer." Mondo looked and felt relieved, as relieved as he could be hours before his Rex tuck-in. He went up to hug Harris. They had not hugged before, but Harris opened his arms and the men embraced. "Thanks, pal," Mondo said once they had separated.

"There's one thing you might do to protect yourself, however," said Harris.

"Yeah? What's that?"

"Fully charge your phone, keep it in your pocket, and hit *video record* just before you enter his room. At least you'll have an audio recording if he should try to distort the truth."

"Buena idea," Mondo said spritely.

"Good luck. You'll be fine."

"I'll be fine and I'll let you know all about it."

"By the way, Miranda asked for a tuck-in. Tonight."

"You rascal," Mondo kidded. "I knew you'd come on-board."

"I'm not on-board."

"I'm glad I didn't call it *Mondo's Tuck-in*. Tonight's the first of many for you. Good luck, pardner."

"Breakfast at 8:00 tomorrow?" Harris asked. "Compare notes?"

"See you then."

CHAPTER TWELVE

"I'm here," Mondo announced tepidly.

"I'm in here, honey," Rex countered in a falsetto voice that confirmed to Mondo that things would be different this tuck-in.

Mondo walked cautiously into Rex's place. Not seeing him in the living room or kitchenette, he continued toward the bedroom fearing what he might discover. What he found was Rex sitting up against the headboard of the bed, with a dark tee-shirt on and the rest of his body under the covers. Mondo looked around for a chair. There was a simple wooden chair next to Rex's bureau that had his pants draped across. "Mind if I move these?" Mondo asked while lifting up the pants.

With the lamp on next to his side of the bed, Rex had no problem seeing what Mondo was referring to. "Sure, knock yourself out," he said. "I'm not sure what you expect. I decided not to get naked right away."

Mondo put Rex's pants on the bureau. He hadn't planned on revealing this, but after he put his guitar strap on over his head, but before he sat in the chair, he said, "You know Rex, if at any time I feel just a little more uncomfortable than I do already, I'm leaving."

"Whatever you want, honey. I just can't wait for you to play me something I like," he said continuing his poor female impersonation.

Mondo reached into his pocket. Again, he hadn't planned on this. He pulled out his phone and said, "I should probably let you know I'm recording this…to protect myself."

Rex was quiet for only a second or two while taking in what he'd just heard, then realizing what had transpired so far. His eyes bugged out, as did the veins on his neck before for he threw back the covers, made a motion like he was getting out of bed, and said, "You fucking asshole. I ought to kick your priest's ass all the way down the hall." He slid his legs out over the edge of the bed revealing his old-school whitey-tighties.

"That's it! This tuck-in is over," Mondo replied while quickly moving out the bedroom door.

Rex stayed seated on the edge of the bed, his bare feet reaching the floor. "That's right…get the fuck outta here."

Mondo reached for the front door knob to the apartment, and realizing Rex had remained on his bed, glanced over at the kitchen counter. A ten-dollar bill rested on it. Without thinking at all, but sensing there would be *some* ramifications, he took three steps toward it and snatched the money.

From his position on the bed, Rex could see what Mondo was doing. With this, Rex leapt out of bed and moved stiff legged toward Mondo. Mondo pulled opened the door and rushed out and briskly down the hall. As the door was closing, he heard Rex yell out, "You fucking thief. Give me back my money."

Mondo looked back just once, from about 50 feet down the hall. The door never reopened.

CHAPTER THIRTEEN

The following morning, Mondo was waiting in the dining room for Harris at 8:05. He had slept as unevenly as Harris had. When Harris arrived, they ordered breakfast before comparing notes in hushed tones. Mondo was pleased that Harris' encounter had gone much better than his own had. Harris was dismayed but not surprised that Mondo's experience with Rex had turned out the way it had.

While the men were nearly finished talking and eating, Rex sauntered in and sat at his regular table. Setesh, Mrs. Hannigan, and Diana were also just finishing up and about ready to head to their rooms." You're a bit late this morning, Rex, aren't you," said Mrs. Hannigan. "We just about gave up on you."

"Well, after the horrific experience I had late last night, I'm surprised to be here at all," he said in a loud voice for all to hear including the neighboring tables. "As soon as I order my bacon and eggs, I'll tell you about it…that is if you're interested. Setesh pushed himself back from the table and departed without saying a word. The women lingered.

"How about we get out of here?" suggested Harris after he and Mondo had heard Rex's pronouncement. "He's going to try to embarrass you."

"I'm good here," Mondo replied as if bracing for a fight.

"You really want to sit through it?" asked Harris.

"Bullies want to see you run," said Mondo with a tone that convinced Harris to stay.

After Rex had ordered, and his breakfast mates had shown a sufficient amount of yearning to hear his story, Rex began, "Well, I can tell you won't leave until I tell ya' what happened with my tuck-in from the padre over there." He tilted his head in Mondo's direction, while not making eye contact with him.

"Being well within my rights, I set up 10:00 last night to see what these tuck-ins are all about. I know many of you have tried them. I just wanted to see what you was getting yourselves into and whether you might be in danger." Diana and Mrs. Hannigan listened patiently, having been fully indoctrinated previously by Rex's b.s.

When they did not initially respond, Rex continued loud enough for Mondo and Harris to hear, as well as any others within that radius. "Not only did he charge me an exorbitant rate of a dollar per minute, he took off without playing one song and stole my $10 to boot. I don't know if he got cold feet performing for a man, but he suddenly bolted out of my place like a frightened kitten. Strangest thing I ever saw."

All eyes turned toward Mondo from Rex's table as well as the others within earshot.

"Stay here," Mondo said softly to Harris as he stood and headed the 12 feet or so toward Rex's table.

"Well, looky here. Are you going to fight me, Father Armando?" Rex bellowed as Mondo got close to him. "I thought you fellas were trained to turn the other cheek."

Mondo reached into his pocket, pulled out some paper money, and laid eight dollars in front of Rex. "You didn't have the exact amount. I'm guessing it was two minutes. Is that about right?"

"I reckon, before you skedaddled so fast, I didn't know what hit me."

"There's your change."

"Can't say I really got my money's worth…even at two dollars," he said while forcing a chuckle and repositioning himself in the chair. "In fact, I'd have to say your little side show is much ado about nuthin'."

Mondo nodded his head very slowly in mock agreement. There was the slightest smirk on his face as he held Rex's stare. "Ladies," began Mondo as he looked at Diana and Mrs. Hannigan. He pulled his phone from his left front jean pocket, held it high, and glanced around the room as he continued, "This is what really happened." He pushed the *play* button on the video he had queued up for this moment. Though there was nothing to see, the audio was clear. The dining room got very quiet except for the sounds of some dishes coming from the kitchen.

The audio from the phone began with Mondo's voice, *I'm here,* followed by Rex saying *I'm in here honey.*

Diana's jaw dropped immediately. Both she and Mrs. Hannigan turned to look at Rex. Rex jumped up from his chair and said, "You recorded that without my permission." He was speaking louder than normal, attempting to overwhelm any of the sound that was coming from Mondo's cell. "If you continue playing that, I will have my lawyer sue you for every one of the few dollars you have."

Mondo touched the screen to make it stop. He said firmly and calmly while looking at Rex, "You will lose, and you will lose the defamation of character lawsuit I will file, because, what I have here," he held the phone higher, "greatly contradicts the lies you have just spread about me to all these witnesses."

"You'd better not play it," said Rex as sternly as he could. All eyes turned to Mondo.

The two men glared at each other.

"Well, I'd like to hear it," said Diana after a brief silence.

"Me too," said Mrs. Hannigan.

"I think we all ought to hear it," said Harris approaching Mondo and settling at his side.

Mondo, looked at his phone, slid his index finger over it, and said, "I believe we missed a couple of things." Mondo played the entire recording. There were sighs and gasps at the *I decided not to get naked right away* part. When they heard Mondo say *I should probably let you know, I'm recording this…to protect myself,* several heads nodded. When they heard *you fucking asshole,* and *that's right…get the fuck outta here* from Rex, Mondo shut it off leaving them to wonder if there had been more, though there had not been.

Rex stood there motionless. Harris would later tell Mondo he actually felt sorry for Rex while watching this all unfold. When that last part was played, Rex pointed at Mondo and said, “Expect to hear from my lawyer, mister,” and hobbled, stiff-hipped away. When he had gone 20 or 25 feet, he turned and red-faced hollered, “You’re going to regret this!”

CHAPTER FOURTEEN

Miranda called Harris later that same morning. She had not walked at her normal time. Harris knew that, because he had been looking for her from his chair. "Can we schedule another one…tonight? The same time?"

"Why, yes, I believe my schedule permits that."

"Great, I'll see you then."

"See you then."

Harris let her lead the way. He had hoped for more conversation about last night, whether it was on a walk today or during the unexpected phone call he'd just received. Instead, Miranda was brief…friendly, but brief.

As he half-heartedly watched television in his tiny apartment that afternoon, his mind kept flitting back to *can we schedule another one…tonight?* He thought about his age and how he shouldn't need approval. He also thought about how he'd gotten almost no affirmations from his wife during their entire relationship. He felt like he was 16 again and suddenly hoping a girl would send him a flowery note. But as he sat there that afternoon, waiting for 9:30 to come, and rehashed the previous night's twenty minutes with Miranda and her call that morning, he realized two truths: wanting approval most likely never ends for *anybody*, and the words *can we schedule another one* were approval… absolute approval. Perhaps they weren't as flowery as the scripts from television shows, movies and novels that he had experienced throughout his life, but they were Miranda's way of doing things…and he liked her way.

9:30 did come. The second tuck-in went as smoothly as the first one had. Harris chose three different songs, all soft and soothing. How she positioned herself on the bed, where he sat, and what they said to each other was nearly identical as the previous night. He left satisfied and joyful.

The following morning Miranda called again. "Good morning Mr. Archibald. Thank you for last night. I enjoyed it."

"You're welcome. I did too."

"I was hoping today we could do a walk instead of a tuck-in?"

At first, he felt crushed, wondering why no tuck-in, but he responded, "Sure, sounds good. What time were you thinking?"

"How does 11:00 work for you?"

"I have a conference call with Michelle and Barack at 11:00," he said, "but I'll reschedule. 11:00 works perfectly."

"Great! Look for me as before. I'll see you then."

"See you."

Mondo had survived Rex nicely. Harris mentioned it briefly to Mondo the following day. "You handled it well," is all Harris needed to say. Mondo knew how he'd done, but still welcomed hearing it from his friend.

Mondo resumed his busy evening schedule. He had lost no business after Rex's tuck-in and their ensuing encounter. Word spread throughout The Ridge of the recording with Rex, with only minor embellishments. The community's perception of Mondo the man and minstrel, rather than Father Armando, was only enhanced with the recent Rex developments. Mondo hadn't thought this well of himself in many years. How others looked at him and spoke to him was different and better. The pecking order of males at The Ridge had flipped. The Ridge senior facility was becoming Mondo's domain, with Rex sliding toward the bottom rung. The latter was pitied by some, and labeled a foolish buffoon by others. Mondo and Harris still got together for some ball games, but not past 7:30 as before. Playing guitars together also tapered off as each was getting in enough music on his own.

Miranda took to eating meals in her room more often than not. Mondo and Harris rarely ate together. Rex tried his best at meals to act like nothing had happened after the incident with Mondo, but it was several days before he found his opinionated voice again. No one at his table ever brought up Mondo or the tuck-in service in his presence.

When Miranda appeared at 11 o'clock sharp outside Harris' patio, she was walking without a cane. "Good morning," she said with a smiling face. "Isn't it lovely?"

"Good morning. It's is lovely. Supposed to be the warmest day of the year so far," he responded.

Miranda had dressed with the weather in mind. She had a form fitting white blouse with its collar turned up to go with tight black jeans. He thought *she doesn't dress like however old she must be*. And while the bare front of her neck looked like the 78-year-old that she was, other parts of her conveyed something different.

"Where's your cane?" he asked.

"Oh, I forgot it."

He looked at her skeptically and said, "Really?"

"Yes, I really forgot it…on purpose. I figured if I'm walking with you, you can pick me up and dust me off, or I can grab your arm if I need some steadying."

He smiled then said, "You wouldn't be trying to flirt with me now, would you?"

"I'd say *yes* unless you thought I'd done it wrong. I'm a little out of practice."

"No, no. I think you did just fine."

"Good. How about we go in the opposite direction today?" she asked. As they turned to go in the counterclockwise direction around The Ridge property, she stuck her left arm around the crook of Harris' right arm.

"Do you text, Mr. Archibald?"

"I do."

"Good. I've decided that I'd like to contact you that way in the future, rather than phoning you. I didn't feel right calling you this morning."

"How's that?"

"It made me feel like I was in high school, nervously calling a boy."

"O-kay," he said drawing it out.

"Thank you. At my age, I'd rather not feel that way…ever again."

They walked the perimeter of the property twice. It took about 40 minutes with a rest built in. When they resumed after the rest, Miranda did not grab his arm, but they walked closely, brushing up against each other occasionally. He was not causing the contact with his straight stride, but he didn't mind.

When they reached the end of their walk, Harris glanced at his watch. I think I'm going to grab some lunch now. Do you care to join me?" When she paused with her response while looking at him, he too felt back in high-school…as an unpopular boy asking a cheerleader to the Prom.

"Thank you, but I've arranged to have my lunch brought in today. It's probably just about there."

He tried his best to hide any disappointment, and said nothing, hoping she would suggest a tuck-in.

"Perhaps we can schedule another walk and talk tomorrow," she suggested.

"Of course," he said with some relief.

She rubbed the side of his right arm with the back of her left hand and said, "Great. I'll find you at the same place, same time."

Harris ate lunch by himself, trying to connect the dots. There weren't enough to render any picture of what this was. He was beginning to feel something, but was it all just his imagination? The forgotten cane; the acknowledgement of flirting; the touching; the blouse. It was warm, how was he to know what she would have worn if she had walked by herself?

Back in his room he cycled through the same things, adding that she didn't want to go to lunch, that she hadn't booked a third tuck-in. Had he done something wrong? He had never been good at this…never gotten it right. In his pre-marriage dating life he either went too cautiously and the females lost interest, or was too aggressive and they took off. He wanted to do more tuck-ins, but only with Miranda. What was happening? It felt like high school, senior living style.

The next day they met a few minutes after 11:00. Miranda made no mention of running late. It was warm, already above 75 degrees.

"Which way?" he asked.

"Let's change it up each day," she suggested.

As they began walking clockwise again, she grabbed his right arm with her left. She was wearing a fresh yellow tee shirt with some embroidery up near the neck and shoulders. As she grabbed his arm, she leaned into him in a way that pushed her left breast into his arm before she straightened herself and walked as if nothing had happened.

When they had walked less than a lap, she asked if they could sit at the nearby bench. He helped her position herself on the bench before he sat, wondering to himself just how much help Miranda really needed. He then situated himself close to her but not quite touching. Within 30 seconds she turned away from him to admired the nearby roses. "Aren't they magnificent?" she said more than asking.

Before he could answer, "Pretty nice," she had turned to face him but somehow repositioning herself closer. Their legs and arms regularly brushed each other the rest of their time on the bench. He made a mental note of this and resolved to not moving a millimeter in any direction while they sat.

"I want to tell you something, Mr. Archibald."

"Why do you call me Mr. Archibald?"

"I like the sound of it."

"Not keen on Harris?" he asked.

"Harris is fine, but I like Mr. Archibald. It sounds so dignified. Did you like your name growing up?" she asked, willing to defer what she was inclined to talk about.

Harris thought about it, then said, "When I was young, certainly before high school, I didn't like it. There were no other Harris' around, and Harris combined with Archibald just sounded old, stodgy."

"I can understand that."

"But some time in high school I started to like having a different name, and the sound of it."

"Well good," she added.

"But I noticed as an adult that people had expectations for someone called *Harris Archibald*. I just had the feeling that they expected someone smart or worldly or dignified. I wasn't any of those things. I always thought they were disappointed once they got to know me."

"Oh dear," she said. "Well, I think it's a terrific name, and it's one that suits you just fine Harris Archibald."

It was from then that Harris felt like a better person whenever he was around Miranda. He stood taller. His voice sounded better. He was even more comfortable being quiet or picking his spots when he tried to say something insightful. He believed this person, Miranda, thought that not only his name was terrific, but he was as well. It had been a long time since he'd thought that.

But on this day, Miranda had something on her mind that she wanted to get out. "Relationships are tricky things," she began. "It seems like they can make you want to be a better person or break you, or a whole bunch of things in between." She stretched her legs out together in front of her and raised them a few inches before returning them to the ground. "I had a good marriage. I'm not going to badmouth my departed Ken. But like so many women of our time, I followed his lead on everything...where we vacationed, who we entertained, when we had sex, how we had sex. I was a good wife."

"You make it seem like it being a good wife isn't all that great," Harris interjected.

She sat quiet with her thoughts for a moment starring at her knees before saying, "Maybe I was different than most other wives, but I think not. Women put up with a lot for the sake of the marriage." Her head turned to look at him directly. "I think I loved him, but I also enjoyed a comfortable lifestyle. Those things blend together and I bit my tongue a lot to keep them going. I don't regret it and I'm not going beat myself up over anything about it. But since his death, I've had a lot of quiet time…you know, to reflect."

"And you'd do it differently next time."

"I'm not sure there will be a next time, but yes, it would be different." She paused a good while. "I'm a breast cancer survivor, Mr. Archibald. A single mastectomy when I was 59."

"I'm sorry to hear that," he offered. "Is everything okay?"

"They've made significant headway with breast cancer. I just take a pill a day now. It seems to be in remission."

"Good."

"But I ended up with these…" She thrust her chest forward and pulled her yellow shirt taught from the bottom. The mounds were round and prominent. "We had a choice to make. Ken lobbied for reconstructive surgery. It made sense to me as I didn't want to live out my days with only one very sad looking breast."

"Makes sense to me too. It seems like many women have chosen that route," Harris replied, not certain yet why Miranda was telling him this.

"Ken's interest in me…well our sex life anyhow, had tapered off to next to nothing before my surgery. I had been a sagging B, and was intrigued with the notion of going to a C. Ken convinced me how good I'd look going even bigger." Here she paused again, unsure how to continue her thoughts. "It really is the oddest thing, Mr. Archibald, to sit there and order replacement parts for your body out of a picture book. In the end I couldn't resist the opportunity to experience what bigger was like."

Harris just nodded silently, unclear if she had finished saying what she had to say.

"I just wanted to get that out of the way. It seems silly now that I've brought it up, but with the warmer weather, I thought you were bound to notice some irregularities in my physique."

"I may have noticed, but I didn't want to stare. And I'm not the kind of guy who's going to ask *are they real*?"

"I already know you're not that kind of guy. It's one of the reasons we're spending time together."

When they had sat there awhile looking at the nature around them, she said, "Well, shall we continue?"

"Before we do, I've got to ask…I'm not clear if you regret your decision or not?"

"My life changed a lot, from having cancer and having it cut out, to having a body that made me very popular. Ken couldn't keep his hands off of me. He actually became a nuisance. Men and women have looked at me differently ever since, and they treat me differently. I do have more confidence. Maybe I shouldn't say this, but I still like looking at myself in the shower and in the mirror. I can't believe it's me."

"All that seems pretty positive to me, except the nuisance part."

"It is and it isn't. Every other part of me has wrinkled and aged as it was supposed to. I've got these man-made mounds that are pretty firm and still well-shaped because they are just 19 years old. Men still want me. They wouldn't without them. They want to have sex with me. I don't want to have *real* sex, Mr. Archibald, but I do like the attention. It's the darnedest thing."

"I think we all want attention, to be noticed and wanted," he said. "It's one of the tougher things about aging."

"The weirdest thing is that they have around a twenty-year lifespan", she said. "Next year I have to make a decision about them…whether to have new ones put in…what size? I'm really dreading all that."

Harris nodded silently, unable to say anything meaningful. After a few moments he broke the quiet eye contact and stood. She grabbed his arm and they continued walking.

When she indicated she'd had enough and was ready to head to her room, he couldn't help himself and asked, "Are we supposed to eat some meals together or grab coffee or visit each other during the day?" He felt awkward and geeky as soon as he'd asked.

She was quiet for a time before touching his forearm with one hand and saying, "Mr. Archibald, you are very adorable. But I like how things are."

He got into his car and went to lunch downtown by himself. His head swirled with their most recent conversation. What had any of it meant? There were more dots to connect…the new with the old, but again they led to nothing conclusive. He tired of the dot exercise, the futility of it. He sensed he was falling… head-over-heals or in love? He wasn't sure. And yet the person he was falling for seemed content with walks and tuck-ins. He was growing more intrigued and confused by this person, Miranda. His attempts to steer or broaden their friendship were as senseless as trying to connect the dots.

They had ended their walk with him making a minor fool out of himself, or at least he thought so. And Miranda had not only shot down his suggestion for coffee or meals together, but made no mention of another walk or tuck-in.

That evening he watched the Giants-Dodgers game by himself and drank three beers.

The following morning, he received a text from Miranda. *Would like to schedule a tuck-in tonight. Does 9:30 work?*

CHAPTER FIFTEEN

Rex had learned to take on a certain persona on the oil rigs…talk tough, be tough, show no sign of weakness or sensitivity…be a guy's guy. The others would swarm on the guys who didn't fit that profile. Sure, there was the occasional female coworker that was dropped on them, but once the female coworker said something like, *What are you looking at, you ugly fuck?* or *god, your breath smells* she was treated like one of the guys.

He didn't like or understand political correctness. There was no need for it on the rig.

Whenever he returned home from his multi-week shift, he expected sex and to be fed, and lots of both. His mind-meanderings of sex while on the rig drove him to expect it his way when he got home. He brooded when reality played out differently.

When he brooded, he drank. When he drank, he brooded more. Rex knew he was not an easy man to live with, but what was he supposed to do? Go to counselling? Counselling was for humans with vaginas.

He lived in two completely different worlds; his home life and his work life. It seemed only fitting that a helicopter ride was needed to bridge them. The oil rig had its own culture, its own written and unwritten rules. That culture became apparent from Day One of a rigger's career. Whenever a newbie arrived, low-grade hazing that occurred. The young man, often called DAK for dumb-ass-kid, might be told during an intense part of a shift to run over to the man in the orange helmet and get the pipe stretcher. Though confused, amid the noise and activity there was no time for DAK to ask for clarification. The rookie would ultimately do as told. The orange helmeted supervisor would ask incredulously, "Pipe stretcher?" More times than not, DAK would turn, point, and say, "They sent me to get the pipe stretcher" only to turn and find the guys throwing their hands in the air then bending over in laughter.

The latest DAK might also be required to wear a frumpy dress and serve beverages to the other men for a couple of meals. All in good fun, Rex always thought. He believed that traditions were good, and these and other rig rituals had been traditions for decades.

Rex had participated in both of those rituals as a DAK, and some others. His father was on hand observing and laughing while his son went through them as the victim. There was nothing dad could or would do to alter things. It was the rig's rite of passage.

Rex did not have sons that followed his footsteps. He never had to watch them endure these customs that had institutionalized themselves over time. He, instead, had a daughter, Lauren, who was fortunate to be raised mostly by her mother. Her mother never bad-mouthed Rex to Lauren, but she intentionally did everything to encourage her daughter to branch out, to break the cycle of Rex Junior and Rex Senior. As a result, Lauren became highly educated, a professional, and sought out men different than her father.

It could be said that Lauren loved her father, and he loved her. They just never needed to talk about it nor did they really understand each other. During the time of Rex's stay at The Ridge, whenever they spent time with each other, they each silently wondered how they could be related. Rex was proud of his daughter, more than she was of him. Still, she looked after him. It was what good daughters were supposed to do. He enjoyed her visits. He mainly enjoyed showing off his daughter at meal time or throughout The Ridge common area. She knew he was proud of her, so she gladly played that role, visiting weekly, sometimes more if her schedule permitted.

Perceptions were important to Rex. Physically in decline, there wasn't much he could do about that. He didn't like getting old, but to him it's just what happens when you don't die. What he spent his energy on was being the main man at The Ridge. Showing off his daughter was part of it, being informed through FOX News, and sharing his beliefs was another part. He was confident in his beliefs, and why shouldn't he be? They were a lifetime in formation. If the other residents at The Ridge were too insecure or ill-informed to share their insights, then too bad for them. He had his voice, and by God, he was going to use it. What Rex had going for him was his wisdom about the world and his fearless willingness to communicate it.

Sure, he knew he offended people once in a while. He pitied them for being so thin-skinned, and for having been indoctrinated by the recent overload of political correctness and liberalism. If someone was a Jew, why couldn't you mention it any longer? If a woman had large breasts, was he supposed to pretend they didn't exist? Of course not. A Jew was a Jew, and big tits were…well…nice. Most women who had them were proud of them, he thought. Of course, they'd want you to notice them. And if you noticed them, why not say so? Otherwise, you are just pretending that you didn't notice them or they didn't exist. And to Rex's way of thinking, that just wasn't right.

Rex believed most people liked or admired him at The Ridge. He could tell by the way they looked at him or deferred to him at meals. He sensed most women secretly wanted him. How else could he have ended up with the best one in the place… Miranda? She had an amazing, man-made chest. He had seen it many times. That was just another sign that he was king of The Ridge.

Miranda and he had run their course. Didn't all relationships? Two people want and need different things…especially at their age. It wouldn't surprise him if Miranda still needed him sometime. He'd bide his time. He didn't mind that the other residents at The Ridge had gossiped about the two of them when they had been seeing each other. He did nothing to hide his trips to her room. No one needed to know exactly what they did or didn't do there. Leaving it to their imaginations and whispered conversations was sufficient in his mind, and good for the perception of him as The Ridge's alpha male.

That background, that history, was why Rex took his breakfast encounter with Mondo so hard. In a few short minutes, so much changed. He had seen it on their faces when Mondo played the phone recording. Surely, they understood he was kidding when he had said *I'm in here honey* and *I decided not to get naked right away*...but they didn't act like it.

There had been damage, serious damage to his reputation and standing at The Ridge. He was not certain quite yet what his next moves would be, but there was no way this would be the end of it.

CHAPTER SIXTEEN

TUCK-INS THREE, FOUR AND FIVE

For his third tuck-in with Miranda, Harris brought his iPad as well as his guitar. He didn't want the tuck-ins to become predictable and stale. Miranda did not have stuffed animals lying around her room, but he couldn't see himself working those in as Mondo had, even if she'd had some.

This night, he played one instrumental of his own creation, and one Paul Simon song, *Punky's Dilemma*. He had also queued up on his iPad, a piano solo he really liked. He played it as the last song, on low volume. He wasn't sure if she dozed off before it was finished. When it had, he picked up his things without her saying anything or moving. He left with his dollar and without making a sound.

The next morning, she texted, *That was lovely. I rudely dozed off before you left.*

He replied, *I'd call that success.*

Can you do that again tonight?

See you then, he texted back.

When Harris arrived at the standard time. Miranda was propped up in bed against some pillows and the headboard. The top of her black nightgown was above the covers in the dim light.

"I see you brought the iPad again," she said. "I wanted to ask you what it was that was that played on it last night."

"That was the piano version of *Clair de Lune.* Composed by Claude Debussy in the late 1800's. I found it and bookmarked it after Sylvia played it and won the talent contest. I like it too."

"I've heard of *Clair de Lune*, but had no idea that was it. It really is something."

"Glad you like it. I didn't want our tuck-ins to get too predictable."

"Bonus points for that," she said smiling. It surprised and delighted him when she said things like that, things that defied her age.

"Ready to begin?" he asked.

"Yes, please," she replied sliding down under the covers and rolling onto her right side to face him for the first time.

He played two instrumentals this time. She closed her eyes for several seconds a couple of times, but otherwise watched him with the look of a contented woman. There was no drifting off during this tuck-in, their fourth. After the beautiful finger picking, he reached for the iPad, kept it on the floor so that when he turned it on, the light it emitted would not disturb her. He selected *Clair de Lune* again. When it finished, she was still looking at him with a tiny smile. She made a little noise along the lines of "Mmmmm."

"Night," he said softly.

"Can we walk in the morning?" she asked.

"I'll be looking for you."

"See you about the same time."

~

The following morning, she appeared on the path behind his patio. The weather had changed. It was cool and breezy and threatening a final Spring shower. "It's much too cold for a walk," she observed.

"Yes, the weather has really turned," he added. "Would you like to come inside instead?"

"That would be lovely," and she entered his rear door as comfortably as a life-long friend would have. After he moved a tee-shirt and his slippers from the floor, she sat on the love seat, he in one of his chairs.

"I can't get over that *Clair de Lune*," she said. "I just love it."

"I'm glad. Clearly, I do too, or I wouldn't have bookmarked it."

"Last night, I listened to it carefully," she said as she repositioned herself to face him more. "It seemed to have moments in it that reflect the swings in people's lives, my life."

Harris pushed his chin forward a bit, squinted quizzically and asked, "Like what?"

"Most of it seemed to have great energy and life that was intermittently punctuated by lulls, slower parts. The slower parts seem a mix of sweetness and melancholy. That's the way most of our lives are, don't you think?"

"I suppose," he replied.

"And then there seemed to be multiple times, deep into the piece, when it could have ended, but it didn't. Instead of winding down in typical fashion, there were little interludes…little surprises before signing off."

"Wow. You've heard it twice and you came up with that?" he said with admiration.

"It seems like my life. This is a sweet little interlude… you and me… towards the end," she said smiling while her eyes locked onto his.

Harris' chest swelled and his pulse quickened, but he wasn't certain what to do or say next. Should he move onto the love seat with her? Without thinking further, he reached out his right hand toward her. She reached out her left, palm down. He took it and held it for many seconds, running his thumb slowly over the top of her smooth but aged hand. They silently held their gaze, each content with this amount of affection. Eventually Harris gently squeezed then slowly released her hand and pulled his back.

After a brief silence, Miranda asked, "Did you and your wife ever spoon, Mr. Archibald?"

He looked at her with surprise then pondered before answering. "We did, early on…after sex a few times."

"But not at bedtime, before sleep?"

"No. That wasn't us. Most of the time I went to bed after her the last few years, and I thought *I can't believe I'm here... with this person...again*!"

Miranda chuckled. "I'm sorry. You missed out on something beautiful. It was one of the best things about Ken. He spooned my way as we drifted off each night. We called it *baking each other to sleep*."

"Sounds nice. I think you need to have the right person for baking. I didn't."

"Yes, well, that's a pity indeed." She looked away toward his TV and then at the beige carpet before continuing. "We'd bake each other in the middle of the night too, if one of us couldn't sleep. It was marvelous for getting back to sleep."

"You're making me jealous, I'm afraid," he said feeling uncertain why she was telling him this. He did not have to wait long to find out.

"Mr. Archibald, I'm going to ask you something, and I want you to feel comfortable saying *no*. It won't affect our relationship if you do say *no*."

His heart rate quickened again upon hearing her prelude. "My, what a preface," he said.

"I was wondering if you might spoon with me... sometimes during the tuck-in. Not every time, mind you, but maybe we could try it...just to see how it feels."

An impish grin formed on his face. He wanted to say *yes*, but delayed an answer while he processed her request and formed a response befitting it. Finally, he said, "Why, yes, I think that could be part of our tuck-ins, once in a while, just to see how it feels."

"Great."

"But I'm not sure I can be Ken for you," he added.

"I don't want you to be Ken. You'll be Harris Archibald."

He was surprised at her using his first name. He liked hearing it.

"I'd pay you extra," she continued, "this being above and beyond and all."

He tried not to change his expression, but may not have been able to mask his disappointment. The thought of this being a financial transaction changed the moment for Harris.

"I was thinking," she continued, "I'd put two dollars on the counter when I wanted spooning, one when it was a regular tuck-in. You'd check the counter when you came in. Would that work?"

"That seems pretty straight forward," he said without emotion.

"Great. There will be two dollars on the counter tomorrow night, if you're ready to give it a go?"

"Let's try it on for size."

"Harris, don't worry about this," she added before leaving. "Clothes stay on. I'll lead us through it, but we'll figure this out together."

That sounded fine to him, but her suggestion to lead them through it did not surprise Harris at all. She was leading and steering every part of their relationship, or whatever this was. He was just holding on.

The following night, their fifth tuck-in, Harris arrived with his guitar, iPad, and heightened anticipation. He settled in his usual chair alongside her bed, played an instrumental and then Mr. Bojangles. She was laying on her right side in bed, facing him.

Upon completion of his two tunes, Miranda said, "C'mon now, let's get this over with," while she patted the open side of the queen-sized bed that was between the two of them. He did not respond other than removing the guitar strap over his head as she rolled away from him. He took her pat on the bedspread as meaning he should start on top of the covers. When he cautiously got on his left side and scooted next to her, he found where her knees bent, and fit his knees in behind hers. There seemed to be just one sheet and a medium thick blanket on top of her, under him, and now in between them. He wasn't sure if this is what she had in mind, nor what he should do with his right hand and arm. When he put his right hand on top of her right thigh and left it there, she did not seem to mind. She, in fact, scooched herself to be closer to him, against him as much as the covers would permit.

He wanted to reach for the iPad and play a new song he had bookmarked, but he realized any movement would be disruptive. They lay there still and quiet for a minute, before she said, "Mr. Archibald, you're going to need to get under the covers for this to really be spooning."

He did as she suggested, quietly moving to the edge of the bed, removing his black leather loafers, pulling back the covers, and sliding in. Once he moved in next to her to find her backside and bent knees, she moved to be up against him again, her full backside against his full front side. Their bent knees fit perfectly without the covers to contend with. Without delay, he again put his right hand on her left thigh. She was wearing something full length. It felt smooth and silky. Perhaps it was the black nightgown he had seen a glimpse of the previous visit. Within a couple of seconds, she whispered, "That's better. Thank you."

He squeezed her thigh ever so slightly.

They laid there together, his front to her back, spooning, for three or four minutes. Neither of them moved or said a thing. Harris wondered how long he should stay, how was this supposed to go. Was she getting relaxed? He was not. Should he stay in this position until she dozed off? She said she would lead the way. He listened for her breathing. It was difficult for him to pick up, but he was not sensing any change, any sign that she was moving toward sleep. He began thinking that this could get awkward, that maybe he didn't have the requisite experience at spooning. Before much longer, she raised her right arm, and took his right hand from resting on her thigh and led it slowly across her chest. Once there, she had his hand cup her left breast. He was surprised and became aroused. He couldn't believe this was where she led them, but more significantly could not believe what he held in his large right hand. It was a very full, firm, perfectly round breast. He knew immediately he had never felt one so perfectly shaped. He made no attempt to move his hand away, instead he rearranged his fingers and palm until they cupped her breast more on the front and side, between it and the bed. There it felt most right. Her only response was, "That's best."

They stayed in this position another 15 or 20 minutes, baking Miranda. Her breathing did change. Her entire body twitched at one point, then he could feel her relax and drift off. He knew when it was time to remove his hand and slowly slide out from under the covers. He took the two dollars from the counter and left without either of them saying a word.

When he quietly shut Miranda's door, Harris turned to head down the hall. Not twenty feet from Miranda's door, sitting in the hall in one of the two wing-back chairs was Rex. The two men glanced at each other. Harris was startled to see him, but pretended not to be. Rex gave Harris a parted-lips smirk, but did not otherwise acknowledge him. Harris looked straight ahead. When he got closer to Rex, he could see, out of the corner of his eye, the seated man raise his left arm and exaggeratedly look at his watch.

CHAPTER SEVENTEEN

Diana had been married three times. The first one ended because she found her husband boring. He was a journeyman carpenter who arrived home tired most nights. She was young and playful and expected more in every way from a young husband. Early on, she realized she needed a different lifestyle and sex life. After 22 months there were no children. She saw no harm in moving on.

Three years later she married a regional vice president of Motorola who was six years her senior. He had seven-state responsibility and travelled frequently. He had a voracious sexual appetite and attire preferences for her. It was the sexual play she had craved with her first husband. Richard also provided a lifestyle Diana enjoyed.

Diana tried to find work to fill her time and contribute financially, but not being a college graduate, the jobs proved menial and unexciting. She was embarrassed to say, at Richard's work gatherings, that she worked as a clerk at JC Penney's or answered phones for a construction firm. Richard was embarrassed too.

He talked her into being a true housewife. They had difficulty bearing children through no fault of trying. It was of no consequence to her husband who had his career and his golf buddies at Olympic Club in San Francisco. Diana was not sure whose reproductive parts were not working, but it didn't matter enough to her to find out. The thought of becoming a mother did not appeal to her at this stage of her life.

Living 30 miles from San Francisco in the upscale community of Alamo, Diana slid comfortably into the role of homemaker and trophy wife. She relished overseeing home improvement projects and taking care of herself. Health clubs in the 1970's were not what they later became with machines and classes of every kind. To keep her trim shape, she took up running. She ran the Iron Horse Trail most days, while finding pleasure and esteem in 10K races. Her times were in the 49-minute range, usually not winning her age group but placing high enough that it resulted in positive comments from her racing competitors and, more importantly, from Richard's fellow employees and spouses.

Richard and Diana lived on a secluded 2/3 acre property that had oak and redwood trees on its perimeter. One of the upgrades to the property that Diana oversaw after moving in was the installation of a pool with a waterfall and an adjacent spa. It became the centerpiece of their property, so much so that they had held a 4th of July pool party for friends and family, and a Labor Day barbeque for the local Motorola team. For each event, no expenses were spared for food, beverage and decorations. For the work party, Richard would hire a steel drum band or a juggler to entertain. He was proud of his dwelling, his corporate position, and his lifestyle which included Diana.

She relished her role on those two days of the year as well. Her planning had included how far in advance to get her hair cut and colored, so that it looked perfect and not recently done. She also got a mani-pedi the day before, usually in a shade of pink or red that accentuated the tan she had worked on, and the new bikini she had picked out for the season. She believed in real tans rather than spray on or tanning creams. She also preferred no tan lines, and Richard did too. Their property allowed for the requisite sunbathing.

Diana was not an exhibitionist. She always wore an appropriate cover up over her bikini for these events. Because of the time of year and climate in Alamo, guests were encouraged to swim or use the spa.

"We built this for you," Richard would say to his guests the first year or two, until that saying was known by all invitees and began sounding rehearsed. Richard would often throw one of his teen nieces into the pool, or playfully pretend to with one the wives of his co-workers. After another swimmer or two had been brave enough to enter the pool, Diana would join them, shedding her cover up. Males and females could not help themselves sneak glances to watch her splash the others in and out of the pool. Diana rarely put the cover up back on after leaving the pool, even when it cooled in the evening. She would enter the spa when she needed warming up, encouraging others to join her. Early in the evening, she could be seen with three or four men in the spa sipping another drink, while talking and laughing loudly.

Both Richard and Diana received much esteem from these parties. Their guests seemed to have fun and were effusive about their house, backyard, and Diana's good looks. The couple usually had sex after the guests had left while Diana was still in her bikini. "Join me in the spa in five minutes," Diana said once with a wry smile. Richard knew what she meant and turned out all the backyard lights before joining her. Often, they had sex the following morning before rising.

Richard was gone on business a couple of weeks a month. Diana managed the house, the bills, the home improvement projects, ran the trail, and saw her friends. She had the gardeners and housekeepers come on Fridays so everything would look great when Richard returned from his latest trip. The pool service day was Thursday and the young man that worked the route one spring typically arrived between 2:00 and 3:00. As spring became summer, she began watching out for him as he worked in his tank top, shorts, sandals and cowboy hat while his tan got darker. It was then that Diana made certain she sunned herself every Thursday from 1:30 on. The first time she stayed in her orange bikini, and brought out lemonade without asking if the twenty-something wanted any. "You really must take a break," she told him. Though initially resisting, the young man sat at the round glass patio table. After she served them both, Diana sat in a chair near him, rather than straight across the table.

"This is mighty good, ma'am. Thank you," the man said in his best golly-gee, aw-shucks voice.

"You're welcome," she said smiling. "I think labor laws require you take a break every so often."

"I believe you're right, but I have a boss who figures driving to the next pool counts as a break."

"What's your name?"

"Troy."

"Ahh Troy," she said. "I like Troy. Please plan on taking a break every Thursday afternoon at this pool."

"Okay."

"Are you married, Troy?"

"No ma'am. Not married", he replied taking off his hat to reveal a full head of uncombed brown curls just long enough to catch Diana's attention.

She did not probe further, but after taking a sip of her drink, said, "That's good. A handsome young man like you needs to play the field before setting down, don't you think?"

Troy had been down this road before, and believed he knew where it was headed. "Now you all wouldn't be trying to seduce me, would you? I heard about stuff like this," he said playfully with a grin to match.

"I'm not sure yet," she answered. "Would you blame me for trying?"

"Probably not, ma'am," he said.

Diana was unclear on how to proceed. She felt comfortable flirting, but was not yet in the habit of taking it further. She cleared the glasses and pitcher. Troy returned to cleaning the pool and spa with her watching from the kitchen window. When he appeared to be leaving, she went outside and asked, "Time to leave?"

"Afraid so. Got three more stops to make. Thanks for the beverage…and the chat."

"I do hope I didn't scare you off, Troy. See you next Thursday?"

He smiled and said, "I'll see you Thursday."

"Good. And Troy…don't shave for a day or two."

Things progressed as predictably as a soft porn movie over the next four weeks. A pattern had been established and was clear to Troy. When Diana's husband was working locally, she dressed more modestly, and did not bother Troy while he worked. They would steal a kiss and touch on these occasions in a safe part of the house before Troy left; "Just in case," she said.

Soon the signal Troy learned that Richard was traveling was when he saw her sunbathing wearing very little, and the lemonade and glasses were on the table.

Deep into the summer, one Thursday when Richard was traveling, and they swam naked, Diana said, "I never thought I'd be doing this on my anniversary."

"You're kidding, right?" Troy said sounding both disgusted and alarmed.

"He called this morning, wished me happy anniversary, and said he take me somewhere special tomorrow night when he got back."

"Ahh," Troy said, sounding more relaxed before swimming over to her and giving her a roving-hands boyfriend kiss.

What Diana didn't realize was that Richard had rearranged his schedule to arrive Thursday afternoon from Seattle. He wanted to surprise her on this, their sixth anniversary. When Richard walked into the kitchen and looked out to the backyard, he was the one initially surprised to find his wife and another man naked in a compromising position in the spa. Within seconds, Troy and Diana joined in the surprise.

Diana did everything she could to make amends after being caught, but it was never going to work for Richard. Their marriage officially ended less than seven months later. He sold the house, unable to face his neighbors. They split $1.1 million in assets.

Diana felt some shame, but soon embraced the life of a bachelorette. She felt comfortable now in moving a prospective lover through the steps. But she had also gotten comfortable with the lifestyle that Richard had provided, so she pursued men of a certain type. Within four years, she married a banking executive who was ten years her senior. They were married for 22 years before he passed from pancreatic cancer. She inherited a sizable sum. She never had to work and she never married again.

Though her memory played tricks on her now at The Ridge, Diana often thought back on those days when she knew how to attract men and get what she wanted. She never lost her appetite for flirting, though it never amounted to much anymore.

~

One evening, at his scheduled tuck-in with Diana, Mondo was surprised to find her not in bed waiting, but sitting on the couch in the living room in her powder blue bath robe and fluffy white slippers. "I thought we could just have a glass of wine tonight," Diana said after Mondo had said *hi* and looked surprised.

"Yeah, sure. If that's what you want."

She got up from the couch as he propped up his guitar in the corner of the room. "White okay?" she asked.

"For sure. That's what priests drink," wishing immediately that he had not mentioned his occupation.

When she handed him a generous pour, and sat next to him on the sofa, she said, "I was raised Catholic."

"Really?"

"Really. Confirmed and everything. Married in a Catholic Church the first time."

"Good for you," he said while taking in the unexpected turn in this evening's tuck-in.

"I never understood why the altar wine was white," she said. "If it's supposed to represent the blood of Christ, shouldn't it be red?"

"Good question," he replied. When Mondo raised both shoulders in unison and gave a look on his face that he lacked a knowledgeable response, they both laughed.

It was then Mondo noticed the red lip stick Diana had on that overshot some edges of her lips. He also noticed the sagging skin on her face and neck from years in the sun. She was still slight of build with a tummy that all seniors had some version of.

"What day is today?" she asked.

"Tuesday."

"I can never remember what day it is in this place. Maybe Tuesday we can make our wine night," she said more as a pronouncement than an inquiry.

"Sounds good to me," Mondo replied.

After some small talk about dinner and the news of the day, Diana said, "I imagine this part of your life here at The Ridge couldn't be more different than most of the rest of your life."

He looked at her closely before responding, "It is." He thought a bit more then added, "And it isn't. I've always been part of a community and yet have still been alone."

Diana nodded, unsure how to respond but hoping he was going to say more.

He did. "I've always had a room of my own. Most years I was in a parish with other priests and someone cooked for us, so this is no different. As a priest though, there are many obligations and interruptions. Calls from parishioners to administer last rights to family members came at all times of the day and night. Mass schedules, funerals, weddings and wedding rehearsals, visiting the sick, confessions, and participation on different committees took up most days."

"I see," she said.

"But there was enough alone time, sometimes too much. It was hard not to feel like the rest of the world was living life and I was missing out."

"Didn't people invite you over to dinner once in a while? Our family did with a favorite priest of ours."

"Yes, and it was very nice of them. But when a priest walks out their front door after dinner, he is all by himself... and they have each other. That can make for depressed nights and days after a good meal."

"Oh my. I hadn't thought of that," she said.

"This is a nice place. I have meals prepared for me. I think my money is going to last here. That's important. I actually feel less alone."

"I like it here too," she said. "But this a change for me. I almost always lived in really nice places and never worried about money. I got to travel the world. My husbands and I always had many friends and activities. I think it's odd that most of us end up in a place like this...if we're lucky."

"Yeah," Mondo acknowledged but was surprised at the solemnity of the discussion.

"Some of us have died by now or are in need of a nursing home," she added. She poured them some more wine even though neither glass was empty, and moved a few inches closer to him on the long end of the L-shaped sofa.

"What day is today?" she asked.

Mondo looked at her curiously for a moment before answering, "Tuesday."

"Ahh. I can't keep track anymore."

"Do we really need to?" he asked. "Breakfast, lunch and dinner are always at the same time...*every day*. At 9:30 I'm here."

"Yes, and I want you to know how much I love this part of my day. I've had a lot of things in life, and men who said they wanted me, but no one ever sang me to sleep. Thank you."

"I get a lot out of it too."

"You are a sweet man," she said, and as she did, she placed her left hand on his right thigh.

Mondo smiled but his heart quickened and his face felt flushed. His mind darted between thoughts of the priesthood, his vow of celibacy, all that he had missed out on, and wondering what Diana might do next- all in a microchip-processing sort of way.

"Am I making you nervous?" she asked smiling while scratching his thigh with her chipped red nails.

Mondo's upper body was rigid. He kept looking at her hand when he answered, "A little. I'm kinda new to this."

"Good. I'm not," she answered. "I don't mind you being a priest, if you want to know the truth."

Mondo did not respond, but bit his lower lip.

"I'm not as pretty or in as good a shape as I once was," she added.

Mondo's mind raced again. What should he do or say next? What did other men do or say at moments like these? It occurred to him that this was one of those moments he wondered about in the confessional. While he remained silent, Diana smiled and kept her eyes on his face. It had been a long time but she remembered how this script went. She had replayed it in her head many afternoons and evenings the last few years recalling the men of her past. The details of those memories had never needed bending or embellishing. Even though well out of practice, she knew with Mondo's silence she needed to scoot in closer to him, eventually resting her head on his shoulder while moving her fingers a little higher on his thigh.

When she did that much, Mondo awkwardly placed his right arm around her shoulders.

"That feels nice. It's been a while for me too," she said as her hand slowly rubbed his right upper, inner leg.

Diana could feel and hear Mondo's breathing becoming deeper and more irregular. She raised her head from his shoulder and put her mouth next to Mondo's right ear. "It's okay," she whispered, as she reached all the way up and cupped him on the outside of his beige Dockers.

"Oh god," he said nearly stuttering. When she continued moving her hand slightly, he repositioned his body to face her more and kissed her on the mouth. He put his left hand on her right side, leaving his right arm and hand where they had been, and never explored further over the next few minutes. Mondo's eyes were open and wild. He kissed her with youthful exuberance, never opening his mouth and rarely breathing.

Diana did not judge. She knew this was an inexperienced man and there was something exceptional about that for her. While it was not kissing the way she remembered it, she knew not to criticize or instruct, and never rearranged his hands. There was something raw in his kisses, and gentlemanly about the placement of his hands. She contemplated not rubbing him further, but recalled men telling her it was cruel to stop what she had started. As long as he wasn't indicating otherwise, she continued. She touched the man, and moved her hand in a way that excited them both. He wanted to say *stop* but couldn't. They continued until she heard him grunt a breathless *tchehhh* while arching his back.

Afterward, he sat struggling to normalize his breathing while instantly feeling a unique blend of euphoric relief and overwhelming remorse. Soon he reached for his guitar while saying, "I've got to go."

CHAPTER EIGHTEEN

Harris did not see Miranda at any meal the following day, nor did she text him. He was unsure if he was supposed to contact her, but he didn't think so. Miranda had made it clear…she would contact him for a walk or a tuck-in. But that was before things had progressed. This was all new to him and he did not yet feel adept at it. And so he waited. The waiting was difficult. He thought of her almost continuously. She had led the way as she'd indicated she would. And while she led him to her breast, and he had welcomed that, it was so much more for Harris. He enjoyed being with her. Waiting for her next move, her next contact, was difficult, but wait he did.

The next morning, the day after not hearing from her, she texted, *9:30 tonight?*

Yes, please he responded, before wishing he would have simply said *sure.*

When he arrived at the appointed time, he noticed $1 resting on her counter. He hid any disappointment and played three songs from the chair next to her bed. She faced him from her side of the bed, often with a comfortable small smile. Never did she try to sleep. When he finished, he softly said, "It's okay to sleep deep, Miranda. Have a good rest."

She replied, "That was lovely, I will. Can we walk tomorrow at 11?"

"Yes."

As he left her apartment and headed down the hall, Rex was again waiting in the hall chair. When Rex raised his arm to check his watch, Harris slowed his walk, looked at Rex, and said, "Jealousy can be a beautiful thing."

While continuing his walk, Harris heard Rex mutter, "Piece a shit."

~

The following morning, Harris was happy when Miranda appeared near his rear door. Without a cane, she hooked onto his left arm after a short greeting. "I hope you like how things are going, Mr. Archibald. I haven't enjoyed life this much in a while."

"I'm glad you brought it up. I am too. However, I'm finding off days to be excruciating."

"Isn't that wonderful?" she replied.

"Not really. How can excruciating be wonderful?"

"It's good to *want*, Mr. Archibald…and to change the well-worn script couples have. It hardly ever happens that way anymore, don't you think?"

"You do realize our clocks are ticking, don't you?

"Ahh, Mr. Archibald," she said squeezing his arm a bit tighter, "let's not be too predictable."

"Is that why there was just one dollar on the counter last night?"

"You're catching on, Mr. Archibald."

After walking a bit more and admiring the beautiful day, Harris said, "I chose not to bring this up this first time it happened, but Rex has waited for me twice now in the hall after I've left your room."

She gave Harris a brief look of concern then quickly acted nonchalant. "He's just a crochety old man. Likes to be heard and be seen as the *only* cheese around here. You and Mondo have changed that. Ignore him if you can."

"Will try my best."

When Miranda had indicated she'd had enough exercise for one day, she released his arm and said, "Tomorrow is an off day, but can we schedule the night after tomorrow night?"

"You're killing me, you realize that, don't you?"

"I hope not. I hope you're around for a long time."

When he arrived the third night after their walk, Harris smiled at the sight of two dollars on the counter. He played one song, and then queued up *Clair de Lune* on the iPad, before climbing into bed.

As he was pulling back his side of the covers, Miranda said, "Mr. Archibald, if you want you can take your pants off… but no funny stuff, okay?"

He paused to process this unexpected development. But without saying anything, he did as she suggested. She did not watch him remove his pants nor as he entered his side of the bed wearing only his underwear and a burgundy tee-shirt. After they had arranged knees and gotten comfortable, Harris placed his hand on her nightgown-covered thigh. Without hesitation, she took his hand and placed it where she had before. She never had to do so again. Harris now understood what spooning met whenever he saw two dollars on the counter.

CHAPTER NINETEEN

The two of them are roving minstrels...going from room to room...taking money for doing next to nothing. This thought bothered Rex in ways and to a degree more than anyone could have imagined. *If foolish women want to spend their money unwisely, that's their business* he thought. *But this affects me! The only thing the women around here wanna talk about now is Mondo this and Harris that! Heck, even other guys here are interested in the shenanigans of those two! What am I supposed to do, naked cartwheels around here to get a little love and attention?*

Rex mulled over going to The Ridge's management and disclosing the minstrels and the danger they posed to elderly ladies, but he suspected they already knew. Plus, that whole unfortunate incident with the priest may come up, and he didn't care to relive any part of that. He was ticked off, there was no question about that, and rightfully so he thought. He had been displaced at the unofficial main-man of The Ridge by two losers, and had been humiliated by one of them. Rex was not a man to forgive, forget, and move on. No, Rex Hornsby Jr.

was a damned force to be reckoned with at The Ridge and the tables needed a little turning.

What irritated him more than anything was seeing the other dweeb coming out of Miranda's room. They weren't probably doing nothing, he thought, but it irritated him nonetheless. He also realized from his nightly hallway patrols that the priest was bouncing from room to room with his guitar, but the other fella seemed to be only about Miranda. As he thought fuller about this, he realized Miranda musta' gone out her way to request this other guy. Was she in love with him? Naw, Miranda wasn't the falling-in-love type. But she was getting something out of it, he knew that much. And if the others were also getting what they needed from visits with the padre, well then, dagnammit, it was more than Rex could stand. He knew what his next move was going to be. It may not fix everything, but it was going fix somethin'.

CHAPTER TWENTY

Harris hadn't seen Miranda at either breakfast or lunch, nor had she walked, and he decided by mid-afternoon to check on her. Maybe she was feeling under the weather and was unsure whether she would ask him to get her something. Maybe she had a doctor's appointment and forgot to tell him about it.

Yes, she had told him the afternoons were her time—for napping, reading, podcasts, binge watching, phone calls… he didn't know...whatever she wanted he supposed. Maybe her telling him that was just a cute thing to say when people barely knew each other, but they were different now. Still, he had never imposed on her in the afternoon, and felt a little hesitation as he approached her door. What if she were napping? He knocked lightly deciding against the doorbell… just in case. No response. He turned the door handle quietly, just a bit to see if was unlocked. It silently and easily rotated, so he kept turning it all the way. He pushed open the door a crack to listen for the TV. He heard nothing. As he opened the door more, he could not see her in the kitchenette or the living room, but he began to hear something, some minor movement from the bedroom. The window curtains were drawn shut, and for mid-afternoon, her apartment was very dark. Perhaps she was sleeping, so he chose not to call out her name. Curious, but now feeling creepy, he knew he should quietly reverse his movements and exit the apartment. But he didn't. He would later regret this decision, this unexplainable lapse in judgement. Instead, he took another two silent steps forward so he could just make out part of her bedroom, including the end of her bed. On top of the bottom of the bed, he saw what was likely the end of her legs, and two other bare feet and legs straddling hers.

"That's right," a man's voice whispered barely loud enough for Harris to hear.

Harris was trying to process the last thing he expected to see and hear. He was completely confused. Was he even in the right room? Yes, of course this was Miranda's room. What was going on? Was Miranda on the bed? He had never seen her bare feet before. If it was her, who was the man? What was Harris to do? He knew he was not supposed to be standing there right then. She did not sound in distress. He could leave, but there would be so many unanswered questions? How could he ever raise them if he left now?

He took another quiet step forward, not all the way to the bedroom door, and still not yet to where they could see him, but to where he was able to see most of the bed. The woman was wearing a black nightgown and was on top of the bedspread. He was a big man, bare except for some plaid boxers. She had her arms around his neck. He had his right hand on her left breast. She was not being held against her will. He couldn't see either of their faces, but he was certain it was Miranda. Harris was crushed. He froze again, uncertain how to proceed.

The man did not appear to be fully on her or in her. She did not have her legs wrapped around him, but she moved underneath him. She rubbed his back, digging her finger nails in his burly back. Harris became more and more agitated. His confusion, his ability to think clearly was overshadowed by being more pissed than he could ever remember. There was no inclination now to slip quietly back out her door. *We've been open about everything*, he thought. *Surely there had been ample opportunity for her to tell me about an old boyfriend, or part-time lover, or any such thing.* He would have understood…maybe. *She was still attractive, still had sexual energy, and was appealing to men other than himself.* He might have understood if she had given him an indication anything like this could remotely happen.

His heart was pounding. He could feel the heat in his face and ears. He fought an urge to barge in and pull the man off her. What should he do?

A few more seconds passed with not much change in the activity. Finally, he took two more steps forward into the open doorway to the bedroom. They still did not notice him. Miranda continued rubbing his bare back and he continued doing what he had been doing.

"What the fuck?" he blurted out. "What the fuck, Miranda?"

The startled man rolled off Miranda while looking back. It was Rex. He looked at Harris and yelled, "Get the fuck outta here."

Harris froze and said nothing.

"Harris, leave," Miranda said tersely as she rearranged her clothing to cover her breasts.

"Miranda! What the hell? Really? Rex?" He threw up both hands and turned to leave. "Fuck you both." As he opened the front door, the daytime med-tech, Alfonso, was standing there.

"Yeah, get the fuck out of here, you fuckin' peeping Tom," Rex shouted.

"Rex, shut up," Miranda pleaded.

Alfonso and Harris looked at each other in frozen confusion before Harris passed around him. Alfonso asked, "Is everything okay in there?"

"It's great…just great," Harris replied as he moved down the hall.

Alfonso remained in the open doorway and called out, "Miranda, are you all right? Do you need any help?"

"I'm okay. Just a little misunderstanding."

With that, Alfonso turned and left.

That evening, despite wanting to remain in his room, Harris sheepishly sauntered into the dining room for dinner. He sat with no one. After some time, Rex joined his usual table, which always had a couple different people than his lunch table. Harris ate slowly. He was curious whether Miranda would show, and if she did, how she would handle things. This was hers to fix, not his. Would she stumble over herself trying to make amends? Not likely, he thought. Not in front of others. More likely, she would act as if nothing had happened.

Neither occurred, at least that evening. She did not appear for dinner. Silently, Harris was glad, thinking she must be mortified. She should be, he thought. How could he have judged her so wrongly? Had Harris been misled that she was different…that what they had was the beginnings of something special?

After the longest time he had ever spent over a meal at The Ridge, he got up to leave. He purposely walked close to Rex's round table, taking the side that allowed him to look directly at Rex's face and have Rex look directly into his. Harris slowed as he got to the round table, looking only at Rex's eyes. Harris slowed even further, barely moving forward for a few seconds. He thrust his jaw forward while glaring at Rex. Rex met his stare, never breaking eye contact, turning his head ever so slowly to match Harris' walk.

The others at the table stopped eating when they noticed. Diane cheerily said, "Hello." Harris said nothing, rather holding his glare, barely stifling his rage.

When Harris had finally moved beyond the table and out of the dining room, Setesh, the man in the wheelchair, broke the silence asking, "What was that?"

They all turned to Rex who thrust his chest up and out, rearranged his napkin, and then said, "That, my friends, is the look of a loser…a lost soul."

The truth was that Rex was accurate for once. Harris was lost. He spent most of that evening and the next day in his apartment, working his remote to no satisfaction. *Do people really watch this crap*, he thought. He skipped The Ridge's lunch, instead choosing to hit *In & Out* ordering a double-double animal-style, fries, and a strawberry shake. Afterward he swung by Safeway and bought two six-packs of *Fat Tire*.

When he returned to The Ridge, it was nearly two o'clock. He checked his mail. There was nothing. *Perfect,* he thought. *Junk mail doesn't even want me*. Rather than return to his room, he sat in the sofa next to the piano in the common living room, and near the white painted brick fireplace that had candles in it that had never been lit. With it being well after The Ridge's lunch, there was no one in the dining area, which he could see from where he was seated, only an occasional staff member moving to their next task. He noticed how the place smelled. It was different than any other place he'd ever been. There was mix of cleanser and disinfectant odors, not as strong as in a hospital, but unmistakably present. Mixed with that was the smell of old age and that was what was all around him. Did all flabby, decaying skin turn this way or was it just the skin that wasn't cleansed and scrubbed enough? Was it in their clothing? Harris had noticed it before, especially whenever a larger group gathered at Ridge. Age had its scent, and today, right then, he didn't care for it.

As he sat, he also became aware and irritated by the piped-in music that always played at a low volume within the common areas of The Ridge…Perry Como, Johnny Mathis, old blue eyes…even instrumentals of Beatles tunes. God, every day. *You'd think these people never heard of music after those guys. Would it kill them to play a little Petty or Seger or Springsteen?* he'd wondered more than once to himself.

His fingers played with the fabric on the armrest, his thoughts bouncing from Miranda to Rex to his own pathetic life. What had he expected from this place, this phase of life? He was who he'd always been…a disappointment…an underachiever. Business success was meant for others. Love, esteem, a wide social circle… pretty girls… had always missed his universe.

To his immediate right was the end table with the chess board set up. He had seen it before, but had paid little attention to it as had most everybody else at The Ridge. He did recall seeing the man in the wheelchair, the one who was usually at Rex's table, on rare occasions playing chess by himself. How could anyone play chess by themselves? *That's almost as pathetic as my life,* he thought. *Is white really going trick black through an unsuspecting sequence of moves?*

Harris had played chess many times over beers at S. F. State. He still remembered some opening-game tactics based upon whether he chose to be aggressive or to play conservatively. He often chose the conservative route, setting up a defense while anticipating mistakes from his opponents. This served him well considering the skill-level of his beer-guzzling challengers. He couldn't, however, recall much about the middle or endgame strategies. Back then he had known some of what to do when the game was reduced to three or four pieces on each side. He might have even once known the sequence of moves if he was left with two pawns and a queen, or a knight and a rook, to tip the game his way, but no longer. And while there was no way to access that level of detail these many years later, he still recalled the principal that endgames favored an aggressive king used as an attacker, advancing him to the middle of the board after protecting him for much of the game.

Sitting there letting his gaze and thoughts center on the board with it carved wooden pieces, he realized what a metaphor chess was for life. Many different players, moving parts, and roles. Some pieces acting like others, but some were so completely different... not at all equal in shape, size, mobility or stature. The need for the player to act and react... the need to plan and anticipate. As he sat there starring in his depressed state, he understood there had been no way he could have anticipated what he had witnessed in Miranda's room. But still, it hit him hard to acknowledge who the queen was in this Ridge melodrama, and, more importantly, who the king and pawn were. *Yes, a metaphor*, he thought. *What will Miranda's next move be?*

The following afternoon, Harris was strumming his guitar in his apartment, barely audibly singing James Taylor's *Long Ago & Far Away*, the most melancholy song he knew. *"Long ago a young man sits and plays his waiting game,"* he sang.

There was a knock on his door. He got up, thinking it was Mondo or housekeeping dropping off his laundry from the day before. A fleeting thought of it possibly being Miranda passed as he grabbed the door knob. It was. His shoulders slumped as he stood there saying nothing.

Miranda forced a little closed mouth smile before asking, "May I come in?" Harris did not reply, but opened the door all the way and motioned with his free hand for her to enter. She walked to the nearest Barcalounger, placed her cane on the side of it, and sat. He walked to the other Barcalounger, creating the largest space two seated people could have in the room.

She crossed her legs at the ankles and folded her hands on her lap. Nothing about her seemed nervous or rushed. For the first time, Harris noticed she was wearing jeans, brown boots, and a high necked, forest green sweater. He had never seen her in denim.

Harris placed both his forearms and hands on the arms of his chair. He thought of offering her a beverage, but decided against it. He felt more uncomfortable than she appeared.

After a few long seconds of neither of them speaking, she looked at him squarely and calmly said, "I told you my afternoons were mine. What I do with my time is my business. You entered my apartment without being invited, and without knocking."

He watched her closely, wondering if she had finished what she wanted to say, or at least wanted to start with. Certainly, he thought, there must be more.

When she offered nothing more, he emphatically dropped his jaw for two full seconds before saying, "That's it? That's your explanation, your apology? You broke my heart, Miranda. I thought we had something special."

"We do have something special."

"We did. What you did with the biggest asshole around here…well, we will *never* be the same."

She uncrossed her ankles and leaned forward a bit. "Rex and I have a complicated relationship. It's not a healthy one. We had a physical relationship last year. I got something out of it until I didn't. Then I ended it."

"And yesterday? It didn't look like you were putting up much of a fight!"

"He blackmailed me. I was taking care of things."

"He blackmailed you? What could he blackmail you about? How about telling me or management so somebody could do something?"

"He did blackmail me. The tuck-in episode with Mondo, and then finding out you were doing tuck-ins with me, was too much for him. He has pictures of you leaving multiple nights with your guitar or iPad. He was going to go to management to stop you and Father Armando."

"He can't do that! I can come into your room anytime I'm invited. There's nothing to blackmail!"

"You don't know that! It might be something the general manager feels he needs to end." She stopped looking at Harris, became quiet and focused on the carpet. Miranda folded her hands and rested them on her lap. After many seconds she said in her calmest voice, "Everything about the tuck-in, your visit, is perfect... even paying you, as silly as that sounds. I didn't want *anything* to change. Rex bought me a new nightgown and said, '*just once*' and he wouldn't go to management. He and I had been through that before, long before you got here. It was not a big deal to me. I did what I thought I had to do to end it."

Harris sat there trying to make sense of what he'd just heard. He wanted to believe Miranda and her convoluted logic about being coerced yet it not being a big deal, but was struggling. "And you believed him? Just once?" he finally asked. "You don't think a week from now or a month down the road, he won't demand it again."

She crossed her arms tightly across her chest. "This happened suddenly, Harris. I was taking care of it... my way. It was something I could handle. Losing the tuck-ins, I couldn't."

He stood, crossed his arms, and turned away from her, looking out through his glass backdoor. Her irrational un-explanation...even her calling him *Harris* seemed so odd. All of this had gotten so far out of whack, so quickly. After some quiet, he said without turning back to her, "And you expect us to go back to just the way things were?"

"I know my behavior must seem odd. I'm sorry you saw what you saw. I didn't expect you to walk in at just the wrong moment."

He turned to face her, still standing and said, "Well, I'm glad I walked in at just the wrong moment."

"Harris, you have every right to be mad, to be confused."

"I'm *not* confused," he said angrily.

"You are. You saw something disturbing. We're not married. We've never vowed fidelity. You may not believe it, and this isn't the best time to say it for the first time, but I care about you…deeply. I'm very much in love with *us*. Even though our relationship is young, it is special and important to me. I had hoped it would continue until the end of one of us. I'm sorry if I ruined it. That will be a horrible loss for me if I did, and a terrible burden to bear."

He sat back down, this time in the love seat closer to her chair. He leaned forward, elbows on his thighs, hands clasped, thinking. She waited. She knew his next words were important. It was their moment of truth. After nearly a minute, he sat back, put his hands on his thighs, and looked at her directly. "It's a loss for me too. But you and I will never be the same, because of what happened. I'm going to struggle with this because I've become invested in our relationship. Right now, it seems like it was a farce, a lie. It really does. Right now," he paused, "it seems like I'll never get over seeing you with him."

She took all this in. She knew what he'd just said was raw and real. This man who had seemed unsure of himself early in their relationship, who had not had much confidence and luck around women, had been finding his way with her, and it was never more evident than right then. While this moment was uncomfortable for both of them, seeing how he was handling it made Harris seem even more special in her eyes. After letting there be some quiet to let his words settle, in her calmest voice, she said, "You're so close to it, to what you saw. This doesn't make a lot of sense right now, but *we* weren't a farce. I have never lied to you and intend to make this the one relationship in my life where I never even partially bend the truth. You are important to me. I don't want to change anything. I don't want to spend more time together. I don't want to spend less time together. It's been perfect. If you can ever trust me on that and get beyond this moment, I'd like to try again. And yes, we have this now in our memories."

"Okay, so now what?" he asked.

She squeezed her lips together in a way that made them almost disappear before saying, "I think we need to give it some time. We can't fix this today. I've said what I've come to say. Thank you for listening to me."

"You're welcome," he said in a kind voice.

With that, she stood and he did too. She stepped toward him with her arms out summoning him to hug her. He did. She held him tightly and did not break it for many seconds. While doing so, she said, "If this is the last hug, I want it to be a good one." She pulled away a few inches and put both of her hands on his upper arms. She smiled a similar smile to when he first opened the door and said, "I want to resume the tuck-ins if you ever do...a week from now, a year from now. If all you want to do is talk further about this, I can do that, too."

He nodded silently. She left through the door without turning back to look.

CHAPTER TWENTY-ONE

The two men did not talk about the developments in their lives. They sat, drank, and watched games occasionally, but seldom ate together.

Separately they tried to make sense and put some order to what had transpired. Mondo was conflicted. What had occurred with Diana had never happened between him and another person. On Wednesday, the day after the couch episode, he felt remorse. He prayed and asked God to forgive him and his lustful ways. He did not, however, believe he had broken his vow of celibacy, after all. He had not engaged in intercourse. He had been human. He had experienced a woman's touch and kiss for the first time since before the seminary, and was glad for both. Was that so wrong? At that moment, it seemed like it was.

What would 9:30 bring that very night? He assumed that it would be a more normal tuck-in, that Tuesdays would be their wine night as she said. He wondered about next Tuesday. If Diana remembered it was Tuesday, would something similar occur? He would have six days and nights to think things through and decide whether he would let things go as far as they had, but at this point he felt equal parts of shame and excitement, dread and anticipation. He would first go through tonight's tuck-in. While he fully expected 'normal', Diana had surprised him last night. He knew that this Wednesday night and the tuck-ins that followed would shape this phase of his life. It was possible, he surmised, that Diana would feel some remorse or embarrassment. Not likely, but possible.

Harris, on the other hand, brooded. For the two afternoons following their talk, he sat in his chair in his tiny living room without the television on or guitar in hand. He replayed, rehashed, reviewed, re-everythinged about the bedroom incident, Miranda's visit, and their conversation. He hated what he had witnessed in Miranda's apartment, and he knew he would always hate it. But he was also absolutely disgusted with himself for having intruded. *What was I thinking to walk in on them and then shout? Stupid idiot!*

As the days passed, he felt less disgust for Miranda, though more confused with her explanation. Her feeling trapped by Rex's threat to go to management didn't seem entirely plausible or believable to him. How could she be so naïve, to think that was the solution? The longer he sat there, the more he realized her lapse in judgement was no worse than his own. Perhaps it had been the truth…for her. If so, then what she did with Rex to save the tuck-ins could almost be considered honorable and noble. But he was so rattled, *so close to it* as she said, to throw *noble* onto anything about this… that was a leap too far.

The replays of their conversation included *I want to resume the tuck-ins if you ever do...a week from now, a year from now.* Really? How could she suggest that, even think it might be a possibility? Things were too messed up. He had spoken the irrefutable truth too: *things will never be the same.* Resume tuck-ins? He couldn't see how.

Then he remembered, *I care about you…deeply. I'm very much in love with us. I'm sorry if I ruined it. That will be a horrible loss for me if I did, and a terrible burden to bear.* He wanted to believe her, but that went against everything he knew about relationships. Weren't couples supposed to break up after something like this?

As he sat there those two long, sad afternoons, Harris was introspective enough to realize that any headway the last few months he'd made feeling better about himself, his life, and being able to relate to even one woman, had come about through his relationship with Miranda…because of Miranda. But suddenly, he now sensed he was back to where he'd been for years… an aging man without a woman in his life, lacking the most basic capabilities of relating, connecting, and moving a relationship along.

He was filled with regret. *Why did I open her door and then shout?*

Wednesday night's tuck-in with Diana did happen. Mondo was relieved it did not include wine and red lipstick. Diana never mentioned Tuesday's wine tasting or their heavy petting session, nor did she act uncomfortably or remorseful. After the Friday, Saturday and Monday night tuck-ins, Mondo was a little disappointed when they too turned out to be simply guitar playing while she lay quietly curled on her side, and he departing by saying *nigh'-nigh'. Maybe it was a one-time deal…an aberration*? he wondered. Then…*Maybe I did something that had disenchanted or disappointed Diana?*

When the next Tuesday came around and he saw Diana at Rex's table during lunch, he fought the urge to remind her it was Tuesday. With her forgetfulness about the days of the week, he doubted anything would happen.

As he opened the door that evening, he noticed there were no lights on in the kitchenette or living room. This was not unusual. Sometimes there were, often not. There was low light coming from her bedroom. "Diana? Hello," he said in a voice not meant to alarm her. As he peeked through the door jam, he could see her propped up in bed reading a magazine with her nightstand light on next to her.

"Oh hi," she said looking up at him.

"Is now still a good time?" he asked holding up his guitar with his right hand to remind her why he was there.

"Oh, you brought your guitar. How nice," she said in way that befuddled him.

"Did you still want me to play?"

"Sure. That would be lovely. Do whatever you want to do."

Armando wasn't quite sure what was going on, but as she seemed comfortable with him being there, he decided to sit in his usual spot near her bed. He kept an eye on Diana as he brought the guitar strap up over his head and let the guitar rest on his right thigh. Taking off the capo and setting it aside he embarked on a flamenco tune he had played for her before. Though it should be played with gusto, he always toned it down considering the time of day and his reason for being there.

When he finished, she clapped and said, "That was wonderful. Have you played long?"

He played two more songs, one that he sang, and another instrumental.

Diana sat upright in her bed the entire time, something she had not done since the first time he had played for her. Before leaving, he grabbed one of her stuffed animals, gave it to her, and said, "nigh-nigh, Diana."

"How nice of you. Good night."

As he left her room, he noticed there was no dollar on the counter, and as he opened her front door, he heard, "That was so thoughtful. Bye."

CHAPTER TWENTY-TWO

Four weeks had passed since his world stopped making sense. They had been excruciating days and nights for Harris. He had replayed every walk, every tuck-in, every touch, every word of every conversation, and every text over and over in his head. He tried to make some sense of it…she said this and this…and did that, and yet here they were. Harris couldn't believe where they had gotten to in their relationship…at this impasse.

It was a frustrating exercise… the replaying of the loop. It consumed him. It never led to a different outcome. He knew it was futile, but he couldn't stop himself. Perhaps, he thought, he was connecting the dots in the wrong order or overlooking some. It was what drove him to perseverate. At the end of recalling everything yet again, he tried on different conclusions: *She does love me. She does think I'm special. We do have a long future. I want her with me at the end.* None of those felt true and logical conclusions. He then flipped to more negative conclusions. *She wanted things only her way. Seeing her with Rex was more than stunning, it showed me who she really is. She is not a good person. It is better that I cut my losses and move on*. None of those seemed accurate either.

The only things he knew as true at the moment, were that he felt disappointed and blue... *very* disappointed and *very, very* blue. There was a large void in his life after things had been going so well. That is what he knew.

One evening while eating alone in the dining room, he recalled the podcast she had recommended on one of their first walks. He had listened to it back then out of curiosity as to what Miranda would find interesting. But now there was a little voice inside his ear telling him to listen to *Rethinking Infidelity* again; this time more closely.

That evening with the lights low, television off, and nursing a beer in his favorite chair, he heard Esther Perel, the author, being interviewed for the podcast say, "*We definitely have higher expectations of marriage today than we have ever had. We want everything we expected in a traditional marriage in terms of companionship, economic support, and family life, but also want what the romantic marriage brought us which was belonging, and connecting, and intimacy, best friend, trusted confidant, passionate lover.* ***And now*** *we also want self-fulfillment in our relationship, and to find a soul-mate…forever…and forever keeps getting longer.*"

No wonder people end up disappointed! he thought. And this wasn't even marriage. This was just a simple little, later-in-life friendship. And even that had hit a bump.

Other things caught his attention that Ms. Perel said. "*The definition of infidelity is not agreed upon and it keeps expanding. Is porn infidelity? An emotional affair?"* These words caused him to pause and think about himself and Miranda... Rex and Miranda. Is it really any of his business what went on between Rex and Miranda? And besides, it didn't look like they were having real sex. And equally important, Miranda didn't seem to be emotionally involved in Rex now, even if she had been before.

There was one more line that Ms. Perel spoke on the podcast that hit him hard. *"Unless there is rape or coercion, it is the person who wants less who has the control, has the power."* That had been his marriage in a nutshell. His wife had withheld sex. She had withheld taking care of herself. She withheld even trying. As a result, she had assumed all the power. There had been an imbalance in their relationship because of that. It was not until he filed for divorce, to withdraw himself from the marriage, that the balance shifted.

He thought about what implications, if any, were at play in that regard with Miranda. There was one he thought of immediately. He knew that if he and Miranda ever spoke seriously again, this one thing would need to be addressed.

As the podcast ended and he sat alone in the nearly dark, he doubted that a serious talk would ever happen. He also found it more than strange that of all the podcasts out there, she had directed him to that particular one. Had she known something like this might happen between them from the onset?

CHAPTER TWENTY-THREE

As the days and weeks went by, Armando prayed more and asked God's forgiveness nearly every day. He could not suppress the knowledge that he was still a priest nor that what he and Diana had engaged in that one Tuesday night was wrong. What they had engaged in had also led to lustful thoughts and actions ever since.

On the nights of their normal tuck-in, Armando could not get over how Diana now acted. She never mentioned that one Tuesday, never flirted or came on to him. For nearly half the tuck-ins, she was asleep before he finished playing, before he bid her 'nigh'-nigh', before he looked for the dollar which was never on the counter anymore, and before he quietly left. He also couldn't get over how comfortable and guilt-free she seemed on *that* Tuesday. Perhaps, he thought, that just comes with experience, and experienced he was not.

One Saturday he drove to Stockton nearly 50 miles away, made the sincerest confession of his life, repented, and promised silently to not give into the flesh again. For many weeks, Father Armando was a tormented man. Every day was an inner battle with himself. He wanted touch, passion, release, and yet he did not. How could one moment's pleasure lead to this much angst? It could. It did.

He slept poorly most nights. This too was new to him. He realized that most of his adult life, for all the demands that had been placed upon him as a priest, it had been simple...and his sleep had reflected that simplicity. A little sexual pleasure changed all that.

Besides forgetting to leave payment, Diana no longer asked for tuck-ins, and yet her door was always open and Armando kept showing up. She seemed to enjoy it even if some nights she was surprised by his presence, and Armando derived some simple pleasure from singing to her. The possibility that he was working something out by continuing to sing to her was not lost on him. That cycle showed little signs of breaking until one Friday. He had not seen Diana at all that day or evening, although it was not all that unusual. So, when Mondo opened her door Friday evening at 9:29 holding his guitar, he was surprised to see lights on and Diana fully clothed seated on her sofa. He was rattled more when he noticed a much younger black man seated in the chair near her.

Before he could process what he was seeing, or apologize for intruding, Diana said, "Come on in." When Mondo hesitated, still holding the door open, she continued, "No really, please come in. There is someone I want you to meet."

Mondo closed the door gently and stepped into the small living room.

"Mondo, this is David. David…Mondo." David stood and extended his right hand. Mondo leaned forward, extended his and the men shook. It was then that Mondo noticed a handsome man in his mid to late forties, with a fashionable three-day beard, wearing a navy, cable-knit turtleneck sweater, and pressed jeans.

"I'm so glad you came by tonight," she said looking at Mondo. "David and I have been catching up." Mondo's mind raced. When she added, "David took me out for some nice pasta and I told him all about the nice man that comes by sometimes to sing me to sleep," it did not ease Mondo's mind or slow his heart rate.

"Are you in town visiting?" asked Mondo trying to be polite but keenly interested.

"You might say that," David replied in silky smooth, nearly baritone voice.

"Mondo, I want to tell you something, and I'm afraid it may shock you," said Diana. She a let a long second go by. "David is my son. This afternoon is the first time I've seen him since birthing him." Mondo sat speechless, before Diana continued, "David searched for me and contacted me last week to ask if we could meet. I wasn't completely sure he would show, so I didn't say anything."

"It's nice to meet you David," said Mondo smiling warmly at David.

"It's great to meet you," replied David. "A tuck-in service, huh?"

"That's me," said Mondo. "And you…" he said turning to Diana, "wow. You are just full of surprises."

"Well, I'm afraid this might be the last one, but isn't he a nice one?" she said clearly happy.

"So…a first-time visit? That's pretty huge."

"Yep," said David. "Feels like my birthday."

"David was raised by some wonderful people in… where was that?" Diana asked turning to David for help.

"Marin County, mostly San Rafael. I've been blessed," David added.

"My, oh my," is all Mondo could say while smiling and shaking his head. "This wasn't on my radar walking in here this evening."

"David's married and lives in…well, nearby," Diana said, wanting to tell Mondo more of what she'd learned that afternoon.

"We live in Berkeley. My wife works for Genentech in South City. We have twin boys who turn 18 in a couple of months. Things have turned out well for me. I just got the calling to find my birth mother."

"I'm glad you looked for me, dear," Diana said while reaching out to pat David's knee.

"I'm glad I found you and that you agreed to see me. It would have been crushing if you would have said *no*."

There was a brief, warm silence in Diana's little apartment. Armando had been surprised and uncomfortable initially but was now glad for what he was witnessing. He also knew it was time. "I think I need to be getting back to my place," he said. "David, it was great meeting you," while extending his right hand."

"It was nice meeting you, sir," said David.

"It looks to me like you've made your mother happy. It took some courage to find her. Well done."

"Thank you," David replied.

Diana stood, leaned forward to give Mondo a hug, and said, "Thank you for coming by. Maybe you could bring your guitar tomorrow night?"

"Sounds good," said Mondo unsure of Diana in so many ways at the time.

"See you then," she added.

"G'night," as he let himself out.

The following evening, Mondo took his guitar to Diana's room after having completed three tuck-ins for other residents. Diana was waiting for him on the couch, in her normal daytime attire, and no wine glasses in sight. "I was wondering if we could talk tonight, friend to friend," she asked.

"Sure. Of course," he said while leaning his guitar against the nearest wall. He sat in a nearby chair.

"Yesterday was a big day, as you might imagine," she began.

Mondo nodded, listening and looking intently, waiting for her to continue.

"Yesterday I became a mom, a mother. Of course, I knew all along there was a child and then a man out there, but I successfully pushed that aside, believing he had found a good home…a good family to raise him.

Obviously, he did. Look at him!" she exclaimed with a voice of pride and relief.

"Looks like he turned out great," added Mondo.

"He doesn't need me to be his mom, someone else is that for him. And she must'a done a terrific job. But I'm his birth mother. I'm a mother with a son in her life! God…it's overwhelming."

They sat quietly. Mondo thinking while Diana began crying softly.

"I think he does need you," said Mondo. "He went to considerable effort to find you. He took a big risk, maybe the biggest risk of all by asking if you'd see him. You gave birth to that big guy. You are his mother. He wants you in his life."

"He didn't even ask me… why I gave him up," she blurted out between sobs.

Again, Mondo sat quietly. Years of counselling had taught him it was better to listen more, speak less.

Diana reached for the box of tissues on the coffee table, then dried her eyes and blew her nose. When she felt more composed, she sat more upright with her hands holding the tissue in her lap, and looked at Armando. "I was between marriages. Wild and carefree. It was just some guy I met at a party. We were together just one night. Unprotected sex."

"It happens. A lot."

"I knew I was unfit to be a mother at the time. And I knew I could not abort what was growing inside me."

She threw her hands up a little when she said, "The father wanted no part of this. He offered to pay for an abortion, but that was it. When I told him I couldn't do that, he disappeared. I don't even know the father's last name. How pathetic is that?" she said beginning to cry again.

"I wasn't there," said Armando. "And I only know part of the story, but it seems like you did the right thing. You gave birth to a healthy boy and you changed a couple's lives for the better. It seems like you did something wonderful."

Diana smiled a little smile and said, "Thank you for saying that." She tilted her head forward a bit and began rubbing her face with her left hand. After she blew her nose again, she said "I'm so happy he came into my life, that he showed up yesterday like he said he would…that he didn't yell at me or make me feel bad. He could have done that, you know."

"Yes, I suppose that happens too," Mondo replied nodding his head ever so slightly.

"But I'm so confused. I feel like a different person, just like that. I'm a mother, but I didn't raise him. Someone else did. What do I say to that person if I ever meet her?"

"I think you might be getting ahead of yourself, but *thank you* seems like a good place to start. *You did a great job with David*, might also be appropriate."

This time it was Diana's turn to nod.

"Did he mention yesterday that he wanted you to meet his parents?" asked Mondo.

"No. In fact, he said he hadn't told anyone except his wife about calling or meeting me. He wanted to see how it was going to go with me first."

"David's got a good head on his shoulders," Mondo said.

"Just before he left, he said he'd like to tell his sons, if I was okay with that. When I said *sure*, he said he'd like to wait until they were 18, when it seemed like it was a good time for them to hear it, and give each boy an adult decision to make. Individually they could choose to meet their other grandmother or not. The choice would be theirs."

"David's got a *great* head on his shoulders. And you don't need to sort this all out on the first or second day of your life changing."

Diana sat without moving or making a sound, looking at her lap. When she looked up, she said, "Thank you. You're right. And you're such a good friend. I feel so different." Again she paused, seemingly to see which thought would come forth. "I value our friendship. I hope we can continue tuck-ins."

Mondo said nothing. This surprised him. It seemed she had forgotten about tuck-ins or was surprised he was there sometimes. He didn't know what to make of so much of this. But this evening she seemed so alive, so conversant, and able to remember details of her life long ago. It was what she said next that surprised him the most.

"I'm sorry about the one wine night, I forget what night it was. I may have behaved inappropriately. I'm sorry, Father." She stood and held out her arms. He folded into them and hugged her tightly. She held on for a good while, then asked, "Tomorrow, 9:30?"

"9:30 tomorrow," he said as if chiseling it in stone. "And bring your guitar."

"Will do."

"Oh, and there's a dollar on the counter…for your time today…even though it was worth so much more."

He looked at the dollar on the counter, then back at her a little disappointed. "I don't think so. Tonight was two friends talking." As he pulled the door open to let himself out, he smiled and said, "Save it for tomorrow."

As he walked back to his room, he couldn't have been more perplexed about Diana, especially her memory. He'd been certain she'd been slipping, showing signs of dementia. But after the last two encounters with her and her ability to recall things related to her son and also to *that* Tuesday night, he wasn't certain about anything.

CHAPTER TWENTY-FOUR

Three days after her friend-to-friend talk with Mondo, Diana went to breakfast wearing her bathrobe, slippers, and one hat. The waitress, alarmed at Diana's attire, tried to stop her and said, "We can bring breakfast to your room, if you'd like."

"I just need a cup of coffee, please. Black."

Diana saw Harris who was halfway through a plate of scrambled eggs and overcooked bacon. Since the middle of the night, she'd had an urge to talk to him. Like some urges, this one led to action. More than coffee, finding him was her intent this morning. She approached his small table and said, "Good morning. Mind if I sit with you?"

"Of course, not. Good morning," he replied with feigned energy in his voice. "I don't think I've ever seen you at breakfast before."

"Thanks," she replied while pulling out a chair to sit on. "I try my best to not be seen at this hour." Harris noticed how she was dressed as well as looking like she'd just crawled out of bed. He understood why she'd said what she had.

The waitress brought Diana the coffee. "Thank you."

The two chatted about the weather and Diana sipped her coffee before she jumped into what was on her mind. "Have you talked to Mondo lately?" she asked.

"Not really. We watched a game the night before last."

"Did he say anything about me?"

Harris shifted in his chair, suddenly feeling back in eighth grade before saying, "We don't really have that kind of friendship."

Diana unaware or uncaring of how her question might have sounded said, "He met my son. I had given him up for adoption. It's changed my world. You should ask him about it."

"Wow! Good for you…I think. How are you feeling about it?"

"I feel great about it. I'm still stunned, but that's not what I came to talk to you about."

Harris lowered his fork without finishing his bite. He raised his eyebrows while thinking *you're kidding, right? It sure seemed liked you came to tell me that.*

"I checked in on our friend, Miranda, who I hadn't seen much of lately and who hadn't seemed herself when I did. She told me something happened between you two. She didn't tell me the details, but she feels rotten about it."

"So, she sent you down here to talk to me?"

"No. She's not that way. This is my own doing."

Harris thought for a second. He knew what he'd say next might well work its way back to Miranda. He also realized he and his breakfast companion had not had many conversations, and certainly not about anything serious. "I appreciate your concern, Diana, but it is truly complicated. It's not something I feel comfortable at all getting into with others."

Diana looked at him, regretting her impulse to find Harris at breakfast. She took a final sip of coffee before pushing herself away from the table and standing. She looked at him then walked away without so much as *have a nice day*. She stopped suddenly, spun around, took a step back towards him, and said, "You want to know what complicated is? I'll tell you what complicated is." She began punctuating some words with a raised and pointed right index finger. "It's having a 47-year-old black man show up at my door and saying *hi mom*…and then discover he's a great guy that must have been raised by a great mother who wasn't me. That's complicated!" She continued after collecting another thought, "And then I find out I've got two grandsons that are almost 18… that I've *completely* missed out on. That's even more complicated."

Harris sat stunned, not taking his eyes off Diana. She then added in calmer voice, "And after talking with him...my gosh he's a great guy… I've decided I want him to be part of my life. I don't know how, but it needs to happen!"

Harris said nothing, but instantly realized that he had just received a crash course on perspective.

She continued, "The two of you guys seemed to have something special between you. Everyone could see it."

"Really? Everyone?" he asked, truly surprised.

"*Really…everyone.* Lately you've both been moping around like two lost souls. I suggest you get your butt up there to see her soon and figure somethin' out. Whata'ya waiting for? The clock's a tickin'."

Diana walked away, not waiting for a response, and this time did not turn back.

CHAPTER TWENTY-FIVE

The following evening, during a baseball game and over beers, the two men sort of talked about it, the way that only men can talk around the edges of things. Mondo acknowledged that he had been introduced to Diana's man-son, and that he seemed like a fine man. "Diana seems pretty consumed by this," Harris observed.

"Consumed, rattled, smitten…I'm not sure what it is, but it has altered her life," Mondo answered.

"You guys still going to do the tuck-ins?" Harris asked.

"Yep, tuck-ins are still on."

That was the extent of their discussing Diana, her son, and how Mondo fit in. That discussion slid neatly into one muted car commercial, and a portion of a Burger King ad. There was no need to belabor the facts. Mondo never felt the need to inquire about Harris and Miranda, for all he knew things had never changed. Harris had never indicated anything different, so Mondo assumed their tuck-ins were still occurring. It may have been obvious to others at The Ridge that

Harris had been in a funk, but Mondo wrote it off as Harris having finally settled into the boredom of the place and resignation that this is what life was for him.

The following morning Harris sent Miranda a text: *I'm ready to chat, if you are.*

Her reply read: *Ready.*

Does 2:00 today work at your place?

Yes.

That afternoon Miranda greeted him warmly but without touching. "Please come in."

He sat in a chair, she on the small couch in her tiny living room. He looked around, noticing pictures and knick-knacks for the first time before saying, "I'm a little nervous. Any thoughts on how we do this?"

"I'm nervous too and feeling a bit vulnerable," she added. "You called this meeting. I think you need to go first."

"Yes, I suppose so," he said business-like.

"Before you start, I have to say that I may need to take a call if my land-line rings in a while. You can stay if you want… if I do get a call."

"Okay," he said only minorly flummoxed, before realizing he had asked to see her on short notice. "I've been doing some thinking," he began. "A lot actually. And people…at least one person…has said that I seem like a lost soul."

Miranda smiled and said, "She told me that too."

"Ahh, yes. Well, I was intending on doing this. Diana just nudged me at the right time in the right way, I guess."

"I'm glad she did."

"The thing is, I felt good around you for a long time…maybe the best I've felt around a woman ever." He paused to see if she would respond. She was attentive, but did not react. "There were things that perplexed me about you, things I wished were different, but it was still pretty stinkin' great up until the Rex incident."

"It was great for me too," she added.

He was leaning forward in the chair, hands on his legs occasionally rubbing his knees, trying not to fidget, but feeling jumpy inside. Hesitantly he said, "I think there's something here." He watched her face and looked into her eyes as he spoke. She was careful not to interrupt this moment, but he could tell she liked what he'd just said. Her head nodded up and down almost imperceptibly. "I'd be open to starting over… slowly, if you're open for it. Maybe an occasional tuck-in or walk, and kind of feel our way through this."

She waited a couple of seconds to make sure he had finished his thought before smiling just a bit and saying, "I'm good with that."

"Good," he said leaning all the way back in the chair. "There's one other thing," he said while locking his eyes back onto hers. "I've relistened to the podcast you had me listen to."

"*Rethinking Infidelity*?"

"Yes, that one. I can't help but ask…did you know that something like Rex was going to happen between us… and that you were just trying to warn me?"

Miranda let out a little laugh. "No, I'm really not that clever or clairvoyant or manipulative or however you want to put it. But I can see how you might think it's a little weird."

"It's more than a little strange," he said, "that out of the universe of podcasts...you had me listen to that one."

"I simply liked what she was saying is all. There were some profound insights that caught my attention." Miranda straightened out her legs in front of her, the way she did on their walks when they sat, then asked, "That's it? That's the one thing you wanted cleared up?"

Harris looked at her for a moment, shifted his weight in the chair, and said, "Actually there was one part that caught my attention the most. It was when Miss Perel said that the person who withholds in the relationship has the power."

Miranda nodded her head a couple of times with furrowed brow, not quite sure where Harris was headed. "That's what happened with my wife," he added. "She withheld a bunch of stuff, and my fear is that is what is happening between you and me…maybe to a lesser extent, but it's still happening."

"I'm not sure I follow. I invite you to my room," she said with some agitation. "We don't have sex, but we are intimate, very intimate I'd say. We communicate freely. I feel like I can tell you most anything. I've never lied to you. I'm not exactly sure what I'm withholding."

"Miranda, you decide where, when, and how we will see each other. I have little or no say in that. I've wanted to see you every day once we started to get close, but you decided to throw in off days. There were no excuses or reasons given. It's what you wanted, so it's what happened. You have held the power in our little relationship."

Miranda was quiet for a long time before responding, "I see."

"I need that to change. I'm not sure I get how Rex coerced you into getting together, but I'm willing to put that behind us. It seems like you don't really care for him. But I need to have a say if and when we get together."

Miranda sat quietly again, not having expected the conversation to go this way. She hesitated saying what came into her mind. She knew it might come across as contentious, but it was important to her, the center of her and Harris' relationship, so out she came with it. "Do you know why I suggest off days for us?"

"No idea. To drive me nuts? To make me want you more? I thought I was past that stage of my life," he said with an edge.

"We have or did have something special," she said. "I thought about you all the time. I looked forward to our next encounter, whatever and whenever it was."

"Same here."

"I didn't want that to end."

"It doesn't have to," he added.

"But it does... it will, Harris, whether people want it to or not." She had called him Harris again and it sounded strange to both of them. "Couples who like each other and pair off, start hanging around each other *all* the time. They start doing *everything* together, and pretty soon it's *bor-ing*. They get too used to each other. I didn't want that. I needed to go about it differently... to hold onto that special feeling for as long as we could."

It was Harris' turn to sit quietly, to ponder her words. He was beginning to understand her. It made some sense, her view on how couples went from infatuation to boredom, but he was unwilling to turn complete control back over to Miranda, to let things simply return to how they had been. He said, "But isn't there a middle ground...without getting bored with each other?"

"I don't know. I don't think there is. It seems to happen *every* time, to *every* relationship. I look at it as this is my last chance to get it right...to go about this one differently, in a way that feels correct and proper to me. I haven't been in that many relationships, but I've observed a lifetime of them."

"I see."

Just then her land-line telephone rang. She looked at him dejectedly knowing the timing was poor. "I'm sorry. I have to take this. You can stay if you want, but it may take a while."

Harris sat. Her thoughts about relationships circulated in his head. His curiosity about the phone call was piqued when she moved to sit next to the phone, put a headset on, punched a button on the phone, and said calmly "Hello, my name is Miranda. Whom am I speaking with?"

While Miranda listened, Harris watched her reach under the phone's charging station to pick up a brightly colored, 8.5 x 11-inch laminated sheet.

"I'm glad you called, Tiffany. You can tell me as much or as little as you want. This is not being recorded. It's just between the two of us, okay?" She paused to listen to a reply that Harris could not hear, then continued, "But I've got to ask, are you contemplating hurting yourself today?"

Harris shifted nervously in his seat, stunned at what he was hearing, believing he understood what kind of phone call it was. He was surprised, curious of course, but suddenly felt like he was intruding on something very private even though he couldn't hear Tiffany's side of the conversation.

"Can you tell me a little bit about what's been going on, Tiffany?" Miranda asked in her calmest voice. "What are those things that have been happening in your life that have gotten you to this point?"

While Miranda listened for multiple minutes, only interjecting with an *I see* periodically, Harris found a scratch pad and pen on Miranda's end table. He wrote:

You have important work to do.
How about I catch up with you tomorrow?
Btw, I enjoyed our chat.
H

He got up, walked the note over to Miranda, laid it in front of her, and patted her right shoulder.

She looked at the note while reaching up to his hand with her left hand, squeezed his, and mouthed *thank you.*

Before he left, Harris walked to the kitchenette, found a glass and filled it with water. He placed the glass in front of her before giving a tiny, barely above-the-waist-wave good-bye. Miranda smiled, watched him head toward the door, and turned her full attention back to Tiffany.

CHAPTER TWENTY-SIX

David came out to see Diana every week or two. When he visited, they always worked in a lunch or dinner for the two of them. He wanted to get her away from The Ridge, even for a couple of hours, though he found nothing overtly disturbing about the place where his mother lived. David always insisted on paying. Twice he took her to afternoon movies, and once on a clear, crisp day, he drove her to the top of Mt. Diablo to witness the stunning view.

One lunch, over a panini sandwich and fries at a nearby fashionable restaurant, Diana informed David, "I'm in the process of drawing up a will. I've never had anyone to leave anything to. It's not that much, but I want you to have whatever I leave behind."

"That's not why I found you," he said with some sternness for the first time.

"I know it isn't. That's why it's easy for me to do it. It would be much more complicated if I thought that's why you found me, don't you think?"

"I suppose it would be," he said smiling, eager to put this topic behind them. He fiddled with the silverware at his place setting before changing the subject. "The boys turned 18 last week. I didn't want to tell them about you on their birthday, but two nights later over a family dinner…those are getting more rare in our household by the way, I told them about you… about finding you."

"And?" she asked.

"Of course, they were stunned, and, of course, they'd like to meet you! I knew they would. There was never a doubt."

"Good. I'm so glad! That makes me happy," she said.

"I'm thinking dinner at our house, some Sunday, when it all works out. How does that sound?"

"Oh my…it sounds thrilling. I'll be nervous about it, about meeting my grandsons and your wife. I never would have imagined this could happen. Not in my lifetime."

"Good then, let me look at our multiple calendars and button something down for the next month or so. I don't want any of my clan surprising me with, *I forgot to mention I had this meeting or practice…*".

Diana chuckled then asked, "What are their names…your sons?"

"Ladaniel and Marques," David replied. My wife's name is Keshia."

"Beautiful names. I'm gonna jot those down so I don't forget."

Diana found a pen and a scrap of paper. David helped her with the spelling.

Diana began hopping on The Ridge shuttle van every Wednesday for shopping excursions. She no longer drove, nor did Miranda. She thought she needed new clothes, and she wanted to get something for David, his wife, and their boys. Toward the end of one shopping outing, the van driver had to search for her. Diana claimed that she'd lost track of time, but the driver found her sitting on a bench a hundred yards from the agreed upon meeting spot.

Back at The Ridge, Mondo still did tuck-ins for Diana four or five nights a week. They were always platonic. Sometimes Diana propped herself up in bed and they chatted between Mondo's songs, never intending to be sung to sleep. One evening, Mondo noticed while playing to her, that some things were missing from her room. "Where are the stuffed animals?" he asked.

"Oh, I tossed those silly things out. It seemed like they were part of the *old me*. I've got a son who comes to this place now, and someday my grandsons may too. I want them to see me differently."

"I see," Mondo responded.

"I'm not sure you can understand how wonderful this all is, but I feel like a different person."

"I'm happy for you," he said.

"Thank you. You're a great friend." She smiled at him before rolling onto her side, a signal to Mondo that she was done with chatting for the evening.

CHAPTER TWENTY-SEVEN

11:00 o'clock work to continue our chat? he texted the following morning.

Yes, she quickly responded. *My place okay?*

Harris wanted to finish up their discussion. He had given it more thought, and was certain Miranda had too. He also had many questions about her hotline calls. When she opened the door, she smiled warmly. He moved to her for a hug with his arms outstretched this time. She wrapped hers around him. They held each other like reunited friends.

"Please come in, sit where you want," she said finally.

He chose the small couch, sitting to the right portion of it just to see if she might join him there. She did.

"I'm not sure where to start," he said. "We kind of left off at a key point in wading through our stuff, but I want to know more about the calls you take."

"How about we wrap up our stuff first?" she asked. "I'm thinking that we can do so pretty quickly and painlessly."

"Quickly and painlessly works for me."

"You need more say in when, where, and how we get together," she said. "And I see this as a last chance for this incredible relationship that is floating in my head...one that never gets stale. One where I can tell you everything and no part of it is even a tiny lie. It's probably unrealistic and unfair to both of us, but I really felt like I could navigate us through it…and it seemed like it was working for a while."

"Except you didn't know I was starting to build up some resentment and secretly wishing things were different."

"You were being so compliant with me directing my little fantasy," she said with a devilish smile.

"Classic case of passive man--aggressive woman, I sense. I was mostly happy to be in your presence."

"And I in yours, Mr. Archibald," she added. "It would be such a loss, a large hole in my life, if you weren't in it. I'm willing to bend, to give you an equal say in when, where, and how."

"Thank you," he said exhaling deeply through his nose. But I kinda' like your idea of striving to *not* become like most other couples. I think it's an honorable fantasy you have there."

"Why thank *you*."

"What if every *other* time you let me initiate getting together and I will be sensitive to keeping things spaced out a bit? You gave me a good model to work with. I'll never lose sight of it."

"Deal. But you can put your own spin on things."

"Deal," he added.

"I'll be anxious to see what it looks like with you driving this half the time."

"I initiated this gathering," he pointed out, "so the next one is yours. But before I leave, I want to hear about whatever it is I caught a glimpse of yesterday."

Miranda walked stiffly over to the little desk area with the telephone on it and grabbed the laminated sheet from underneath the charging station. As she reseated herself, she said, "I volunteer to take calls for the suicide hotline twice a week for three hours at a time. I used to do it more at their call center in Walnut Creek, but when I stopped driving and told them I could no longer help, they said they would make an arrangement for me to do it remotely. Now they forward some calls to this phone," she said as she pointed to the land-line set on the small desk in the living room.

"But when did you get into this? Why?"

"After my husband died, I floundered. I had little purpose and was in a funk. I read an article in the local newspaper about some of the work volunteers were doing, and how they were always looking for others who might have that calling. I contacted them. They said that if I was interested and willing to commit to six hours a week, they would train me. I decided to do it. Initially, I was doing three four-hour shifts a week. The calls can be very draining. It's been over eight years."

"Did anyone you ever know, friends or family, commit suicide?"

"We've all had some heartache in our lives, some of us even tragedy," she said slowly and not exactly answering the question. "It's not a job requirement… having that in your background. Once I thought about it though, I was just pulled toward doing this. It was like my calling."

"You sounded so calm yesterday, the little bit I heard."

"Yes, well, that *is* a requirement. Some of these people are in bad shape. Some are getting counseling, many are not. We can't fix them. We just try to talk them away from the edge if they are on it, give them a caring voice at the other end of the line. The goal is always to get them through this day, to seek some kind of other help if they are willing, but to always know this is a number they can call."

"Wow. I would have never guessed in a billion years that this is what you did with some of your afternoons. What great work you do!" he said.

"Thank you!"

"And I can see why you didn't tell me."

"It's kind of messed-up if you go around saying, *Yes I volunteer for the Suicide Prevention hotline…aren't I wonderful?* Or worse yet, if people at The Ridge knew I did this, they'd want to know all about the last call I took."

"Rex would!" he said chuckling.

"Ha. He'd only ask about it to then tell me how he would have handled it differently."

"Yeah," he said. "*Listen here you stupid son of a bitch… put down that knife! Do you know how goddamn stupid you are to cut yourself?*"

She slapped her thighs with her hands, bending forward while laughing heartily. "Oh man, that's probably pretty close to how it would go too!"

As Harris left that day, they hugged again at her door. "The ball is in your court. It's your fantasy," he said.

Miranda texted the next morning: *9:30 tuck-in tonight?*

When Harris arrived that night in Miranda's dimly lit apartment with his iPad and guitar, he glanced at the counter of her kitchenette. There were two dollars lying on it.

CHAPTER TWENTY-EIGHT

Rex willed his way back into prominence, at least in his own mind. He never missed a meal. Never missed showing off his daughter. Never felt shy about telling management how they could run the place better. Never overlooked an opportunity to share his educated insights on the latest political issue. "Them lib-tards are nuthin' but socialists. Free healthcare and free college tuition! Who the hell they think is going to pay for all of that? It sure as hell can't be us…we're all on fixed income."

"Does Medicare work pretty well for you," chimed in Setesh, the man in the wheelchair.

"It does," replied Rex with an edge. "But I paid into that goddamn system my whole working life. Why should 20-somethings who just starting their working lives get the same healthcare? You're not thinking it through, See-tesh. Gotta use that noggin' of yours."

Setesh remained calm when he said, "Healthcare costs have been rising 10-20% for decades. Why do we have to pay insurance companies billions of dollars to push paper around? Hundreds of millions of dollars go to stock dividends. You have some CEO's making more than $40 million. Why not let the government run it without profit?"

"You ever seen the government ever run anything right?" Rex said putting down his fork.

"They've done a fine job with the postal system," responded Setesh.

"Are you kidding me? You're kidding me, right?" asked Rex.

"The National Park system."

"Have you lost your mind, man? The government already outsources big parts of the park system like lodging, restaurants, the reservation system. And besides, if you give the government healthcare, you'll have these death panels making decisions you don't want them making about you and your family."

"Nobody ever has denied me the healthcare I've needed since I've been on Medicare. But some lowly paid rep at the end of the phone line did multiple times when I had private insurance."

"See, that's what I mean. Medicare for all will just be filled with waste…providing everything to everybody. That's why it'd be too damn expensive."

"I thought you were concerned about death panels?" asked Setesh while smiling and looking straight at Rex. Rex had no comeback. "I think you are talking in circles, Rex. I think you can't keep track of your own arguments."

"I keep track of my own arguments just fine, thank you. If you had any sense of what you're talking about, or what's good for this country, we could have an honest discussion. But seeing's how you don't, I'm just going to eat my damn ravioli. You're ruinin' my dinner."

Mrs. Hannigan and Diana sat quietly eating. They wanted no part of this discussion and knew better than to arbitrate. Silently, each liked the way Setesh argued with Rex. The way he went about it almost made his point of view more reasonable, more appealing, but neither of them said so.

~

Rex knew he had won the healthcare argument when he went back to his room after dinner. How informed and intelligent could an immigrant be expected to be on today's issues, anyhow? For all Rex knew, Setesh got his daily dose of uninformed propaganda from one of those liberal networks like CNN or MSNBC.

Rex's daily routine consisted of three treks each day to the dining room, reading the local paper immediately after lunch, and watching television from his favorite chair, mostly hunting and fishing shows. After his dinner at 5:00, he'd settle into watching Hannity and the others on FOX News until he made his evening rounds. Like a couple of other men at The Ridge, he left the front door to his apartment open most of the day. He liked to hear the activity of the hallway, sometimes noticing who was walking by, occasionally kibitzing with them. Often, the passersby would see him slouched over in his chair snoozing with the tv on. He liked beer at night, every night. His daughter would bring him a six pack or two when she visited thinking that would tie him over until her next visit.

Rex still roamed the halls after 9:00 PM. There had been no activity to and from Miranda's room in the evening for a while, which pleased him. He could see Father Armando leaving Diana's room most nights around 10:00, but even that seemed to have tapered off a night or two a week. Diana's business never had concerned him much, but he still felt some satisfaction sitting in the chair in the hall near Miranda's room when night after night Harris neither came nor went.

When it changed and Harris came out of Miranda's door unexpectedly one night, Rex didn't hide his derision offering a snide, "Get lucky?" and, "Didn't think so," when getting no immediate reply.

The second time, Harris was prepared for that question, and decided to nod affirmatively with a wry smile and say, "She's amazing." He felt bad later, knowing those words could be taken different ways and he didn't want Miranda to be seen as something different than she was…even to Rex. He relayed the entire incident, verbatim, to Miranda the following day.

"He's such an ass," she said after listening. "Tell him anything you'd like. Embellish it. But make sure you include my breasts. He's enamored with my breasts."

"I won't be doing that," Harris said. "He seems bothered enough by seeing me just come out of your room."

"Good. I'll make sure I give you a long, passionate kiss sometime at the door just to really flip him out."

Harris smiled at the thought. They had not gotten to the point of kissing, let alone passionate kissing, though the thought had crossed his mind. Maybe Miranda's mentioning it was her invitation, her suggestion to move things along.

Every once in a great while, Harris and Mondo would cross paths in the hall around 10:00 PM when heading back to their own rooms. While Diana's and Miranda's rooms were not near each other, they were both on the second floor.

One night, Harris had just left Miranda's room and encountered Rex sitting in the hall.

"You're still a loser. Always will be," Rex said.

Harris stopped this time, four feet from Rex and said, "This really is pathetic, you must know that… sitting here night after night… getting all worked up about what Miranda and I are up to."

Before Rex could fire something back, the door nearest them opened. Initially no one came out, but it appeared as though someone was holding the door open from the inside. A few seconds later, a gurney rolled out. Harris looked at the nameplate next to the door…*Rose Hannigan*. Two men, dressed in brown suits whom Harris had never seen before, carefully squeezed the rolling gurney through the open door without scratching the door frame. There was a covered body on top. Brian, The Ridge's General Manager, was the last to come out of the room. After shutting the door, he made certain the door was locked with his master key.

Harris and Rex each had perplexed looks on their faces trying to process what they were seeing. Brian, noticing their expressions whispered, "She passed last night or this morning."

"We didn't see her at lunch but nobody thought anything of it," Rex said.

"When our staff hadn't seen her at breakfast or lunch, we decided to check in on her," Brian said as he turned to follow the men charged with removing her body.

Just then Mondo joined them, holding his guitar, approaching from the direction where the gurney and men were headed. "What happened?" he asked looking at Harris and then Rex.

"Mrs. Hannigan passed," said Rex. "Sometime in the last twenty-four hours."

"Why are they removing her body now, at ten o'clock at night?" Harris asked.

"It's the way they do it around here," Rex said with feigned authority. "After hours, when they think we're all in bed, they bring the morticians in, hoping nobody notices."

The three men looked at each other, then the floor, saying nothing more. Slowly, Harris turned and headed down the hall with Mondo following, watching the gurney enter the elevator in the distance. Rex remained seated until everyone was out of sight.

CHAPTER TWENTY-NINE

After several weeks of their new shared routine, Miranda texted Harris. *Take me to a Drs app't tomorrow AM? Would need to leave about 10:40.*

Sure. Everything ok?

Annual check-up. Lunch on me afterwards.

Sounds good. Meet in lobby 10:40.

Harris arrived in the lobby at 10:35 with Miranda, using her cane, arriving moments later. They chose not to hug.

On the drive there, Harris asked what kind of doctor she was seeing.

"My oncologist. I've been with him since it all happened. I picked out one much younger than me, figuring I would never need to find a new one."

Harris glanced at her while driving in the slow lane, respecting her logic.

"He's a good guy. I have a lot of confidence in him. He wants to see me twice a year now, but I've been giving him one. Arranging for the shuttle is a bother."

"I don't mind driving you if you'd like to go twice, although I can't help but notice this is taking our relationship into a very mundane, ordinary place."

Miranda paused before saying "Thank you. Maybe I should go twice a year. This stuff can recur, and usually does if you don't die from something else first."

When they parked in the doctor's office lot, Miranda said. "We're early. Traffic was light. My appointment's not until 11:15. Can we go back to what you said earlier? About being mundane?"

"Sure," Harris said.

"You and I are intimate. We have an intimate relationship."

"Huh? We don't even kiss," he said in disagreement.

"Tis true. I, by the way, think we should do something about that, but that is for another time. I let you touch me in a very special way. I behave in the most open of ways with you. I'm more comfortable with you than anyone. That's intimacy in my book. Healthcare is also a very private matter for most people. It is for me. Having you drive me and be involved in this part of life…well, there's a certain intimacy there too."

"I see," said Harris slowly. After a pause he added, "And I agree about everything you just said. Anyone can fuck, pardon my English. We *are* intimate."

"Well maybe not everyone at my age, but intimacy is so much more than that. If you find the right person, you invite them into your life. I'm inviting you into another aspect of mine…today."

"I'm privileged and accept."

She smiled and said, "We should get going. He's on the 3rd floor."

At lunch, Harris probed more about the doctor's appointment, about Miranda's health.

"They want to do a PET scan next week. It's something they insist upon every couple of years. I'm okay until they tell me I'm not."

"I'll be happy to take you to that appointment," he said.

"Thank you. It's something I try not to think about, but that's not possible, it seems. Once you've had cancer and go through a significant treatment, in my case a mastectomy, you wonder when…" her voice tapering off, not finishing her thought.

"Well, you look great. Your energy is good," said Harris. He had not been down this road. He knew instantly his words sounded trite, but he didn't know what to say, how to act. He was new at this. They ate their burritos mainly in silence. Harris took her to get the PET scan eight days later.

CHAPTER THIRTY

Diana had long stopped asking for tuck-ins from Mondo, and he began going less on his own. He did not take it personally, rather chalking it up to changes in her family situation. One Saturday, while running into her near their mail boxes, he asked if he could play for her again sometime soon.

"Well, I suppose that would be alright," she replied.

"How about tonight? he asked.

Diana paused and looked him quizzically before asking, "What time?"

"What time?" he asked animatedly and amused. "Our normal time, 9:30."

"Oh, that's much too late," she said. "How about 8:00?"

Mondo didn't think much of their exchange and the time change until he arrived at her apartment that evening, only to find the door locked. He knocked softly, but when he got no response and could hear the TV inside, he knocked louder. Diana came to the door and acted surprised to see him.

He was confused but only became alarmed when Diana welcomed him in, and said, "Oh, you brought a guitar? How nice."

Mondo sat while she turned down the TV and asked if he wanted a glass of wine. He could see she had a partially finished glass and he declined.

They chatted as though they were acquaintances, Diana never asking him to play for her, and Mondo never suggesting it either. Diana did tell him, "I have a new family. It's a long story. I still can't believe it." Diana proceeded to tell Mondo most of the sequence of events that he already knew.

When he rose to leave, he thanked her for the visit.

She said, "Next time, play that guitar for me, okay? I bet you're pretty good."

~

David called her the following morning to tell his mother he would pick her up around 4:00 that afternoon to bring her to dinner at his house. It was more than simple courtesy. He didn't want her to forget and not be properly dressed. This was a large day for all of them.

"Oh really? This is the first I'm hearing about this. Did you tell me before?"

David said, "Yes, Mom. We talked about it Thursday when I came over."

He called again at 3:30, under the guise that he was running a few minutes late, just to remind her to wear something nice. Diana didn't say much on the phone other than "Okay," but was waiting in the lobby at 4:02 when David arrived and signed her out. Diana greeted him with a hug. "Hello," was all she said. She wore a nice brown pants suit with a light green blouse and an apricot scarf.

"You look nice, Mom," David said glancing at his mother from head to toe. He was glad to see her not wearing any hats, but was surprised to see how thin her grey hair was.

On the drive to his house, David tried to make small talk, but he was worried about how this gathering might unfold. Had he done the wrong thing by suggesting it, in orchestrating it?

"I know this is a big deal for you Mom. It is also big for my children, your grandchildren, in a different way. They need a little time to process all this, to get used to you."

"Now remind me, what are your children's names?"

"Ladaniel and Marques. They are both 18. My wife is Keshia."

"What unusual names," she said.

David fidgeted in the driver's seat.

"Now where are we going?" she asked.

"Berkeley. My house…for dinner. We live in Berkeley."

"Oh, how nice."

David adjusted the rearview mirror. He tried to bring forth his most calm voice. "How have you been feeling, mom? Are things okay?"

"Oh, I feel fine."

"No falls or anything?"

"Nope, no falls."

"Mom, how about we keep expectations realistic today?" David suggested.

"What are you saying? They might not like me?"

"Oh, they'll like you…in time. This is new for them. Just give them a little time, okay?"

"All right," Diana sounding confused.

"I just hope you don't expect them to come running up to you with outstretched arms saying *grandma*."

Diana was quiet for a while before saying, "I'm not sure what to expect, I'm kinda new at this too, but I guess that might have been in there."

"Let's just take it slow. This isn't a one-shot deal. Let's just give everybody a chance to get comfortable with this new information that we are all very related."

When they arrived in the driveway, David turned off the car. They sat there for a minute, letting her take it in.

"It's lovely," she said. "You must be very successful."

He held her left arm as they climbed the portico's stairs. "We're here," he sang as he opened the tall front door. The first thing Diana saw was three wide-eyed, nicely dressed people standing in the very high-ceilinged foyer.

"Come in. I'm Keshia," she said extending her arms around Diana's shoulders.

There was a stiffness for all concerned during the next two and a half hours. *How could it be any other way* thought David as he observed the proceedings.

"David tells me that you handled his sudden appearance into your life with great calmness and acceptance," Keshia said as they talked in the living room before dinner.

"Well, it's not like I didn't know I had a son out there somewhere. I just didn't know he'd be so handsome and successful, and with such a beautiful family," Diana replied.

"He is handsome, but David was very relieved that you welcomed him back into your life. He was worried about it," Keshia added.

"I'm so glad he found me and took the chance, and that you've all welcomed me into your home." Diana looked at the four black people who were watching her, listening to her closely, amazed that this was her family, her only family. "I'm not a very religious person normally, but this is such a blessing at this stage of my life. I… I just can't believe it," she stammered.

The boys had been quiet while they all sat on the large L-shaped sofa. When Diana looked down and got very quiet, David nudged one of the boys. Ladaniel piped in with, "Do you like where you're living?"

"It's fine," Diana answered. "Nothing special really. It feeds me. There are some people to keep me company. I think one of my ex-husband's was nice enough to help me find it."

They waded through the get-to-know-each-other-talk over dinner, led mainly by Keshia. Diana couldn't articulate it, but she was drawn to how calm and kind Keshia was throughout this time. David poured Frank

Family Chardonnay for his mother, wife, and himself while Keshia served the halibut dinner with a dill sauce. He put the bottle away without ever offering seconds. Before dessert, David could see Diana was losing steam, and suggested, "This has been a big outing for you Mom. We can get you back at any time."

"It has been a big outing for me. I'm sorry to be such a pooper, but my batteries do seem to be fading. What time is it?"

"7:33 mom," David said.

They agreed to call it a day, said good-byes, and David drove her home. Diana had forgotten about the gifts they had placed in the trunk, and David had decided not to bring the gifts in, though he had remembered. When they arrived back in The Ridge parking lot, Diana asked if they could sit in the car for a minute, before getting out.

"You have a lovely home and family," she began.

"Thank you."

"You found a good wife in Keshia. You hang onto her."

"Thanks for the advice. I'm not trading her in," David replied with a grin.

Diana got quiet, and looked down at her fingers that were picking at each other. She then looked up at David and said, "I'm sorry I gave you up. I don't know how a mother could do that."

David thought of a couple of different responses before saying, "It happens all the time. Everyday. I'm sure it seemed like the only option at the time."

Diana's eyes welled up then she said, "You're very kind."

"I've had a good life, a very good life," David said. "And now we have each other. I don't want you carrying any guilt with you, okay?"

She forced a smile and said, "Okay."

CHAPTER THIRTY-ONE

Well into dinner one evening, Rex noticed Miranda at a nearby table place her folded napkin onto her plate, slowly get up, find her cane, and begin the walk back to her room. That evening she had been at the table to his right, dining with two other ladies she sometimes ate with. He had glanced in her direction three times during the previous 15 minutes without making eye contact. "Well, I think I've had about enough tonight," he said to the others at his table while crumpling up his napkin and placing it to the side of his partially finished dinner.

"What, no dessert tonight?" asked Diana.

"Nope. On a diet," he said patting his formidable belly while standing. "At least for one meal."

Rex pushed his chair back in, found his cane, and departed in the direction Miranda had headed, which was not the way to his own room. He caught up to her as the elevator door opened. She was startled to see him walk into the elevator right behind her, as she had not noticed him before.

When she pushed the button for the second floor, Rex asked, "Everything okay?"

"I don't know. What are you doing here?"

"I'm just checking on you. I've been noticing your little boyfriend is back with his evening activity in your room." The elevator jerked to a stop and the door opened onto her floor. Miranda immediately moved into the hall.

She continued on toward her room, not looking at him but stating sternly, "I know you think otherwise, Rex, but it's *really* none of your business."

Rex moved at her pace, just trailing her right shoulder when he said, "I'm always interested in your safety, Miranda. You know how boys can be…even the ones who start out nice. I know Brian, the General Manager of this fine establishment, is interested in your safety too… and what the roving minstrels are up to."

She looked around as she got near her door and recalled Harris' prediction. The hallway was empty in both directions. "You're an ass," this time looking into his eyes as she spoke.

"I may have been from time to time in my life," he said with a little chuckle. "But I think it's time we got together again, for a little visit, to keep your little tuck-in service going…if you know what I mean."

"That is *never* going to happen," she said as tersely as she could. "I'm going inside and if you attempt to follow me, I will scream my head off."

"Suit yourself. Just trying to protect you and your friend."

Miranda turned the key to her apartment, opened the door, entered, and closed it quickly behind her. Her last image of Rex was him leaning on his cane right in front of her door, smiling.

She did not sleep well that night, mulling over the implication of Rex's last couple of statements. She vacillated whether she should tell Harris what Rex had said, or perhaps go to the General Manager this time. When she awoke about 3:30 and went to the bathroom, she returned to bed only to lie there unable to drift off. There and then, she decided that she would not tell Harris. What would he do but act all chivalrous? That could play out weirdly or badly. Contact Brian the General Manager? That's probably what she should have done the first time, but how would she word it? It was possible he'd make Mondo and Harris stop. She was restless until almost dawn, when she fell into the deepest sleep. When she awoke again at 8:40, her first thought was that handling this the correct way, once and for all, was critical. She and Harris were back again on good footing, and she wanted to preserve that most of all. She also wanted Rex to be gone, to give this up. He was a horrible human who was good at finding ways he could get next to her. It had worked once, and as Harris had suggested, Rex was trying again. If successful this second time for Rex, a third would be inevitable.

Days passed. The new routine for Miranda and Harris seemed to be working, at least for him. When it was his turn, he held off for a day, sometimes two, before texting her with his suggested plans. He now had some say in how things flowed, just what he had been looking for. She was less in-charge, and noticed herself being edgy, waiting for the next text to arrive, feeling like a disappointed, desperate damsel whenever he skipped a day.

One text from him was for a lunch invitation at a very nice place in town called Piatti's. They sat near the lit fireplace and shared a good meal. To Miranda, it felt like a date. It did to Harris as well.

When he drove them back to The Ridge, Harris walked her back to her room. They hugged and said awkward good-bye's not knowing quite how to do the next part of the date.

Harris went back to his room, and he'd had the Golf Channel on for only 20 minutes when his phone pinged. *9:30 tonight please* it read.

Two dollars were on the counter. He never let her know in any way that he was disappointed whenever there was only one dollar, but he always was. He'd grown fond of the two-dollar nights.

This night he arrived carrying only his iPad. "Hi," he said softly as he sat in the wicker chair in her bedroom. "Didn't I just see you a bit ago?"

"I think you did. But not like this," she replied smiling, covers pulled up around her.

Harris smiled too as he sat there, not moving in the dark. The only light coming from underneath the microwave.

"No guitar? I'm not sure I'm going to get my money's worth."

"Pay me whatever you wish…or nothing. I want to try reading to you, to see if you like that."

"I see," she said with a hint of playfulness. "I think I like it already."

"I brought one of my favorite books, *Plainsong* by Kent Haruf." When she didn't respond, he continued, "It's a simple story, slow moving. I'm puzzled why I like it so much, but I do."

"Well let's hear a dollar's worth of *Plainsong* then," implying there was a second part to this visit.

Harris stayed in his chair while he opened the Kindle app on his iPad and found *Plainsong*. He began, "Chapter one:

> *Here was this man Tom Guthrie in Holt standing at the back window in the kitchen smoking cigarettes and looking out over the back lot where the sun was coming up."*

Harris' voice and cadence fit the writing well. It was as though he had written the story. No wonder he liked it. Within a few minutes he wrapped up the short first chapter with:

> *Then he got into the pickup and cranked it and drove out of the drive onto Railroad Street and headed up the five or six blocks*

> *toward Main. Behind him the pickup lifted a powdery plume from the road and the suspended dust shone like bright flecks in the sun.*

Harris figured that he had taken it far enough, this first time reading. He looked at Miranda who was still propped up in bed under the covers.

He readied himself before sliding under the covers. Harris moved slowly as she turned once again to her left side. He never rushed this, never wanted to appear too eager, though he was. He placed his bent knees just so, behind her bent knees. And as always, he took his right hand and placed it momentarily on her right hip on her nightgown before remembering that was not where he needed to start. This night, however, she had taken down the top of her nightgown. Harris cupped the skin of her breast. Blood rushed to his head as it had done all his life whenever there was skin on skin. He pulled her back closer to him and she skooched against him, spooning more tightly this night. After many seconds, he removed his right hand, place it on her shoulder and gently rolled her onto her back. They kissed for the first time, and then many times.

For both of them, this was the moment they became different friends. This moment of unmistakable and mutual surrender was orchestrated by Miranda. She knew it came with risk, not that she was worried Harris would expect to take it farther than she wanted, but that it might jeopardize or complicate things. She had decided the two of them could handle it, this addition to their relationship. When she kissed him that first time, it was every bit as exciting and consuming as any other first time. Age played no role. When she kissed him over and over, and he responded without shyness or hesitancy, she knew it one of the best decisions of her life.

While initially surprised once again at her leading them to new territory, Harris didn't fight it. He had an instant and overwhelming feeling that life was good again. Maybe more so than ever. And it did not stop when they did.

Harris did not leave until ten minutes after eleven. The hallway was empty when he did.

CHAPTER THIRTY-TWO

Don't come by this evening, okay? she texted to Harris late one morning a couple of days after their first kiss.

Wasn't planning on it. But okay, was his reply.

When she didn't come back to him for several minutes, he texted back *Everything alright?*

Yes. Fine. There's something I need to take care of.

Harris had never received texts from her like these. There was something cryptic about them and a little disturbing. She didn't ever seem to work the Hotline in the evening. He decided that, while curious, he would honor her request.

Rex opened the door to Miranda's apartment. It was well lit by a lamp in her living room as well as one in her bedroom.

He approached the open entrance to her room to find her lying on her bed in a long pink nightgown. "Hi there," he said.

"I need you to know this is a bad idea and that I'm not at all for it," she said.

"I'm glad you came to your senses. This is best for everyone."

"I don't know about that," she said with a sigh.

"You don't mind if I look around, do you? No funny stuff tonight." He walked over to her mirrored sliding closet doors. He slid one open and looked inside. Then did the same with the other door.

"This will be the last time, you know that?"

"Whatever you say, Miranda. Where's your phone?"

Miranda reached over to her night stand and picked it up. "Right here. Why?"

Rex hobbled over to that side of the bed and took it from her. He looked at it, made certain it was off, and then walked it into the kitchenette where he placed it on the counter. "Not gonna get burned by one of these again," he mumbled loud enough for her to hear. He then walked to her front door and locked it.

He reentered her room and stood at the foot of her bed, smiling as he took off his long sleeve shirt and then his undershirt. He made no attempt to hide his flabby belly. He then sat down at the edge of the bed to remove his shoes, socks, and trousers. He left on his white underwear. As he crawled onto the side of bed opposite hers, he said, "I guess this is how your little minstrel does it."

"Keep him out of this, Rex," she said.

"Oh, struck a nerve, did I?" he said smiling again. After a pause he added, "Pull down your top."

"No."

He jerked his head back in feigned disbelief. "Well, I'm afraid that is a deal breaker. I may have to see Brian after all."

She said nothing while glaring at him.

After some time, he reached over to her and with the back of his right hand brushed the top of her right breast while saying, "You're a nice gal, Miranda, you really are. But, quite frankly, this is the best part about you. The two best parts, actually," he added as he slid his meaty hand across and squeezed her left breast.

She remained quiet, inwardly satisfied with her assumption that this was how it would play out.

When he said again, "Take your top down," this time sounding more like a command than a request, she bit her lower lip while looking at him. He remembered this from before and knew she was beginning to give in. Her face softened and she smiled when she reached for her left spaghetti strap with her right hand. It was at that moment Rex knew he had prevailed. He breathed in deeply through his nose and felt stimulated where he hadn't in a long time.

He watched her slowly remove the second strap over her shoulder.

"That's a good girl."

She kept smiling before saying, "I should probably take this off." She removed the emergency pendent that each resident wore on a chain around their neck. "Take yours off, too. We don't want any accidents," she said playfully.

"Good idea," he said rolling onto his back and removing his own pendent. While he turned and threw his on the floor, she balled hers up and placed it on her night stand.

He rolled back onto his side against her and started touching her again.

"This is the last time, you understand that?" she felt compelled to say again.

"Of course," he replied as he rolled on top of her and began kissing her gently at first. He straddled her right thigh and let his hands move where they wanted. After a minute, his kisses and movement became more assertive. Though her arms were around him and her hands touched the back of his neck, she did not move them.

Rex's breathing changed, becoming deeper. Once he said softly, "Oh yeah." Less than two minutes later, he was startled upon hearing a loud rap on the door and unsuccessful attempts at turning the door knob.

"Miranda, are you alright?" a man shouted from the hallway.

"Help!" she screamed. "Stop it!"

When the evening receptionist and the night male nurse used a master key to unlock her door, then rushed into her bedroom, they saw Miranda trying to push a burly man off her while yelling, "Get off me."

The two employees ran to pull the wild-eyed man away from the woman. "Thank you," she said to them breathlessly when they had succeeded.

"What the hell!" Rex shouted. "This was consensual."

"I told him I didn't want that," she said while pulling up the top of her nightgown.

From the edge of bed, while the two employees held his shoulders, Rex looked over at Miranda and whispered, "You fucking bitch."

Brian was called at his home and arrived back at The Ridge a little after 9:00. He headed directly to Miranda's room and made certain that she was physically okay, that Rex had not penetrated or left any semen. He then asked her if she wanted to tell him about the incident tonight or wait until morning. "It can wait until the morning. I think I need a glass of wine."

"Of course. Does anyone else have a key to your apartment, including Rex?"

"No."

"Good. Here's my cell number. Call it anytime. Otherwise, come to my office in the morning and we'll talk about what happened here."

Rex had dressed and stormed off to his room. Miranda locked her front door and checked her slider out to the back deck. Brian pulled both employees into his office where he was told that the receptionist and nurse both got the alarm from Miranda's pendant about 7:45. They explained they had rushed to her room, heard her screaming for help as they opened the door with the master key, and saw Rex on top of Miranda.

Late the following morning, Miranda went to Brian's office and told him her version of the incident, leaving out the pieces that had led up to Rex being in her apartment.

"Rex says it was consensual, and that you invited him to your room," said Brian.

"Did he mention that he coerced me, kept suggesting we *get together* or that he would tell you some slanted version of Father Armando's and Harris' tuck-in service," said replied.

"He did not," Brian responded while writing notes on his yellow pad. "I've heard bits and pieces about the tuck-in guitarists. No one has ever said anything negative, in fact, what I've heard has been pretty positive."

"All I know is that Harris has been nothing but a gentleman when he sings and reads to me right before I go to sleep. It has added so much to my life. We have a special relationship as a result."

"So, Rex was jealous or something and wanted the tuck-ins to end?"

"He hated all the attention Armando and Harris were getting. He likes being the big cheese, the only cheese around here. I'm sure he didn't like Harris spending time with me either."

"I see. So, you hatched a little plan to take care of things yourself rather than coming to me."

"I did," she said suddenly feeling like she was in the principal's office with a less than stellar excuse. "It may not have been my best thinking, but Rex needed to be knocked down a couple of notches. He kept pestering me, suggesting we get together. When we took off our pendants, I pushed the alarm button. I figured it would be a couple of minutes before someone checked on me."

Brian sat there quietly behind his desk making more notes while they talked. After a few seconds of a forced, closed-lip, half-smile, he asked Miranda, "Do you want to press charges? I'm not certain what the police would make of this sequence of events, but I'll call them if you'd like."

"No, she said. "that's probably not necessary. But I wouldn't mind seeing Rex gone from here. He's a predator and a trouble maker. I'd like to see him given the boot from The Ridge."

Brian's forehead crinkled and his lips rolled inward. After some time mulling over her request, he said, "I'm going to need to talk to Rex again. I can't make any promises, but I've heard you, Miranda. I'll see what I can do."

Brian did meet with Rex again that afternoon. Rex soft-peddled his coercion to Miranda and laughed at the notion of the threat to come to Brian and speaking unkindly about the tuck-in duo. "I could give a good goddamn about what those losers are up to."

"Then why do you sit outside Miranda's room most nights waiting for Harris to come out? Why did you hassle Father Armando?"

Rex had no reply, caught off-guard with how much Brian knew.

"Miranda has decided not to press changes, but that is still on the table as far as I'm concerned, as is your dismissal from The Ridge. Your behavior is serious and crossed multiple lines. Something has to change, Rex."

The next day, Rex's daughter Lauren asked to meet with Brian who suddenly felt he was caught in a web of he-said, she-saids. Brian greeted her and calmly said, "Thank you for coming in," while extending his arm in the direction of one of his two guest chairs.

Lauren was in no mood for pleasantries and with arms folded across her chest led with, "She set him up!" When Brian did not respond, she added with more volume, "That was entrapment, and you know it! The police will laugh this off if they are called in, and we will sue you and The Ridge if you threaten to remove my father."

"Your father coerced a woman for his own pleasure. That behavior is unacceptable around here. We're not going to brush this under any rug. I need to take some action to ensure nothing like this happens again. I'll let you and your father know my decision as soon as I've made it."

"When will that be?" Lauren asked tersely.

"When I've made it," Brian said ostensibly ending the discussion.

The police were not called. Rex was not asked to leave under the signed, agreed upon conditions that he not initiate any written, verbal, or physical contact with Miranda, Harris, or Father Armando. It included him not sitting outside their rooms any time of the day or night. There was also a stipulation that Rex was, and would remain, on permanent probation at The Ridge. Any further incident on his part would result in his dismissal from The Ridge.

Rex and Lauren weren't happy when Rex and Brian signed the document. *Coercion* is a word they both used with Brian in regard to signing it. "You are free to find somewhere else to live if you choose not to sign," Brian said flatly. He continued with no emotion when he added, "And I am free to still involve the police or to insist on immediate removal. There is no coercion. We all have choices."

The afternoon following Miranda's talk with Brian in his office, she texted Harris. *Any chance that I could have some time before dinner?*

When he arrived in her room and were seated on her sofa, she told Harris the entire story, leaving out no parts, and trying hard not to slant anything.

When she appeared to be finished with the story, Harris with his right leg crossed over his left said, "Okay then."

Miranda looked at him, surprised that Harris wasn't more upset or had more to say, and said, "Okay then? That's it?"

"You took care of things. I wish it would have been a little different, but maybe it had to happen just the way it did. Let's move on."

Miranda paused to think. She was still discovering this man, and as she discovered more aspects of Harris, the more there was to like. She took his right hand in both of hers, smiled, and said, "Yes. Let's move on."

He simply nodded.

"There's one more thing you need to know…I pushed the button on the pendant the first time too. You just got there before the med-tech did."

Harris was perplexed trying to process this new information while recalling the sequence of events of that disturbing afternoon. "So that's why Alfonso the med-tech was at the door when I went storming out?"

"Yep."

"Oh man, do I feel foolish! This all might have been over earlier."

"Yep on that too."

"Why didn't you tell me after that first time?" he asked.

"Because you'd have tried to talk me out of what I needed to do."

He looked at this woman seated next him with awe and respect, then leaned into her for a hug. Not all hugs are equal even if some are in duration. This one said things words could not. When he pulled back, he asked, "Moving on?"

"Moving on."

CHAPTER THIRTY-THREE

Mondo spent most of his days alone. Tuck-ins tapered to a few each week, none of them being with Diana. He stopped going to Friday Happy Hour, thinking himself a buffoon for wearing his checkered sports coat, embarrassed for telling Harris that it set up his whole weekend.

It was more than just the Happy Hour regrets. His days were filled with shame about his near-end of celibacy transgression and that now, at this advanced age, most of what he thought about was sex. He was still a priest after all. He and Diana had not had real sex, but even the version they'd had made him want to relive it or think about it with minor adjustments.

"Come by for a beer and ball game tonight?" Harris asked Mondo one day while running into him at their mail boxes. Harris had watched Mondo withdraw, had noticed the change in him.

Mondo dropped two pieces of junk mail in a green plastic tub on the floor. "Yeah, I don't know. Haven't been feeling myself for a while," he replied.

"I can tell," Harris said. "That's why I think you need to come by. Is six-thirty okay? Any tuck-ins tonight?"

"Just one, 8:30." Mondo realized what Harris was doing and appreciated it. "Thanks, buddy. Six-thirty sounds good." He felt better just being asked to do something, to break the cycle he was in.

"Grab one out of the fridge," Harris suggested once Mondo arrived.

Before coming into the small living room, Mondo turned to the refrigerator and pulled out a Fat Tire. He didn't know much about these new beers. Coors and Budweiser had been the ones he was familiar with, but even just trying a Fat Tire tonight with Harris, who always seemed to have beer he'd never heard of, made him feel like he was living again.

They watched the Sharks hockey team skate against Phoenix in Phoenix. The men didn't comment too much about a scoreless first period that didn't even have a good fight. It really didn't interest either one of them much. "Has Phoenix always had a professional hockey team?" Mondo asked during the first intermission.

"No, they got one a few years back, once the city of Phoenix grew big enough to support a team."

"Seems like an odd place for hockey," Mondo said.

"Gretzky coached them for a few years."

"Wayne Gretzky? No way!" said Mondo.

"Afraid so. Don't think it turned out that great for the Great One. Under .500 if I recall." Harris got up and grabbed two more beers even though he knew

Mondo rarely had a second. During the intermission, Harris turned down the television and asked, "So how's it been going? Don't see you much anymore."

Mondo fiddled with the faux leather arm of the chair before offering, "Been keeping to myself a bit these days. Think it's a winter funk."

"Yeah, that happens to a lot of us. More than most people care to admit, I believe," Harris added.

When Mondo went quiet and clearly wasn't going to add anything to this conversation, Harris asked, "So, how are you and Diana doing?"

Mondo adjusted himself in his wing-backed chair rubbing his back in it. "We don't see each other much either." He took a long pull from the bottle, was pensive, then added somberly, "I'm ashamed to admit, we may have gotten too close."

There was a manly pause. Harris decided not to speak, but waited for Mondo.

"There wasn't sex. Not real sex anyhow. There was touching. Sexual touching," he said in a cadence that wasn't normal. "We put an end to it. I'm not sure it was a big deal to her, but it's all I ever think about."

"I see," said Harris. "That can be a rough thing to stop…the thinking part."

"Does it ever stop? It's kinda making me crazy. I'm a priest for gosh-sake."

"You are priest by profession, but still a man, Mondo…always a man, with male needs and drives."

"But I'm supposed to be above this sort of thing."

"Really?" Harris leaned forward, putting his beer down on the coffee table and added, "Above it all? You're kidding, right? How does that work?"

Mondo sat silently in his chair before making little I-don't-know hand movements before looking away.

Harris reached for his bottle, then took a swig. He contemplated his next words. He was getting tired of having to choose his words carefully. He hadn't had to when he ran his business or in other parts of his previous life. Finally, Harris said, "Listen to me. Please," he said lowering his volume, "I don't know what is taught in seminaries about all this, and I'm not very experienced myself, but this I know for certain: men, and women for that matter, are wired genetically to keep the species going…above everything else. As part of that, men, besides being the hunters, have been programmed to fuck indiscriminately, pardon my bluntness. Women, I believe, wanted to as well, but most became more selective over time, choosing only sex partners they felt would not leave them high and dry if they became pregnant. It wasn't until recently that society, with the help of religions, said *wait, hold on, we're all supposed to be monogamous*…you know, marry and just have sex with one person. This after millions of years of having a free-for-all. Our genes, our wiring, still think it's a free-for-all."

Mondo snickered then said, "I don't know…"

"Well, I do," added Harris. "And the priesthood… them asking you to be celibate for your entire life…it's just not human."

Mondo raised his eyebrows before saying without emotion, "Some of that may be true, but it's what we signed up for."

Harris leaned back in his chair then said as calmly as he could to match Mondo's energy, "I think you need to forgive yourself. And ask your God for forgiveness, if you must."

"I've already done that…the last part anyhow…over and over again."

"You need to do that first part too. You aren't given some special dispensation about having a sex drive just 'cause you became a priest. There's all those years of human behavior and genetics crammed inside all of us, Mondo. I'm serious. I don't know too many things, but on this I'm really, really certain. You may not be able to stop thinking about it, but you need to stop feeling bad about it."

Mondo sat quietly. Harris leaned back into a normal sitting position. Mondo wasn't sure if he was talking to the devil or not, but it made some sense. He wanted to believe all of what Harris was saying, but it went against so much of what he had been taught, what had been required of him. Finally, he just said, "Thank you, my friend."

"You're welcome."

Mondo now looked at the floor in front of him. "The funny thing is that I just got a little taste of it. Not even the real thing, and it's all I can think about. I mull it over, perseverate how it was, what had happened. What if it was a little different next time? There's this endless loop playing it in my head." He turned to look at Harris before adding, "It's driving me a little crazy. Does it ever stop?"

Harris could tell his friend was troubled and he wanted to soften his answer while providing some hope, but he needed to tell Mondo the truth, as he knew it. "In my experience, no, it never really does. Maybe over time, the script gets a little weaker, plays a little less often. I don't know how it is for women."

Mondo tightened his lips and nodded his head almost imperceptibly before saying, "I was afraid you'd say that."

Harris shifted in his chair, crossed his legs, and said with a smile and a lift in his voice, "Hey, that's what solo sex is for."

Mondo paused, then blushed, having never heard that expression before realizing what Harris was referring to. "But that's a whole 'nuther thing to feel bad about," said Mondo drawing out the words.

"It's really not," said Harris. "Without it, we'd *all* go crazy or be locked up in prisons."

"I don't know, my friend," Mondo said before taking another pull from the beer bottle. "You're throwing a lot at me to absorb."

The men returned their attention to the game, never to speak again of the subject. Mondo left a short while later for his scheduled tuck-in.

CHAPTER THIRTY-FOUR

He said, "This chapter is called McPherons" and began reading. *"When supper was finished, they sat in the dining room in the quiet. The table had been cleared already and the dishes washed and rinsed and left to dry. Raymond sat at one end of the table bent over the Holt Mercury newspaper before him, reading, licking his finger when he turned the pages, his wire glasses low down on his nose. While he read, he rolled a flat toothpick back and forth in his mouth without once touching it. Harold sat at the other end of the table. He was turned out from it, his knees spread open, and he was rubbing Black Bear Mountain mink oil into the thick leather of a work boot."*

Harris read every night they got together now. Miranda had told him she loved the book *Plainsong*, the characters, the pacing of the story, and the story itself. He typically read six pages or so. Sometimes her breathing became deep before he was finished, occasionally with little snores. Other times she rolled on her side, a signal to him to play a song or two on his iPad and spoon. Never during the reading of the book did he bring his guitar to her room in the evening.

I'm sorry. I really like the book, but your voice and the cadence of the writing may have caused me to slip off last night, she texted the next morning.

I noticed. It's okay. Not offended, he replied.

Hope I didn't miss much. I really like it.

I stopped reading once your breathing changed, he texted back.

The frequency of the tuck-ins increased. There were now only rare nights when he didn't open her apartment door at 9:30. For Miranda the unfolding of the *Plainsong* novel, Harris' reading voice, possibly hearing some beautiful music, and spooning was an addictive package. For Harris, he enjoyed every element of it as well and wanted to keep the conveyance of *Plainsong* moving. Six pages a night was an odd way to read a book. Nights off frustrated him, so when it was his turn to arrange the next visit, he always suggested a tuck-in for that night.

This was a golden time for Miranda. There had never been another like it in all her life. Controlling the frequency of their encounters no longer mattered, though daytime visits had tapered off.

"Can you take me to a doctor's appointment tomorrow?" she asked Harris. "It's at 11."

Harris liked driving her anywhere and was never alarmed or inquisitive about the appointments. "*Cancer survivors must certainly monitor things,*" he thought.

~

She was not surprised by hearing the initial words. She had been feeling nauseated for the last seven or eight days, not wanting to eat for fear of throwing it back up. Miranda had also been napping more, even in the morning, something she had never done. Processing that *it* had returned was enough, but hearing *stage four* shortly thereafter, rattled her core. Her heart began racing and her face felt hot. It seemed dreamlike one moment and hyperreal the next. The doctor apologized for breaking the news to her and her having to deal with this. She initially wasn't sure why he'd said *I'm sorry*, until she remembered that she usually said the same on her hotline calls. She'd suspected it would bounce back sometime. While she sensed over the last few days that it might be now, she didn't think it would be worse than ever. *Stage four.* Two life-altering words, considerably more jarring than hearing *you have breast cancer* for the first time.

Her oncologist went through the options after he had told her what she hadn't wanted to hear. He told her to think it over, but not too long. When she went back to the car that Harris was waiting in, she did not break down, nor give any indication what she had just heard. She simply said. "Glad that's over with."

Quieter than normal on their drives, she reached over and put her left hand on Harris' right thigh as he drove as she had done several times before.

When they got back to The Ridge, she declined his offer of escorting her to her room, smiled, but asked "9:30 tonight?"

Miranda took her scheduled Hotline shift at 2:00, skipped dinner, ate some toast in near darkness and waited for 9:30. She cried a little before Harris got there.

When he arrived, he was surprised to see her fully dressed and sitting on her sofa in the fully lit room. "Sit with me, Mr. Archibald," she beckoned while patting the space near her.

Harris complied, his mind now spinning.

"It's returned," she said calmly while taking his right hand into both of hers.

"Oh Miranda," he said compassionately.

"It's stage four," she said, eyes welling.

"Oh dear," he said putting his arms around her and pulling her close. They stayed that way for a good while. He stroked her hair and rubbed her back, until she sat back.

"It's spread into my liver and other places. I'm not going to fight it."

"What do you mean? There have to be treatments! Chemo, radiation…they've made strides. Of course, you're going to fight this."

"No. There is no beating this, only a futile, senseless appearance of a battle so the obituary reads well."

Harris sat there, not really sure how to process the combination of horrible news and worse yet, her resignation.

She reached for his hand then added, "Mr. Archibald, I want to enjoy this remaining time that

I have with you rather than be in a horribly weakened daze, not really living."

"Did they say how long?" he asked.

Miranda rubbed the knuckles of Harris' left hand with her right thumb and then using her most calm, this-is-what-I've-decided-voice said, "This time is precious for me with you. I didn't think it was possible at this stage of my life. I have two to four months left, a little longer if I begin the debilitating treatments now. It's going to end badly either way. I'd like us to continue the way we've been and when it becomes just too much for me, we'll end it."

"End it? What does that mean?"

"Assisted death, my dear Mr. Archibald. That's what it means."

"But you can't do that!" he said loudly. "You do the Suicide Hotline."

"I do. I took some calls today," she said. "A couple of very troubled people who see no other way out."

Again, Harris sat there not knowing what to say next, not knowing how to counsel a counselor.

Miranda continued, "There are no rules here. I won't be doing anything rash. It will be planned out, orchestrated, following California's rules on assisted death. You'll be there, I hope. I need you there. I'm going to request some things of you."

"I'd say this is pretty rash. You just heard the news today."

"I did hear the news today. But I've known this day was coming. I've thought about what I might do if the doc said *stage four* for years."

Harris was silent and Miranda knew it was best to let him be so. It took a while, but finally Harris submitted. "I'll do whatever you want."

CHAPTER THIRTY-FIVE

When David was signing the visitors log in the main lobby of The Ridge late one Wednesday afternoon, Brian came out of his office and approached him.

"Hi, I'm Brian, the General Manager" he said while extending his right hand. "You're related to Diana?"

"David Ramsey. Yes, I am. I'm her son."

"Great. I've wanted to meet you. I was wondering if I could get a few minutes with you in my office?

David was confused, said nothing, and followed Brian, sitting in the chair that Brian motioned toward.

"What's this about?" David asked.

"David, we've enjoyed having your mother at The Ridge for several years now. She's been almost trouble free. But our staff has noticed some increasing issues with her memory lately."

"I've noticed she's losing track of what day it is a little more often, but I thought that was just part of aging," said David.

"It is," Brian replied. "We can live with that and a lot of other minor things that go on here, but we've found her a couple of times in the laundry room waiting for the machines to stop. When pressed by our staff as to which washer or dryer she was waiting for, it turned out she had no clothes in any of them."

"Okay, but how does that affect you and your staff?" David asked uncertain where this was going.

"She wandered off the property last week. We avoided a large problem when I was driving into work about 8:25 one morning and saw her near downtown unattended. I'm not sure she could have found her way back."

"I see." David adjusted himself in the chair by grabbing both arms of it before asking, "What do you need me to do? Are you kicking her out?"

"This is not a memory care facility. We're not equipped or licensed to have residents with Alzheimer's or even dementia. Something they call mild cognitive impairment, a condition of normal aging is permissible, but nothing more severe. Before we consider any action, can I ask you to set up an appointment with a neurologist who can assess her? We need a copy of the evaluation. I know I'm catching you off-guard with all this, but it's not something I can sit on. If something happened to your mother while she wandered off..."

"I get it," David said.

"I'm sorry we had to meet this way, David," Brian said while standing and extending his right hand.

"Yeah, me too," said David while shaking Brian's hand before turning to leave.

When he reached the doorway, David stopped, and said, "Can I ask which apartment Father Mondo is in? I understand that he's been a good friend to my mother."

"128, I believe. His name should be on the door."

~

"Hi, sorry to disturb you, Father. I'm David… Diana's son."

"Yes, of course, David," said Armando. "Please come in."

After being seated in the living room and a brief exchange about how long Armando had lived at The Ridge and whether he liked being there, David said, "Of course there is something else on my mind to stop by like this. I just met Brian, the General Manager. He said that he and his staff are concerned about my mother and her mental health. It seems like you've been friends with my mother. I wonder if you've noticed any changes lately, you know, with her memory?"

"I see," replied Armando, stalling to choose his words. "So, Brian is wondering if Diana is fit to live here? Is he kicking her out?

"Not yet. That's what I asked. I think his chat with me served as a warning. He asked me to get a neurologist's assessment. Brian said she wandered off recently."

"Wandered off?" Armando asked. "I don't know anything about that. That's not good." He paused and before continuing. "She has seemed different…more forgetful. But its more than just what day it is. I used to sing her to sleep most every night… at her request, of course."

"Of course."

"Awhile back she seemed surprised that I played the guitar. She seems to have no recollection of me playing it in her room five nights a week for months."

David listened with a furrowed brow before asking, "Any indication of falls? Any bruises that you can recall that surprised you?"

"No sir, nothing that I can recall."

David thanked Father, then headed upstairs to find his mother sitting quietly in her room in the twilight. "Not watching tv?" David asked.

"Naw," she replied. "I think the service is out. It is what it is."

David sat next to her and noticed the stack of mail on the coffee table before saying, "Well that's not good. Should I call the front desk?"

"Do whatever you want. They told me it should be working."

David decided to walk to the front desk to have the conversation. Arquelle, the person working then, told him that all residents have Comcast, that no one else was complaining their service was out. She also mentioned that residents were responsible for their own Comcast bills.

When David got back to his mother's room, she was sitting on her sofa holding six envelopes. She sat there speechless and dazed shuffling through them while David looked through the other 10-12 envelopes, some opened, others not, on the small table in front of them. He grabbed five with "Past Due" and "Final Notice" prominently in red on the outside. Two were from Comcast. "Mom, I think they shut off your cable service for nonpayment."

"No, I just paid that last week, dear."

"Where's your checkbook, mom?"

Diana put the envelopes down on the sofa, got up and walked to the kitchenette, looking around, opening drawers. Not finding anything there, she wandered into the bathroom. "Now what am I looking for?" she asked.

"Your checkbook and register, mom. I don't think it would be in there."

"Ahh," she said. "I guess not." She eventually found both lying on the top of her bedroom bureau.

David looked through the checkbook register and then called Comcast using his cell phone while standing near her front door. Nothing had been paid for over three months, they explained. When he finished the call, his mind raced on how to kindly and delicately word what he had discovered this day, the various troubling things that were going through his head. He went over to the sofa where she was again seated holding some of her mail. He sat next to her. "Mom," he began.

"I used to be able to do all this," she said flatly looking only at the envelopes in her hand. "I did it for years and years."

When leaving an hour later, David inquired at the front desk if they could tell him how his mother paid her monthly bill for The Ridge. He learned that payment was taken automatically from her checking account. The receptionist said, "It was probably set up that way years ago."

He wondered how much was actually left in checking, and knew he needed to get more involved with his mother's finances and healthcare.

~

"What day of the week is it?" asked Dr. Tressman.

Diana smiled and said, "That's not fair. I never know what day of the week it is."

"Do you know what year it is?"

She thought for a few seconds and asked, "2017? No, 2018?"

Dr. Tressman made a quick notation after each answer. "Which city do you live in?"

"She smiled nervously, searching her brain for the answer before saying, "I know this one. It's not Walnut Creek. It's not San Ramon. Danville," she blurted out with delight at having retrieved the correct answer.

The questions continued with David keeping a loose score of some correct answers and some remarkably, to him, inaccurate answers for things like who the current President was and Diana's own age. He was relieved that she had remembered David's name.

Doctor Tressman probed for information on falls, strokes, trips to the ER, and checked her reflexes. When Diana had not twitched at the taps, the doctor said it was pretty typical of the elderly to not react when stuck near the ankle or knee.

The doctor then probed about her current situation as an independent resident at The Ridge. Specifically, he wanted to know if she needed to cook any meals for herself, needed help bathing, or did the laundry herself. David responded that The Ridge provides three meals a day, and from what he could tell his mother got herself to and from the dining room just perfectly at least twice a day.

"I never miss a meal, well, sometimes breakfast," she said with pride before adding, "I shower every day and they do my laundry."

"She really seems to like it there," David added. "Is that true, mom?"

"It's as good as I could hope for," she said. "They take real good care of me."

Dr. Tressman made another note before turning to David and saying, "This is really good. You're fortunate she likes it there. It doesn't always work out that way."

"I've heard stories. It would be messy if she didn't like it there or if they made her move." David caught the doctor's eyes before adding, "I imagine you know the drill. *Mild cognitive impairment* seems to be the magical phrase. They won't let her stay with dementia or Alzheimer's."

"I know the drill," replied the doctor. "She clearly does not have Alzheimer's. There is normal aging forgetfulness and inability to recall names and dates. I see no evidence of strokes. She seems to not only like where she is, but functions with the basics of bathing and getting meals without assistance. She is still quite mobile. As long as she's not driving and getting lost…"

The doctor let that hang before David fudged just a little saying, "Nope, thankfully none of that. She doesn't have a car. I'm able to take her to doctor appointments and be involved in her finances."

"Well, good then. I'm comfortable writing *mild cognitive impairment* in my report. Do you or someone else have durable power of attorney for property and healthcare?"

"Not yet," David said.

"I'd recommend getting those going."

"I agree. Mom," David said turning his full attention to his mother, "the doctor is giving you a good report, but recommends us taking care of some legal documents so I can be involved in your healthcare decisions and finances."

"Whatever you say, dear."

In the car, on the drive back to The Ridge, David said, "That went as well as it could have," knowing that his mother had missed the full significance of the appointment.

"It is what it is," she offered back.

David felt relieved, knowing things could have gotten considerably more complicated for them during the previous hour. He also realized he would have legal financial and healthcare obligations for his mother that went well beyond the legal documents that would soon be drawn. Contacting her a few months ago had seemed like such a good idea. And whether a good idea or not, it was something he'd needed to do. He hadn't realized or thought through what the ramifications could be. Those were now becoming clear. He couldn't and wouldn't walk away from any of this. He had his birth mother in his life and he was willing to do what needed to be done. He just had to wonder how all this would be playing out for his mother now if he hadn't popped into her life when he did. She had no one else who could take on any of this.

CHAPTER THIRTY-SIX

Rex had volunteered to be a welcoming buddy for new residents. After many weeks and two new male residents, he had yet to be assigned. He did, however, make certain his lunch and dinner tables were filled, often making a spectacle of inviting new and selected long-time residents to his table. "What… you're not sitting with us anymore?" he beckoned to Diana one dinner and two lunches when she sat alone at a nearby table.

"Oh, alright," she said each time before sidling over to take a seat.

"I just don't get having those sanctuary cities like San Francisco," he said to break the silence one evening. "You can be a damned illegal alien, a criminal, and nobody can touch you. Can't get arrested, put in jail, deported, or nuthin'. I'm not sure what this country is coming to, honest to God, I don't."

When no one felt any urge to participate, he prodded Setesh. "See-tesh, what do you think about sanctuary cities?"

Setesh didn't respond initially, instead choosing another fork full of his small green salad with Thousand Island dressing. He chewed deliberately continuing to look at his plate.

"That's what I damn thought. You all have been brainwashed by the liberal media. Heck, I bet you all watch CNN and MSNBC."

Setesh dabbed his mouth with his blue cloth napkin then looked up at Rex before saying, "I do watch CNN and MSN, but I watch some of Fox too. Maybe not in all equal amounts," he continued with deliberation. "I do believe there is some brainwashing going on with Fox, as well."

Rex was unusually quiet, respectful even, to see if the man in the wheelchair had finished speaking. Setesh added calmly, "But on the matter of sanctuary cities, I agree with you. I don't get them either."

Rex dropped his fork on the ceramic plate for effect while saying, "Well, good goddamn! I do believe that's the first time ol' See-tesh and I ever agreed on something political-like." He raised his water glass and said, "I'm going to toast to that...me and See-tesh agreeing on sanctuary cities." Only Diana, smiling, raised her glass and clicked Rex's.

"How long we been eatin' together, See-tesh?" What, three, four years?"

"Four and a half very long years," Setesh answered evoking chuckles from the others at the table.

"Four and a half years the man said. And we made history tonight...agreein' on somethin'. Well, I'll be damned," Rex said loudly. "Hell, I thought it was going to be just another boring dinner. We made some history tonight, See-tesh."

In the privacy of his room, Rex did little besides drink beer, watch his news/commentary station, and occasionally check out websites on his computer that he even knew he probably shouldn't. The last interested him less and less, but he did so out of boredom or habit or longing. Once, when he did so, he wondered if he, Miranda, Diana, and the others there at The Ridge were the only ones in the entire world who had never made one of them adult videos.

He still walked the halls on occasion, but stayed away from Miranda's room. Whenever he crossed paths with her, Father Armando, or Harris, he always looked down or to the side, never saying *hi* or even nodding. Embarrassment may have been part of it. Animosity too. But the overriding factor was his signed agreement with Brian and The Ridge. The thought of being kicked out and moving did not settle well with him these days, and that is what drove his restrained behavior.

Walking for Rex became more difficult, even with a cane. His left hip hurt a lot. The right one was only a bit better. He tried to talk his daughter, Lauren, into getting him a motorized, 3-wheel mobility scooter that he'd seen others at The Ridge using. "They're only $649 on-line. I Googled them," he told Lauren.

"Those things are death sentences, daddy," she told him. "I think you need to get your old butt out of the chair more often and keep walking."

Lauren could tell his hips were bothering her father. She took him to an orthopedic doctor. After an MRI, the doctor said, "You're going to need your left hip replaced as soon as you can't stand it, and probably the right one later."

"What about physical therapy or cortisone?" Lauren asked.

Though it was a burden for Lauren, she took him took him to a PT session later that week. The therapist had him use stretch bands tied to a door knob, but balancing on one leg quickly became out of the question. Rex made faces and noises when they tried some exercises from a seated position. She saw that PT was not a viable, long-term solution for her father, knowing that he would never do the work on his own.

On the ride back, Rex whined and Lauren caved. "An early Christmas present," she called it. They split the cost while giving him a new toy and delaying the inevitable replacement. Rex was soon riding to and from the dining hall on his red and black motorized 3-wheel scooter. He liked it. Made a show of it, in fact, carrying his cane in one hand and pointing it at others while he road past them, sometimes bellowing, "Watch out...senior driver."

CHAPTER THIRTY-SEVEN

In 2015, the California legislature passed the *California End of Life Option Act*, sometimes referred to as the Death With Dignity Bill. Governor Jerry Brown signed it and it went into effect June 9, 2016. The Act allowed terminally ill patients to request medical assistance in dying under clearly defined parameters. The patient had to be at least 18 years of age, mentally capable of making and communicating this health care decision, and have a terminal disease that would result in death within six months.

In addition, the patient must make two separate verbal requests to their doctor at least 15 days apart, followed by a written request signed by two adult witnesses. The patient then must meet with a second doctor who documents the patient's formal intentions. That doctor also assesses the patient's ability to make such a decision. If either doctor is less than fully certain, they can request a psychological examination.

Part of the process is that the prescribing doctor, the one willing to prescribe the end-of-life drugs, must attempt to ascertain that the patient is not being unduly influenced or coerced into making this decision, and informs the patient of any alternatives including care to relieve the pain.

The next to last steps call for the prescribing doctor to ask the patient to notify the next of kin of the prescription request, although this cannot be required or enforced, and that same doctor must offer the patient the opportunity to withdraw the aid-in-dying medication request.

Once all those procedural steps have been taken and are documented, the medicine can be prescribed.

Of course, there were legal challenges to this law being signed, and some remained while Miranda contemplated her death with dignity. The California courts determined that patients will continue to have this legal avenue to assist in their deaths while the legal challenges were heard and decided upon.

Originally, The California Medical Society opposed assisted death legislation but changed their official position to neutral in June 2015. Individual doctors are free to choose to participate or not in the process.

Harris had found most of this information for himself in order to be educated if Miranda brought it up again. The next step, Harris thought, was to ask Brian for a meeting. "What's on your mind?" Brian asked as they sat in the General Manager's office one afternoon.

"I was wondering, just wondering, not planning on doing anything like this myself…but I've been reading and hearing about it…this assisted death stuff. It's kind of intriguing."

"I see," said Brian wondering if there would be a question coming.

"Has The Ridge ever been involved in something like that?" Harris asked. "Or do you have to discourage it? I guess what I'm asking is, if one of your residents was going to embark on something like that, would they have to do it secretly or off-site, or would you want to know about it?"

Brian studied Harris sensing that there was something more than random curiosity for Harris at play, and decided not to ask his obvious question, rather replying, "Yes…to most all of your questions. We have had two situations like what you're alluding to, and we would prefer being involved. Once we know about a resident's intentions, and have been assured they've taken all the requisite steps, then we ask to take possession of the medicine. We lock it up, and release it at the agreed upon date and time. We can't leave it in the resident's room to be used on impulse."

"Makes sense," Harris replied, instantly relieved that Miranda would not need to do this secretly or somewhere else if she decided to proceed.

"Is there anything I need to know?" Brian asked.

"Not at this time…but there might be down the road. It's good to hear your position. Thank you for sharing it and your time."

Miranda continued to take an occasional hotline shift. She needed the activity, this particular work. It was during the second shift she took after having told Harris about being stage four and her plans for assisted death that she knew there was one more thing she had to tell him.

She was seated in bed at 8:30 when he entered, propped up a little more than normal, her head and upper back on pillows. They had moved up the start time because her energy was waning and the need for sleep came earlier. The lighting was dim with only the kitchenette's under-cabinet lighting helping with sight in her bedroom.

"Hello Mr. Archibald. Were we scheduled for tonight?" she asked coyly.

"I may have mixed up my calendar. I can come back another time," he said matching her playfulness.

"Well, I guess you might as well stay, you big lug. You came all the way from the first floor. That's darn near the edge of the world."

"Thank you. I did walk a long way and had to take that scary elevator. You know sometimes you can get stuck in those things." He crawled onto the bed next to her, using the one remaining pillow to position himself high against the gold cloth, padded headboard.

Miranda took his left hand in both of hers. "I've prided myself, patted myself on the back really, with the notion that I've always told you the truth, no matter how much that hurt either one of us." She paused then turned a little to see into his eyes better. "But there's one pretty big thing that I've left out. That's not really being a great truthteller now, is it?"

Harris was now on edge, listening intently, wondering what he would hear next. There couldn't possibly be anything more of significance, he thought. She had always been so forthcoming.

"I haven't told you much about my daughter. It's painful for me to do so, that's why I haven't. But I feel I must now. You're entitled to know more. I think you should know everything." She glanced down at their hands, moving her fingers around his, then looked back up at Harris. "I loved Beverly very much. Maybe I gave her too much. She was a highly anxious girl growing up, though she had not been any trouble until she entered college. She was bright enough to get into UCLA. There she stumbled into drugs, minor ones I suppose at the start. Somewhere along the line she tried meth. She washed out of school pretty quickly. It wasn't until then that we knew there was a problem. She was in and out of four different 30-day programs, leaving early during two of them. She just couldn't beat it. Ken and I struggled mightily, willing to do whatever it took to get her back on track. I did all the wrong things... checking up on her every day, paying all her finances, suggesting little plans for the day that I naively thought she would follow, and worried about her every moment I didn't see her."

Harris rubbed her hands with his while she paused to collect her thoughts.

"We brought her home to live with us, but she relapsed under our roof. We didn't know how she'd gotten it. We'd check everywhere, but I guess they become very good hiders besides adept liars. It was killing Ken and me. We went to Al-anon, then found a personal counselor who convinced us we had to let go…that this might truly kill us, and that there wasn't anything we could do to save her. Beverly had to save herself. He explained that our daughter, no doubt, loved us deeply, but that addictions were stronger. Those suffering from an addiction can make all the promises you want to hear, can swear up and down that they'll do the right thing, but they just can't do it. The substance of choice is stronger than any promises, than any of those words. Addictions are mightier than a love for parents, a spouse, a job, a favorite animal. That's when we learned what addiction truly was.

"The counselor told us, in order to save ourselves and possibly her, we had to let her hit bottom, to not be around her unless she was sober. So, we explained our position to her the best we could, that we loved her dearly, then asked her to leave. We told our own daughter that she couldn't live with us unless she was clean and sober. Can you imagine that? Our own daughter. It goes against *every* instinct a parent has."

Tears were rolling down Miranda's cheeks now, but the crying did not affect her speech or breathing. Harris' eyes were welling up.

"We weren't sure where she went when she left, but she apparently couch-surfed. But her solid, longer-time friends could only take so much. She was apparently stealing to feed her habit, and god know what else. I hope nothing else. Her suppliers kept her supplied. Once every few weeks, she'd call. Sometimes strung out, sometimes not. She was always apologetic, always so ashamed. It was beyond belief what our daughter had become in less than two years. We'd ask her if she was ready to try another program. She'd hem and haw, non-committal. After a while, it became clear that she was in a relationship with someone who wasn't good for her. Once we asked her if she was safe. She only said *momma* while crying just before the call was disconnected. We asked around and thought we'd discovered where they were living. Ken went there one night to get her. There was some altercation with the guy, some yelling at the door. Ken never saw her, but the man shouted him down. When Ken said he wasn't leaving without her, the man punched him three or four times hard, sending Ken to the ground. We went back after calling the police, but there was no sign of them."

Miranda paused again, this time grabbing a Kleenex to blow her nose and wipe her cheeks.

"You don't need to continue," he said.

"Thank you, but I do," she said forcing out the smallest smile. "Someone called a week later, we don't know who, and said she had overdosed…and gave us an address."

Miranda stopped for a long time. Then she began crying hard. Jagged sobs. Harris wrapped his arms around her. He was crying now too, without sounds but his chest heaving. Finally, Miranda, in the middle of her sobs said, "She was our ba-by," before crying more loudly.

Harris spent the entire night, spooning until it became too warm between them, resuming when they cooled. During one of their spoons, he wondered how many more of these there would be. She did too. They both slept poorly. At one point, Harris heard Miranda crying in the living room after having reached unsuccessfully for her in bed. He left early the next morning to shower, shave, and brush his teeth before breakfast. He no longer cared who saw him leave her room or what they thought.

Later that afternoon, he went by her apartment. She was on a hotline call. She motioned for him to come in and sit. Her voice was calm and clear. After much listening on her part, Miranda said, "I'm really sorry you are going through all this. It's a lot for a person to bear. I'll stay with you as long as you'd like, but do you have someone you can be with tonight or at least talk to?" She listened to the response, which seemed surprisingly lengthy to Harris.

After another 25 minutes, the call wound down. Miranda had encouraged the caller to find a therapist or counselor. "There are so many good ones out there. And please don't isolate yourself. Be around people, or call people who are kind and compassionate." Miranda didn't look over at Harris when she finished that thought with, "It makes all the difference," but Harris believed she was thinking of him when she said it.

The caller seemed to be thanking Miranda for her time and words. When she had finished, Miranda said, "It's been my pleasure, my honor, that you trusted me with your story. But before we hang up, I want to just say one more thing… no matter where you are or how bad it seems, you are important. You have value. I know that for absolute certain just by talking to you this once. Please remember that. I wish you the best."

When she placed the phone headset back down, she sat quietly looking down at her desk. Harris let her, of course, thinking she must need a moment. Little did he know that Miranda was saying a silent prayer, thanking God for giving her good words on that call, and asking God to watch over the young woman. After a bit, she rose from the chair and stiffly walked over to the couch with the help of her cane to sit next to Harris.

"Rough one?" he asked.

"They're all rough," she replied.

"Did they teach you that closing statement?"

"No, they give suggested phrases to use at the start and the end, and what you can fall back on if things aren't going well in the middle, but that ending was mine."

"It sounded great to me. Raw and real."

"Thank you. It needs to be real. You try to make a connection. It doesn't always happen, but we try. I've used that closing before. I thought the woman needed to hear those words before we hung up. Hopefully, she'll get some help and get through this."

"I couldn't do what you do."

"Aww…I think you could. You may not want to, or like it, but you'd be quite good at it, I suspect."

They sat without speaking for a time. Miranda reached for the remote and found a soft music station called *Soundscapes*. She kept the volume low. After a while, Harris said, "Your story last night of your daughter was tough to hear, but thank you for sharing it with me."

"You're welcome. Clearly, I needed to get it all out."

"Does telling it like you did really make you feel any better?"

"It doesn't change the story, doesn't make it go away," she said. "But, yes, physically, mentally, I feel better today. I read somewhere that a hard cry like that actually releases toxins from your body through the tears. I don't know if that's true or a bunch of hooey, but it might be true."

"You may not know the answer to this or feel comfortable talking about it, but is that why you started doing the hotline work…what happened to your daughter? Not that she committed suicide…clearly she didn't."

"I suppose. It's hard for me to say for certain." She reached for the remote and turned the volume even lower, barely audible, before continuing. "She may or may not have overdosed intentionally. There really isn't much difference. She's dead either way. Beverly certainly felt trapped, hopeless, and that there was no way out. That's what most every call I take is about. Our daughter must have known using meth in the amount she was using might kill her, but it just didn't matter to her. She couldn't stop."

For Harris, this was all new, but he was getting a crash course on addiction. "I am beginning to see that addictions are more powerful than love for a spouse or dog or job. It's kind of amazing that anyone ever beats them."

"It's the hardest thing in life. I'm convinced of that. Harder than anything most of us will ever face. And not to be argumentative, but you don't beat them... *ever.* You just manage them one day at a time."

"Miranda," he hardly ever called her Miranda, "while we're talking so candidly, I've got to ask...how can you end your life prematurely... and I get the whole dying with dignity thing...but how can you consider ending it, when you've done the hotline for so long? You talk people out of ending their lives, but here you are planning..." he fell silent not sure how to end his thought without sounding harsh.

"I don't really have any control over whether my callers ultimately commit suicide or not. I just give them someone to connect with when they are desperate and know of no one else to talk to. My job is to listen, be compassionate, get them through this day or night. But I also believe that for some, suicide might be the only way out. And I don't think less of them if they choose to follow through with it. My real job is that if they are going to do it, wait until they've thought it through, heard what others might have to say about the mess they're in, and consider any options out of it. I'd rather that they not kill themselves, but I firmly believe that for some, it's the only way out. For my daughter, it might have been."

Harris forced a closed mouth smile.

"And as for me," she continued, "I see no conflict with my hotline work and dying with dignity. I'm good with it."

With that, they heard the sudden sound of a heavy rain shower beating against her windows and out on the little patio. They both got up and looked out through the Levolor window blinds. "Isn't it lovely?" she said. Harris made only a little grunting acknowledgement. Miranda then asked, "Will you read to me?"

CHAPTER THIRTY-EIGHT

David hadn't asked nor suggested a thing, but Mondo knew what needed to be done. The morning after David stopped by, Mondo knocked on Diana's door. "Good morning. Sorry to catch you off guard, but I was going to take a little walk outside. I was wondering if you cared to join me?"

"Well, yes," she responded. "How nice of you. Let me find my shoes." Diana turned to get her shoes and let go of the door thinking it would stay open, but the door swing shut, leaving Mondo on the other side. "I'm sorry," she said reopening it. "Come in."

Mondo entered and stood near the refrigerator which was next to the front door. "I know they're around here somewhere. She went to her bedroom and looked on either side of her already meticulously made bed. He could watch her movements beyond the partial wall between the living room and the bedroom. "Here they are. I found them," she said relieved and satisfied. She carried them out to her sofa and put them on. She also grabbed three hats, putting *spoiled rotten* on first, the *A's* second, and the *SF Giants* on top.

As they walked out her door and down The Ridge's hall, Diana asked, "Now what are we doing?"

"Going for a little walk…outside…just to get some fresh air and a little exercise."

"Oh, alright."

As they walked on the warm, blue-sky morning, they chatted about the weather and the day of the week. "What day is it?" she asked for the second time. Mondo was patient, never letting on that she had asked and he had answered the question three minutes earlier.

"It's important to keep our legs moving," he added. "I don't want to end up needing a walker or one of those motorized scooters."

"Those scooters look fun. The man I have dinner with...what's his name…well, he got one."

"You mean Rex?"

"Yeah, Rex. That's right. He's got one and it seems like he has a lot of fun with it."

Mondo walked with her every morning that the weather was nice, and on those days when it wasn't, he checked on Diana in the late morning, then escorted her to lunch.

Mondo talked to Harris about it. "I don't know if you've noticed, but Diana's slipping a little bit…short-term memory."

"I hadn't noticed."

"Pretty forgetful, got lost near downtown apparently. Her son talked to me about it. I've been walking with her most mornings. I was wondering if you could watch out for her a little, maybe check on her some afternoons, walk her to dinner once in a while."

"Yeah, sure, I can do that. It's very nice of you to look out for her like this," Harris said.

"This place isn't set up for memory care. If they sense you have dementia and start to see issues, they kick you out of here to one of those other places. The memory care facilities look nice from the outside but they are a little depressing inside… and big bucks. I gave about 10 or 12 last-rights in some of them. I'd rather Diana not end up there, or delay it as long as possible."

"I see. Again, very nice of you. I'll pitch in where I can."

Harris took the opportunity to tell Mondo about the developments with Miranda. When he mentioned *stage four*, followed by *two to four months*, Mondo reacted with genuine surprise and sorrow. "That's horrible," he said. She's such a nice lady. I'll be praying for her."

"Prayers are good. I'm not sure how religious Miranda is, but there might be another role for you."

"Of course, I'll do last rights for her too if she wants. We now call it Anointing of the Sick."

"I'll see if she wants to do that when the time comes, but there is something else she may need. Miranda is choosing death with dignity…to end life on her terms, when she's ready. She's begun some of the legal steps that California requires. She may want some spiritual guidance along the way. Oh, and she won't want anybody trying to talk her out of this. I've gone down that road. She's thought it through for a long time, and her mind is made up."

"Wow. Okay," said Mondo. "I'll do what I can, but my church has been against suicide. And death with dignity is just a nice sounding phrase for assisted suicide. I'm not sure…"

"I understand. I don't want you doing anything you are prohibited from doing, or aren't comfortable with. I just know Miranda likes you and you'd be the only one she'd turn to if she wanted a spiritual advisor on this rather short journey."

"I'll think and pray on this, my friend. I may even seek some guidance myself."

"Thank you, Mondo. I had no idea moving in here would lead to this."

"We deal with what life throws at us."

David, too, was a regular visitor and companion for his mother. After taking care of the Powers of Attorney for both Healthcare and Property, he settled in to a routine of two or three visits a week. One Saturday, Mondo knocked on Diana's door, unaware that David was there too. "Hi Mondo, come in," said David not waiting to see how his mother would handle the situation.

"Sorry, don't mean to interrupt your visit," Mondo said.

“This nice man comes and takes me for walks most days,” Diana told David, surprising both David and Mondo about what she remembered.

“Ahh, I need the exercise,” Mondo said patting his almost flat stomach. The three chatted briefly before Mondo excused himself.

David had lunch with his mother in the dining room that day and afterword swung by Mondo’s apartment. “I just wanted to thank you for looking out for my mom. It’s most kind of you.”

“She’s a good lady. We’re trying to keep an eye on her and spend a little more time with her. Don’t want her wandering off on her own, and getting kicked out of here. Those next places are a bit different.”

“Yes, I’ve checked out a couple of those memory care facilities recently. They are depressing!” said David, his voice rising.

Mondo nodded.

“Anyway, thank you again. You’re doing God’s work, Father. Even here.”

Mondo recalled those last words from David many times over the following weeks. They left him feeling comfortable being both a priest and a tuck-in minstrel. There was still one thing gnawing at him though… death with dignity.

Mondo began looking into the dying with dignity position of the Catholic Church. He chose not to go to the Diocese for input initially. The many online articles he was able to pull up often equated the death with dignity concept with euthanasia. He struggled with that comparison after looking up the definition of euthanasia: *the painless killing of a patient suffering from an incurable disease or in an irreversible coma*. Euthanasia, it seemed to Mondo, often entailed others making the decision about when to terminate a person's life. *Mercy killing* is what euthanasia had been commonly referred to as. This seemed quite different…death with dignity was always patient-driven, with safeguards about the patient's mental capacity. He hadn't really begun forming his own position on the matter yet, he was merely information gathering. His more immediate concern was how to approach Miranda, whether he should wait for her to ask, or if he should pay her a visit.

It suddenly resolved itself, as things often do.

Father Armando had been granted permission to say Sunday Mass at The Ridge over a year earlier. Normally six to twelve residents showed up in the library for 11:00 Mass. The Sunday after Harris had mentioned Miranda's bad news to Mondo, she showed up to his service for the first time. Father's planned homily mentioned mankind's collective need to be kind to one another, for we all have our own crosses to bear, and often those crosses weren't fully apparent to others. Miranda did not take Holy Communion that day, but lingered after Mass to thank Father Armando. She stayed off to the side, pretending to look at book titles on the shelves letting others say their remarks to Father, and thereby ensuring she would be the last in the room with him.

"I enjoyed your sermon, Father," she said while reaching out her right hand.

"Thank you," he replied. "It was good to see you in attendance this morning."

"I know Harris mentioned some things about my health to you, and the decisions I've made regarding it. I was wondering if you might come by my apartment so that I could talk to you?"

"It would be my privilege. I'll swing by however often you want."

"Thank you. Let's try once and see how it goes. Are you free this evening about 7:00?"

~

They sat across from each other in separate wing back chairs. The television had the *Soundscapes* music station turned on low.

"I was raised Catholic and went to eight years of Catholic grammar school," she began. "I practiced for a long time and raised my daughter a Catholic, although we chose the public-school route for her. Eventually, I stopped going to Mass so frequently. In my later years, I didn't attend at all. I'm not sure I have an explanation or reason for tapering off."

"I see," Father Armando replied.

"I never made a conscious decision to stop believing in God or even an afterlife, so now, nearing the end, I'm catching myself thinking that I still believe in both."

"That's good," he said. "It's a personal thing, but I'd say that qualifies as faith."

"Father, I'm very certain I've lived a good life. I'm not perfect, but I never heard that was a requirement for getting into heaven. I have this other thing that I'm certain about…dying with dignity. I can't go through the agony or the highly drugged, semi-vegetative state that are my other options."

"I can do a final confession," he said, "and Anointing of the Sick if you want. Or, if you're not comfortable with me, I can find another priest to do a final confession."

"Thank you. We may go that route. It's more than that, though. I guess what I'm worried about is blowing my chance for heaven with my death with dignity choice. I know that the Church does not look kindly on suicide. Death with dignity seems quite different to me than suicide, but I worry that God might not see it that way." She paused before continuing, "That's my little conflict."

"I'm following you now. Those thoughts would trouble most people. I can't make up your mind for you. It's such a personal thing, the course you're choosing. But I do want to ask why death with dignity? Is it to minimize your pain and grief, or to be less of a burden on others?"

She thought before responding. "Well, since you limited it to those choices, I suppose it's mostly to reduce the pain and agony I would go through. There're really not too many people in my life who this would burden…just one, I suppose. But there's no way he should have to deal with all this."

"And have you asked him how much of a burden it's going to be for him if you don't die with dignity, or what his preference is?"

"No, it's really my choice, isn't it?"

"Ultimately, yes, you are the only one who can or will make this decision. But I thought you implied a minor part of that decision is based upon being a burden to one person. Maybe it wouldn't be the burden you think it would. Maybe his preference is different than ending it early, with dignity as you say."

"The bigger reason is the pain and suffering I'll go through…the indignity of having my diapers changed and being drugged up."

Armando was quiet, while putting his elbows on the arms of his chair and pulling his clasped hands up to his chest. Finally, he said, "I'm not in your shoes. I have no idea how much pain you are going to go through, and what it must be like to die that way, but I do know that Hospice organizations are extremely good at providing pain management and working through the other indignities before dying."

Miranda's elbows found the arms of the chair too before placing her folded hands near her stomach. "You've given me things to think about, Father."

"Have we taken it abut as far as we can or should today?' he asked.

"Perhaps we have, Father. Thank you for coming here and talking with me. I'm feeling a bit tired now."

Eleven days after hearing the bad news herself, life had settled into a routine for Miranda and Harris. He spent time with her every afternoon, until she needed to rest, then usually came back in the evening. Meals were now delivered to Miranda's room. Sometimes she asked for Harris' company when she ate, and sometimes she suggested him visiting about 7:00. He read to her and played music on the iPad, but she always wanted him to spoon her to sleep.

She had asked him not to come by the following afternoon, that she was scheduled to take some calls.

As she sat at her desk, before logging in, she wondered how many more times she'd be doing so. She knew there likely wouldn't be many. He mind raced. She had not asked to speak with Father again, but was struggling with his words about Hospice. Was there really much of a difference in death with dignity and Hospice? Whether there were differences, Father had gotten her thinking that Harris' needs were probably a consideration too. She didn't want to deal with that right new. For some reason, right now she felt compelled to plug-in to the hotline again and take some calls. It gave her purpose, it made her extremely present-centered, and people told her in different ways that she was good at it. Right then she needed to feel good about herself, and to try to do some good for others.

Her first call that afternoon was a middle-aged man, recently divorced, more recently unemployed, *financially ruined* he told her, and fearing there was no compelling reason to continue on. When she finished that call, she waited for over twenty minutes in the silence of her room. She felt bad for the man and his plight. She didn't know if the man had been a good husband or not, a good employee or one that had brought on his own demise. But she, as with all calls, hoped the man would choose to dig himself out, to get whatever help he needed to begin to right himself. She caught herself thinking that life was sacred. She also recycled a many-time-thought of hers… what she wouldn't have given for another week or month with Beverly, another shot at convincing her daughter that she had value, that she could dig herself out.

She knew right then that she would ask Harris soon what his preference was. She was certain she knew the answer, and until now had blocked out any chance of hearing it for fear it would derail her own thinking. She sat awhile longer nearing the end of her shift, thinking that might be her only call that afternoon, when the hotline phone rang again.

"Good afternoon, Hotline. I'm glad you made this call. Whom am I talking to?"

"Tom. You're talking to Tom," the man answered in an irritated drawl. "I don't know why I called this damned number."

It was a voice Miranda thought she recognized, though so stunned to hear it now, this way, affected her certainty.

She paused before continuing, "You can tell me as much or as little as you like, but I need to let you know this will stay between us."

"Miranda, what are you doing on the damned phone?" the caller asked.

"I take these calls sometimes. I've volunteered for the hotline for years."

"Oh well, that's good. I... I... I musta' dialed the wrong number or the lines got crossed or something. Bye."

"Rex, don't hang up," she said quickly before listening if he had. Then she added without rushing, "I think you dialed the right number."

"Well maybe I did, and maybe I didn't. But I sure as hell ain't talking to you if I did."

"I can understand that. My shift was just about to end. You called this number for a good reason, Rex. Now I can transfer you back into the system if you want, and someone else will pick up, or you can call back."

Rex didn't respond. Miranda could hear him breathe differently... deep, choppy breaths. After a few seconds of this, she asked, "Is there a chance you might hurt yourself soon, Rex?"

"Dammit, Miranda," he exclaimed, "I don't want to talk about it with you."

"I understand. I'm going to transfer you now. Someone will pick up that is able to talk to you, okay?"

Again silence.

"Promise me you'll stay on the line until someone answers. It should just be a few seconds."

No response.

"Rex, can you stay on the line?"

After a couple of seconds, she heard, "Yeah… I'll stay on."

For once, Miranda didn't know what to say next. *Good luck* or *please don't hurt yourself* or *I'll check on you* or any number of other phrases that raced through her mind, did not seem appropriate. What came out was, "Thank you."

When the call was transferred, Miranda logged out. She turned off the desk lamp and sat in the diminishing late afternoon light. The extreme unlikelihood of taking a call from Rex was absolutely an act of Providence. How else could it be explained? At that moment, she also realized that she was not the good person she'd fooled herself into believing she was. There's no way, she thought, Rex would get to the desperate point in his life, desperate enough to make that call, if she hadn't humiliated him. Sure, he was a miserable old coot... miserable to be around, and quite likely miserable in his own skin. But like everyone else, Rex had just tried to carve out his own way... in his own bombastic, all-knowing, loud-mouth way. For years it seemed to have worked for him. She knew that for Rex to find the Suicide Prevention number, pick up the telephone and make the call, he'd gotten extremely low. She knew her own actions had helped get Rex to that point. She no longer felt good about how she had lived this last part of her life.

CHAPTER THIRTY-NINE

Harris needed to make a beer run one mid-afternoon. He was also running low on toilet paper, soap, and toothpaste. Part way on his drive to Safeway, he pulled over to the edge of the road near the sidewalk, momentarily frightening her. "Where ya' headed?" he hollered out the open passenger window.

Regaining composure once she recognized Harris, Diana said, "Isn't it a beautiful day. I was just headed back home after a little walk."

Harris decided not to mention that she was headed away from The Ridge, instead saying, "I'm going to the store for a few things. How about you go with me… keep me company?"

"Well, sure, that would be nice."

Once they'd returned to The Ridge, and Harris had walked Diana to her room, he swung by Mondo's.

"This isn't good. What can we do?" Mondo asked after hearing about Diana's latest excursion.

Harris said, "Should we let Brian know about this? He might give her the boot if we do."

"Probably not," replied Mondo. "But are we going to be with her 24 hours a day? She could wander off any time someone isn't with her. I think I should call her son."

~

David took the news stoically. "I'll start looking at the options," he told Armando. "I really appreciate all you and your friend are doing to look after my mother."

David visited three memory care facilities over the next week. He sat with Keshia one evening after dinner when the boys were upstairs. He explained the developments with his mother, the likelihood of her being rotated out of The Ridge, and what he saw the options being.

"You mean they don't have staff that can work with her, be with her at her current place…you know, for an extra fee?"

"They're not set up that way, as a memory-care facility. I'm sure it's a staffing thing, but it's probably how they are licensed too."

"Well can't they at least lock the doors, or something?"

"There're laws against it apparently."

Keshia sat motionless, every part of her face tightened.

"These other places run $8-10,000 a month, and they do have an extra layer of security for exit-seekers," he added. "She's got a little over $700,000 tucked away, but she's also physically pretty heathy. She might live a long time at $100,000 to $120,000 a year, plus annual increases."

"David, I was okay with you looking for your mother. It was something you had to do and who was I to stop you? But this is getting complicated. The boys are headed off to college…very expensive college…I'm not sure I can deal with this."

"I'm sorry, baby. I really, truly am. But I can't abandon my mother now."

Keshia looked at her husband across the table. Among the wide range of thoughts racing through her head then, a new one emerged. This kindness and loyalty that David was showing was part of what she fell in love with. But at that moment she chose to remain silent about the irony of him not abandoning his mother. She believed he too was aware of it.

"There's only one other option that I can think of," he added, "and I'm not going to ask it of you…it's her living with us."

Keshia said nothing, simply opening her eyes wider to the point of wrinkling her forehead.

He finished his thought, "The boys will be gone at least nine months a year. Yes, we'd have to hire a caregiver to watch her when we're at work or wanted to get away. It would need to be costed out, but that's the only other option."

"That's another pretty big thing you've just plopped out there," she said.

"I know. None of the options are that great. I'm sorry."

CHAPTER FORTY

Father Armando wondered if he'd get to talk to Miranda again. That was all settled when Harris knocked on his door late one morning.

"She's having a tough day, but she'd like to see you. She said mid-afternoon would be preferred.

~

"How ya' doing today?" he asked when she motioned for him to sit on the couch with her. She was still in her bathrobe and well-worn pink furry slippers.

"Not too great today, Father. I'm having a full-fledged why-me-pity-party."

"Ahh, a party of one," he responded. "Those are never that fun."

He noticed the whites of her eyes were red, her face puffy. Miranda pulled out a Kleenex from the sleeve of her robe and dabbed her nose.

"It hit me last night and today. This is all very real now. I will die, and I'm not as good a person as I thought I was. It's like I've fallen into that big hole with no way out."

"I'm sorry you are going through this and that you've hit a rough patch." He paused and squared himself more her way, careful not to get too close physically. "Miranda," he added, "I'm not here to offer platitudes."

"Thank you," she said adding, "*It's sooo sad. You didn't ask for this. You don't deserve this*...those clichés just don't help. I know Harris and the others mean well. It just doesn't help."

"He means well," Father said. "The others do too. None of us are good at dealing with this liminal space stuff. Nobody's trained for it. We just repeat what we've heard, read, or seen in the movies."

"Did you say *liminal space*?"

"Yes, liminal space. It's what you're in."

"I've never heard of liminal space. What is it?"

Father Armando folded his hands in his lap and accessed the words he had thought through. "Liminal space is that time betwixt and between two very different realities or conditions. I suspect that when you heard *stage four*, you were immediately hurled into that deep hole as you call it. You left the world you knew and the life you had been living into something quite different."

She nodded affirmatively, listening with interest to what Father was saying.

"And when you heard *two to four months*, then that liminal space was given a human time frame. In those few moments, it became clear what you were betwixt and between...the life you had been living and what comes after that last heartbeat. That is the ultimate liminal space."

Miranda started crying without much sound. She was surprised to hear him say *last heartbeat*, but oddly respected his bluntness, his willingness to say what others were not. Her face scrunched and she used her tissue again. She rocked gently back and forth. He let her continue for more than a minute, wanting to put a hand on her shoulder, but refraining.

After she stopped rocking and sat back against the sofa, she blew her nose and dried her eyes.

"Maybe I shouldn't continue," he said. "I may have misjudged what I thought I should share with you."

"No, no. Please go on," she said with conviction. "I need to hear this." She looked closely at his eyes for the first time. They were dark brown, soft at the edges, and kind. "I want you to go on. Please."

"There've been other liminal times that maybe you've experienced. I've heard you lost your husband. There was a life before his death and then one after. There was probably an uncomfortable, dark time in between."

"Yes, and I lost a daughter too."

"I'm sorry to hear that. You've been through a lot," he said softly.

"Thank you."

Father reached in his pocket, pulled out a neatly folded handkerchief, blew his own nose, refolded it, then placed in back in his pocket before continuing.

"Pregnancy can be a liminal time, especially the first pregnancy. An expectant mother knows her life will never be the same, but she has nine months to think about it, and to prepare mentally and physically. There are role models all around her, good and bad, to help her figure out what kind of mother she wants to be in her new life, or at least start out being. She knows there will be sleepless nights, tantrums, and many new demands placed on her. She also knows with certainty that things will change over time and probably get easier with that child. But what you're going through now is different than that, isn't it, Miranda?"

She sat with her thoughts before responding. She was beginning to understand liminal space better through the examples of the deaths of two loved ones and a pregnancy. She had lived through those. "They say nothing compares to the death of a child," she said, "and it's true. But it is also true that nothing compares to coming face to face with your own death, and having a stupid clock ticking away in your head the whole time."

"I can only imagine," he said.

"This was one of the most glorious times of my life, Father. Harris is a good man. We had carved out a simple yet wonderful relationship that I had no idea could happen at this stage of life. And now it will end… suddenly…rapidly...one way or another."

He had more to say, but he chose not to interrupt. Letting her steer this was important.

"I thought I was prepared to die," she continued. "I've had a few years to think about it," she said with a snicker. "I knew I would not be the first one spared. I've lived a full life, a comfortable life, and I think I've been mostly a good person. So, I thought there's probably a heaven and I'm probably going there. No big deal. But now…face to face with it, it's frightening to think about what comes after that last heartbeat. That is the real, overwhelming uncertainty. And I'm scared about how my death with dignity plan plays into it, as I mentioned to you last time."

Father Armando's research and praying on the death with dignity issue had not led him to any conclusion of his own beliefs. He knew in his heart that he couldn't tell her *it's okay, God will understand, go ahead if you must,* or anything like that. "I can't help you with your death with dignity decision," he said "That's yours to make, but I do know you can worry all you want between now and that last breath, and you're still going to find out what happens afterward. Is that really how want to spend your last bit of time on earth? Worrying about that? Or trying to guess if there is or isn't a heaven, or what it looks like?" When she didn't respond right away, he added, "I don't know you well, but I'm pretty certain you want to spend your remaining time differently."

"You're right, Father," she said softly after some time while fiddling with her left thumbnail. Then with more energy she added, "You do know some things about me, that I need to go about this differently, *and* you knew me well enough that I needed to hear more than platitudes today...that I needed to learn about liminal space...something I didn't even know existed. So, thank you."

He could sense that she was losing steam, that he needed to wind down. He held up his index finger. "There's one more thought that relates before I leave you today."

"Okay," she said drawing it out a bit.

"There's the liminal paradox. It goes like this: on one hand, this is a disturbing and disorienting time for you, one that can be looked at as darkness. You can choose to wallow in it until the next reality emerges, in your case, the afterlife. On the other hand, liminal space offers you the choice to live in it with fierce aliveness, to seek out what it is all about and may have to offer, the uniqueness of this period if you can find it, and to live with the love and companionship that is around you. We must listen attentively to what the liminal space seeks to tell us. It might be as simple as gratitude or making amends. Liminal space is where we are most teachable because we are broken and vulnerable."

She nodded slowly, silently, wondering if he had finished his thought. Eventually she filled the silence with, "Thank you, Father."

"You know, Miranda, the mere fact that you asked for me today, tells me that you are not fully entrenched in the camp to wallow about this. You had no idea if I had anything to offer, but you weren't content in sitting back doing nothing. *You* reached out and made something happen."

"You've given me more than something to think about, you've given me a spark, and I'm grateful, Father. You've nudged me out of my pathetic party of one."

"Good," he said lightly slapping both of his thighs before standing. "You're welcome."

Miranda rose too, extending her arms open to hug him, then saying, "I think I'm going to take you up on that final confession and maybe even the anointing of the sick. No need to find a substitute, either. You're my guy 'til the end."

She sat in silence the rest of the afternoon in her favorite chair gazing out the windows watching the leaves move in the sycamore and oak trees, the skittishness of a squirrel, and seeing a male resident shuffle by pushing his walker on the path. Her thoughts, likewise, shuffled between many positive interactions with people throughout her life, some regretful incidents including those with Rex, places she was glad to have visited, and others she wished she had. She became aware of the movement of air in and out of her nose, the sound it made, and the related expansion of her chest. She wondered how many breaths left? How would she spend those breaths? Should she just curl up in a ball and wait, or grab Harris and frantically visit those places she'd missed? Neither seemed right for her. Father Armando's words came back into her head. How would she spend this last, very small portion of life? She needed to do it right.

Harris tapped lightly on her door at 5:00. Their dinners were brought to them shortly thereafter.

"Are you having wine tonight, madam?" he asked her before beginning their dinners.

"Yes, please."

He went to the fridge, grabbed the half-full chardonnay bottle, and poured them each a glass.

He sat next to her on the couch. There was no room for a kitchen or dining table in their apartments. She raised her glass toward him and he followed. "To life," she said.

"To life," he responded.

"Let's try not to waste it," she added before taking a short sip.

They ate their dry Dover sole, wild rice, and overcooked green beans without much to say. Finally, she asked him, "In regards to my death with dignity plan, what is your preference? Should I go through with it?"

Harris put down his fork, picked up his napkin and wiped the edges of his mouth, before saying, "That decision is not mine to make. Only you can make it."

"Oh, don't be that way," she said in a voice she had not used with him before. "Of course, only I can make it. But what is *your* preference? That is what I'm then interested in."

"Okay," he said placing his fork across his dinner. "You want my preference? I'll tell you my preference," he said sounding equally agitated. "We're two weeks into your two to four months prognosis. I'd rather you not cut that time any shorter...not one week...not one day. There's hospice to make you comfortable. I will help you in any way I can, whatever ways you want me to. You can do what you want, but *that* is my preference."

She smiled the little smile of hers and reached for his right hand with hers. "Thank you. Now that wasn't so hard, was it? I'm going to be on drugs and in diapers, and I'll want you by my side," she said. "That's such an odd combination of words."

"Yes. That is the combination that life has given us. We might wish it were different, but it is what it is."

"Oh, dear God. May I please die on the spot if I ever hear that again. That is my all-time least favorite expression…*it is what it is*."

"Sorry. I won't be using it again," he said.

"I'm sorry too. I'm being a bit of a witch today."

"You're entitled."

She closed the lid to her Styrofoam dinner container, having eaten little more than half her meal.

"I'll tell you what," she said, "I will forget this whole death with dignity thing and contact hospice to get that going, if you agree to stay with me until the end, and you promise to never say my least favorite expression again."

"Are you sure?" he asked. "Of course, I'm with you 'til the end. So, with that said, then your whole decision rests on me eliminating you-know-what."

"Mr. Archibald, I've been leaning this way for a few days. Father Armando said some things today that tipped it for me. It may well be a little selfish of me to end things early, and I just can't get comfortable with what God thinks about it. But, yes, I really like hinging the decision on *it is what it is.*"

"I need to let you know," he added, "that even though I hardly ever use that expression, I am quite fond of it. It has a nice ring. But I will gladly give it up for extra time with you. You get to drive this."

"Thank you. I'm glad you put it that way…me driving this...because what's going to make this last dash for the finish line worth it for me, is some real intimacy."

"Oh really?" he said with surprise.

"Yes, but maybe not the kind you're thinking. I'm hoping you'll play along. It will mean the world to me."

CHAPTER FORTY-ONE

When Mondo returned to his room after his discussion with Miranda on liminal space, he sat and prayed. He thanked God for allowing him to access and convey the right words for Miranda that afternoon. He thanked God for helping Miranda be receptive to hearing those words, and he asked God to watch over this last small part of her life, and make it as painless and pleasant as possible. He also asked God to guide his own life… how to be a good priest and friend, now and moving forward. He thanked God for the creature-comforts that surrounded him, and then sat in silent prayer, letting his mind be as blank as he could keep it for many minutes.

Silent prayer was an exercise Father had practiced in spurts. It calmed his mind, cooled his inner urges. The way he had learned silent prayer was to focus on a white light in the center of his brain with his eyes closed. When stray thoughts crept in, he returned to the thoughtless white light. While the value of such an exercise differed from person to person, most often the outcome sought was meditative calming and relaxation. Often Father

Armando did feel more relaxed when he had finished silent prayer, but he also noticed something quite different on occasion. Never did he go into silent prayer trying to solve a problem or dilemma that he was facing, but sometimes he noticed that after that absence of thought for 20 or 25 minutes, he was more calm and could proceed with his day with more clarity and purpose. Often a solution to a problem or dilemma he'd been struggling with came sharply into focus. It might not be for hours or days after silent prayer, but more than once, he noticed that solutions suddenly and without effort, appeared.

During this late afternoon, after his discussion with Miranda, after his own prayers of thanks and requests were followed by silent prayer, he was overcome with a sense of knowing. He knew right then what he needed to do to be a good priest, to be a good friend. *Of course, there are others.* he thought, *there are many others at The Ridge who needed to hear about liminal space. Not only Miranda.* He knew he needed to start with Harris.

~

"I'm not sure what you said to her, but she's a different person after you talked to her yesterday," Harris told Mondo.

"She's just different than the rest of us, my friend," Mondo replied. "She requires more, something new. The normal stuff, especially clichés, shut her down."

"You've got that right," Harris said deciding not to elaborate on her least favorite expression.

"I'm not sure where she goes with this," said Mondo, "but she's probably going to want to take advantage of this remaining time. You are on the front line, so you're going to get it first. Be attentive. Be open. Don't be surprised if you get requests you don't expect."

Mondo then put on his priest garb, and headed to the main office to see Brian. After hearing Father's spiel, Brian agreed to have Father speak to the larger Ridge community. He told Armando to be ready this coming Friday at Happy Hour.

"Seems like an odd time to discuss liminal space," he said.

"The Happy Hour singer called and cancelled. We're scrambling to find a replacement. You'll have a decent audience, and we'll see where we go from there." Brian was always on the lookout for something new and appropriate to bring to the residents. What little he understood about liminal space sounded like it might be just what many residents needed to hear.

That following Friday at 3:00 with a group of 42 residents, Brian got up in front of them and announced, "Our scheduled entertainment for today called and had to cancel. In her place we lined up something different, but something you may get more out of. We will continue our wine service. I ask you to give him your full attention. Let's welcome one of our own…Father Armando."

After the sparse applause died down, a woman in a wheelchair shouted, "Where's your guitar?" Then she turned to the man sitting next to her and added, "He needs his guitar."

The man turned to her and also said too loudly, "He musta' forgot it."

"Actually," Father began, "I'm not here to sing to you today. I want to talk to you instead. I want to talk about how some of us, maybe most of us, miss that life we had before...and we wonder what is next. Some of us are in this in-between place at The Ridge. Don't get me wrong. The Ridge is very nice. Physically, our needs are met. We get three meals a day, if we want them. We have running water and cable tv. But mentally and emotionally, some of us, me included, miss what our lives were like before this. And we wonder what is next...or we know what is next...the afterlife, and that makes us uncomfortable right now."

The room was quiet. A couple people shifted in their seats, while a few others took a sip of wine. One woman stood up and left with her walker.

For the next twenty-two minutes Father Armando talked about liminal space and the liminal paradox, but only mentioned the term once. When he was speaking, he saw some women dab their eyes, and heard one man blow his nose. When he finished, several came up to him and thanked him for the wonderful talk. One said, "I never knew priests could talk about such things. I thought it was all how God loves me, or we're all sinners, or we need to tithe."

Father had closed by offering to meet with anyone one-on-one if they wanted to talk more about this in private. Three women and one man said they would contact him. Armando's instincts had been correct. So were Brian's. The group had needed to hear this. They were thirsty for something more, maybe not as desperately as Miranda, but they wanted more. Harris had been there and heard. So had Rex and Diana.

CHAPTER FORTY-TWO

The following afternoon before dinner, Miranda sitting on her couch next to Harris reached for his hand and said, "Last night I was thinking about my life. What else, huh? I thought about how my husband and I had lived full, good, upper-middle-class lives. We travelled. We had a nice circle of friends…and at the end it comes to this…The Ridge…where hardly anyone comes to visit me." She looked down at her legs and shook her head ever so slightly. "Are people so busy? Are old friends so easy to forget and move on? It all seems pretty pathetic." She paused before looking back to Harris. "I don't know what I'd do, how much more miserable I'd be if you hadn't decided to live here…at The Ridge. It's kind of scary."

He nodded in agreement then added, "That thought occurred to me too, but you need to know that I would be floundering too…if I hadn't moved into The Ridge."

Miranda squeezed his hand then suddenly shifted the mood by reminding Harris of her intimacy comment. "You and I are already intimate physically, at least as much as I can be. What I'm hoping for from you, if you're willing to play along, is some openness about the corners of our lives, the things people usually don't talk about."

"I see," he said. "Maybe there's some good reasons not to talk about them."

"You silly man. Do you remember when we first met and we shared out favorite podcasts, movies, music, and travel destinations."

"Of course."

"Those were safe and easy and a way to get to know each other a little bit. What if we took it further and shared things less safe…like the most reckless, daring, maybe even stupid things we've done?"

"I can do that," he said emphatically.

"Great. Well, think about it and maybe tomorrow when you come back, we'll start there."

"No. I mean I can do that now. I don't need to think to try and recall. I know which one was the most daring, reckless, and stupid right now."

"Well okay, then. Go ahead, then I'll share mine."

Harris got up and went to the fridge. He pulled out one of the beers he had brought down days before. "You want some wine?" he asked.

"Oh, why not," she answered though it was only 4:15, much earlier than when she normally had her one glass.

He poured her wine and brought it and his beer back to the sofa where they sat near each other. "When I was finishing up at S. F. State," he began without hesitation, "I belonged to the Gator Club. It was not a fraternity, but it was a social club for those of us who didn't live on campus. We mainly drank beer, but we also did things like ski down Lombard Street, streaked in Golden Gate Park, pulled cars over for blowing through stop signs… stuff like that."

"You pulled cars over? What, pretending you were police officers?"

"Yep. Might not have been the smartest thing."

"Definitely not, but sounds like a heckuva lotta fun," she said eager for where this was going.

"It was the late '60's, early '70's. There was a lot going on, but it was also just before the first airline hijacking."

"D.B. Cooper, as I recall," she added.

"Very good! Up in Washington somewhere. It was 1971, but before D.B. was known, one of our Gator Club members had heard that you could go out on the main runway at night at SF International and dodge airplanes."

"Wait…what?" she asked leaning forward then taking a sip of her wine.

"We'd first have a couple of beers at a dive corner bar out on the avenues that didn't card anybody. I was legal by then, but some in the Gator Club weren't. We'd have a couple, then we'd drive to SFO and park near the runways, you know, where parents took their kids to watch the airplanes."

"Everybody did that back then," she said. "My dad took me."

"Yes, well, strangely they didn't have great fencing that went all around the perimeter. There were gaps. It was not maintained. You could just walk out onto the runways then. And if you did it late enough at night, with the heavy cloud cover darkness in South San Francisco, you might not be seen. The main landing runaway, where planes approached from the south, was close to a mile hike out there. We went about 10 o'clock when there weren't many planes taking off."

"And how many besides you were doing this?"

"One car's worth…four or five. It was *very stimulating* walking out there in this unkempt dirt field, hunched over between the sagebrush, stepping over old boards and around puddles. The terminal and tarmac were to our left, the east-west runway immediately to our right. Every once in a while, a security vehicle would drive by, but it was so dark, with only some little blue lights lining the runway, we'd just duck down low. We had no trouble getting out to the north-south runway unseen.

"Once we were out there, we stood at the edge of the runway while some planes landed, whizzing by about a minute or two apart. The deal was, however, for it to count as dodging airplanes, we all had to stand in the middle of the runway once while a plane touched down with their really bright lights on. The landing plane was still a quarter mile away or so, but with the bright lights we were definitely visible. We knew the pilot would be telling the tower that there were some kooks out there, so once we did it, we had to boogaloo back."

"This didn't really happen," she said wanting to believe, but finding the story outrageous.

"It did. I swear. Twice. Then we'd go back to the bar, have a couple more, and tell people what we'd done. And they'd all go *you did what? Why?*"

"Never got caught?"

"The last time was close. After a pilot spotted us on the runway, and no doubt radioed the tower, they sent multiple vehicles out looking for us on our way back. We sprinted left across the east-west runway into the edge of the bay. There were large, discarded blocks of cement along the edge which were placed there to reinforce the shoreline, probably to prevent erosion. They were piled at odd angles overlapping each other which made for great hiding. We stayed there for 10 or 15 minutes until they gave up the search. Again, *extremely stimulating.*"

"And then what? Why'd you stop?"

"D.B. Cooper happened. That's what ended it. The news focused for a week, maybe longer, about how security at airports would be tightened. Very serious signs popped up on the perimeter of the airport announcing it was a felony to go on the runway. New fencing with razor wire happened pretty quickly too."

When he had finished the story, Harris took a long swig from the beer bottle, then sat back. Miranda wondered if there was more but then realized that was it, and she had no other questions. Miranda enjoyed the story. She liked the way Harris had told it, and could even imagine the thrill of being there. "It's hard for me to believe that people did such things," she said. "I was already into marriage then, with a baby. Was probably in bed by 9:00 hoping to get some sleep, while you and others were out dodging airplanes…really big airplanes. Who knew?"

"Yeah, well…" Harris wasn't sure what to add. He didn't want to make Miranda feel like she had missed out any more than she already was. He couldn't say that she'd had it better because that's not what he felt.

After a sip of wine, she patted her bathrobe, and said, "I guess it's my turn." Miranda had enjoyed the escapade of Harris and his friends, although, if honest, she'd hoped for something different…perhaps a secret tryst, public sex, something carnal.

"I don't know if I should tell you this now. Your story was so fun."

"I think you started this by saying we should share things less safe than movies or podcasts.'

"I did, didn't I." She took a deep breath for dramatic affect and then began. "A few weeks before our wedding, Tom and I ended up over at my parents' house. We all had gone out for a nice dinner. I was still living at home. We played cards in the family room and had another drink. After a while, my parents said they were tired and were turning in. I told them we were going to stay up and watch a little tv. Everyone said *good night* and my parents went down the hall to the far end of the one-story, L-shaped house. Tom got frisky after a couple of minutes. If truth be told, I knew how to get him going. It was the era of short skirts and very high heels. I may have had my heels still on and flopped my leg over his while I sat close to him on the couch."

Harris listened intently with the slightest grin.

"Things progressed as they always do when you're young. He started pawing me until I said *wait*." Miranda chuckled but then hesitated, wondering if she should continue with the story as she had planned. She wanted to tell all, to not hold anything back for once in her life to someone she knew she could trust. She still hoped Harris might share something similar. "I pushed his hands off me and stood up. Tom was perplexed. I think he was close to getting crabby, until I started taking my clothes off."

"No," exclaimed Harris. "You didn't…not in the family room!"

"You're right. We didn't in the family room. I did grab him by the hand, though, and led him to the living room, which was much closer to the end of the house with the bedrooms, wearing only my naughty girl heels."

"You didn't! What if they weren't asleep yet?"

"That was a possibility. *Very stimulating* as you say. Right there on the carpet in the living room."

Harris' grin was much larger now. "Why you little…!" he said with just the right amount of playful pause.

Miranda chuckled before saying, "I really wasn't. I was basically a good girl who wanted to do slutty things."

"Didn't get caught?"

"Didn't get caught," she added in a tone that ended her story.

Harris sat there moving his head in little nods, both appreciative and stunned at the same time.

It was nearing the time when their dinners would be delivered. Initially satisfied with the story exchange and Harris' willingness to play along, she wondered to herself *what next?*

When their dinners came, they ate in relative silence. Harris selected their music station on the tv to soften the quiet. Miranda suddenly felt waves of regret reign over her for what she had just told. Nearly 80 and dying…why had she done that? What had she hoped to gain? She had wanted to ask him, had it planned out really, to reveal details and as much as he could about his sexual past. That had been her curiosity for a long time... other people's habits…proclivities...the things that were never shared between even the closest of friends. That is what she thought she'd wanted as though it would make a difference. She believed he wouldn't refuse a dying woman's request. But now after sharing the brief story of her past playfulness, and feeling poorly about it, she knew she wouldn't ask…she couldn't. Some things should never be known, never shared.

While Harris ate, he had no idea of the thoughts running through Miranda's head, but he recalled Mondo's words about Miranda wanting more. He wasn't surprised by her request for his story, but, if truth be known, he was surprised by the telling of hers. Not that he didn't think she was capable of such boldness in her youth...wasn't everybody reckless in their youth? It just caught him off-guard to hear that story from her at this stage in her life. But part of what he liked, loved and respected about her had been her openness and truth-telling. He just hadn't seen that one coming. He wondered if she might regret telling him. He hoped she wouldn't but realized he'd need to respond if she did. He also wondered if this was just a prelude to her asking him for some similar details about his past.

When he had nearly finished his dinner and she had eaten very little, she said, "I wish I hadn't told you that story now. It was silly of me…stupid really, to think that somehow telling you about getting lucky was appropriate. I feel embarrassed."

"It was a good story. It kept my interest. I'm glad you shared it, even though it did surprise me a bit."

"You're very kind, Mr. Archibald. I don't know what I was thinking."

"You were probably thinking it's time to share personal stuff…what am I waiting for?"

"You're very astute too, Mr. Archibald."

Harris had a fork full of au gratin potatoes almost to his mouth. He lowered it, letting the utensil rest on his food, and said, "And maybe you just discovered what it doesn't need to include. We're all life-long learners."

She slowly set her napkin onto the coffee table and then her utensils onto the napkin. She seemed sad and pensive. "I think I'm learning that I'm not the person I thought I was, and that's a tough thing to discover near the end."

He had nothing for that except to place his hand in hers. They were silent and content sitting together on the couch. He broke it by saying with a little playful energy in his voice, "You know, when you're young, getting lucky used to mean one thing. Now that we're older, getting lucky can be just a good morning poop."

"Ha, ha, ha, ha. Ain't that the truth," she said, squeezing his hand tighter.

They sat in silence for a long time, both of them content, each of them accepting. That came to an abrupt end when Miranda said she felt nauseous. "Get the trash can, please." Harris rushed to grab it from under the sink, brought it to her, and she threw up her dinner.

The rest of the night they spooned in her bed, her mind drifting between what the vomiting meant and how she wanted to her remaining days to be. Dying with dignity had seemed so straight-forward, a step-by-step formula for the end. A to B to Z. Sharing stories, especially the kind that people rarely shared had been an impulse. Now that too was off the table. She was uncertain how her final days would play out or how to even steer them now…and steering things was her inclination. She felt anxious and depressed. *This liminal space is no fun.*

Harris lay there trying to think of ways he could make her remaining days better. He believed Miranda deserved a great life, especially this last phase. He knew there was no one in the world who would have a bigger impact on that than himself. He felt the weight of that responsibility.

CHAPTER FORTY-THREE

Mondo knocked on Diana's door one mid-morning. When there was no response, he turned the knob gently. The door was unlocked. He opened it to find her in a wingback chair facing the television which was off. She looked at Mondo briefly without expression, then looked back at the blank screen again. She wore no hats. Her hair was matted, like it hadn't been washed or had had too many hats on it for too long. As he got closer, he could see her eyes were bloodshot and that her face was puffy. There seemed to be a lot of that going around The Ridge these days. He sat on the sofa, the end nearest her chair and said, "What is it?"

She didn't answer, rather turning to gaze out her sliding back door at nothing in particular.

"Diana," he asked again, "what happened?"

She turned her head slowing not to him but to the screen before saying, "I don't know what's going on." She reached over to her lamp table and picked up the *Spoiled Rotten* hat that was lying on it. She didn't put it on, but rather held it in front of her, first running her fingers across the brim and then across the silver sequined lettering. "I used to do everything for myself," she went on. "I just don't know..."

"I'm sorry," Mondo said.

Her land-line phone rang. She looked around then grabbed the television remote and attempted to push some buttons. Mondo watched, surprised at what he was witnessing. As the phone kept ringing, he jumped up, grabbed it, and handed it to her.

"Hello," she said. "Oh, fine. That nice man is visiting with me."

Mondo could hear it was David on the call, checking on his mother. He was surprised how her voice seemed so much more upbeat talking on the phone to her son. When she concluded with, "Everything's fine," Mondo just sat there.

"That was my son," she said after looking around where to place the phone. When she found it, she added, "Just checking on me, I guess."

"What a good son you have to do that," he said.

Mondo wanted to get back to where he and Diana had left off before David called. He knew talking about liminal space didn't fit here. He'd seen dementia at work before with some elderly in the parishes he'd served. Talking it through was always tough for both sides. "Diana," he said, "This aging stuff is hard. It's often unfair. Sometimes we outlive our knees or hips. Sometimes our brains start working differently. I'm sorry what you're going through. I'm sorry you realize that things aren't working the way they did for most of your life. That can't be a great place to be."

She turned to face him more as he was talking. “Yes, it’s not a great place to be. Thank you for saying that.”

“You’re a wonderful person. Everyone seems to like you here. I don’t know all the parts of your life, but I’ve bet you’ve lived a full life, an interesting life, with lots of fun.”

“Maybe I have. What I can remember, I think it was.”

“Maybe it hasn’t gone perfectly, not always smoothly. But that’s kind of how life is, for all of us.”

She didn’t respond initially, choosing to gaze back at the blank screen, sullen again, before saying, “It is what it is.”

Mondo sat with her, uncertain how to proceed, thinking maybe he should leave. In time, he asked to use her bathroom. He shut the door though he didn’t need to go. On her wash basin counter were the normal grooming items: a toothbrush in a clear glass, hairbrush, toothpaste, and deodorant. He decided not to feel the bristles of her toothbrush for moisture, instead placing it at the 3:00 o’clock position in the glass, while pushing the glass completely into the upper left corner of the counter touching both walls. He positioned the toothpaste in a way he could remember next to the cold faucet handle. He then noticed the towel draping over the shower door. He rearranged it in a distinctive, seemingly unreproducible way, then took pictures with his phone of what he’d done. He flushed the toilet, ran the water in the sink, and waited of few seconds before leaving the bathroom and rejoining Diana. He asked her if she'd walk with him.

She said, "That would be lovely," and arranged three hats on her head.

Mondo went by her apartment in the late morning for the next four days, always asking to use the restroom. He always took pictures of the glass and toothbrush, the toothpaste, and the towel draped over the shower door. After the fifth day he called David and explained his concerns about Diana's non-grooming habits, that none of the key articles that he had placed in particular ways had moved in five days. David told Father Armando that might help explain his mother's recent UTI, thanked him for the head's up, and said that he would deal with it.

David went that evening to visit his mother. They chatted casually in her living room and he asked her about things in general. "Are you feeling okay, mom? Any pains?"

"I feel good outside of not knowing what's going on. This is a nice place."

"So, no pains?" he repeated.

"No pains. I feel good."

"Pooping okay?"

"Everything's good," she answered.

"Are you still able to take a shower by yourself or should we get you some help?" he asked.

"I take a shower every day. Everything's good."

He asked to use the restroom, shut the door, and checked out the placement of the things Father had talked about, He went one step further and took the bar of soap that was in her shower and tilted it at an odd angle in the soap tray, something that his mother could not possibly replicate with a wet bar of soap.

When he came back to visit three evenings later, and the dry bar of soap was still at its odd angle, he came out of the bathroom and said, "Mom, how about you take a shower when I'm here some evenings, so I can be sure you're safe."

"Well, okay if that's what you want."

"Good. How about we start tonight?"

"I just took one this afternoon," she said.

"But mom, the soap and the towel are completely dry. I'll start the water warming up."

As he stood and headed toward the shower, he could hear her say with some annoyance, "But I just took one."

He helped her begin to undress, but handled it in a way to preserve some dignity for her, some propriety, "I'll just wait here until you're done, just to make sure you're safe."

She went along with it, resigned to the beginning of this new part of their mother-son relationship that would take place twice a week. During this first shower night, David found a bureau drawer with clean underwear and a night gown. While she was in the shower, he placed the new clothes on the top of the hamper in the bathroom after throwing her dirty clothes into it. He could hear her soaping but hollered "Make sure you shampoo your hair."

When she had finished and dressed for bed, they sat in her living room. He helped her dry her hair. "Now doesn't that feel good?" he asked.

"I guess so."

"You look like a thousand bucks."

She snickered, unsure what to make of his comment.

Before he left, he handed her toothbrush to her with paste. She said, "What's this? I already brushed today."

"It's good to brush before bed too, mom. We're all supposed to do it."

She accepted the brush in her hand and walked toward the bathroom and cleaned her teeth over the sink.

CHAPTER FORTY-FOUR

Harris had not slept well. When he awoke to pee at 4:37, he did not go back to sleep. After being the first in the dining room and grabbing a quick breakfast for himself, he took some oatmeal, a banana, and some black coffee to Miranda's room. Immediately he sensed something was wrong.

"Thank you, but I'm not sure I could keep that down," she said while looking in the direction of the food tray.

"What is it?" he asked.

"I'm feeling very nauseous again and my stomach is bloated." She sat back and stretched out attempting to show the bump under her nightgown.

Harris could see a noticeable rise where only a little had been before. He touched it lightly. It was squishy, like water on the knee, only much larger. Touching it bothered her. "We need to get this checked out," he said in the way that indicated there would be no discussion on the matter.

He called Miranda's oncologist. They were able to squeeze an appointment in at noon. On the drive there, Miranda hardly spoke, changing positions in the passenger seat often to find something more tolerable.

Once in the office, Miranda asked the nurse if her good friend could come into the room. "Of course," the nurse replied.

The doctor quickly assessed the situation, saying that Miranda had ascites fluid around her abdomen. It was common with some cancers and could be easily drained. When the nurse did so, the relief for Miranda was instantaneous. The doctor asked them both if hospice had been called. When hearing that they had not taken that step, the doctor was quiet for a while, looked forlornly, then said, "You don't want to hear this, but the fluid indicates the cancer has likely spread to other places. It might be time to get hospice involved. They can drain the fluid. It will make you much more comfortable, and they will probably need to do so daily."

When they got back to Miranda's room, Harris stood by her phone and said, "Should we call?" Miranda nodded solemnly then went to lay on top of her bed, while Harris called one of the local hospice organizations. They said they would send someone out that evening. They also suggested providing a hospital bed. After dinner, in which Miranda did not eat, a hospice coordinator arrived with an explanation about their program and papers to sign. A nurse and the bed arrived two hours later. They moved some furniture in the living room for space to place the bed. The nurse left six morphine doses and talked through when and how to take it. "Or you can wait for one of us, if you're more comfortable with that. Have ice chips handy. She's going to need them."

Once they were alone, near their normal bed time, Miranda said, "It's even more real now. It's very unsettling."

It was to Harris as well. He moved in, sleeping in Miranda's queen bed by himself, leaving only to get food for himself, a change of clothes from his room, or to run an errand while the nurse was there. The days dragged on in ways neither of them ever imagined or experienced. Over the next five days Miranda slept a lot, ate little, drank enough, and needed the ascites drained every day except one. Her energy seemed to be waning. When she was awake though, she was happy to see Harris. She felt waves of affection for this man who was staying with her through all this. She wanted to talk to him, to be with him, but she needed to sleep and often dozed after a short visit.

He felt most comfortable waiting on her, tending to her needs and requests, but was struck by how exhausted he was too. There was little to do but worry about what each groan or change in breathing meant. Supporting someone in their time of need is a wonderful concept. In practice, when the outcome has been preordained, providing support proved to be draining and wearisome.

But something odd happened the sixth through eighth days of hospice. There were times in these days when Miranda seemed stronger, clearly more alert and talkative. She even wanted to get up and walk to the bathroom, though needing some help.

After it happened the second time for much of the daylight hours, Harris wondered to himself and then to Mondo if they, perhaps, had made a mistake…that maybe hospice had been called prematurely. Mondo suggested talking to the nurse about it. Harris did the next time the nurse came and when Miranda was asleep. The nurse assured him that they see this all the time… there were portions of days when the patients seem to rebound, have a burst of energy and be in seemingly better health. "It usually proceeds the next decline." Harris had no reason to know such things, and no reason to doubt the nurse's expertise. The morning after he had spoken with the nurse, Miranda asked, "Can you see if the kitchen has any watermelon? I really want some."

The kitchen did and he brought her a few small wedges. She ate them with vigor. "That tastes *so* good!" she exclaimed with considerable enthusiasm and delight. When the hospice nurse returned that afternoon, Harris mentioned the watermelon request and how Miranda had reacted.

"Cravings are part of this. Taste buds often get hyperactive," she said.

"I really like watermelon with the black seeds," Miranda added.

Harris recalled that the kitchen's watermelon had been with the smaller white, edible seeds, no doubt with the residents in mind. Later, while a hospice caregiver tended to Miranda, Harris went to Safeway in search for black-seed watermelon. On his drive there, he thought *what if she dies* while I'm gone? He had heard tales of terminally ill people waiting until loved ones left the room to pass, ostensibly to have them avoid the pain of witnessing death. That did not seem plausible given the recent energy bursts and food cravings, but he still rushed as much as he dared, returning with a half watermelon, cut to reveal the black seeds. Miranda devoured two large slices, juice dripping from the sides her mouth, spitting seeds into Harris' open palm. She made hilariously contented noises while she ate. He couldn't believe what he was witnessing. Nobody he had ever seen had enjoyed food as much.

When she had finished, she flopped back, asked for the bed to be lowered, shut her eyes and dozed off. When she awoke 25 minutes later, she said, "Thank you for getting that. It was so good."

"You're welcome," he said, stroking her head.

"How much pain?"

"A little."

"Three?" Harris and Miranda had been trained by the hospice nurse to assess pain one through ten, with ten being the worst imaginable.

"Three or four," she answered.

"Ready to try the morphine?" he asked.

"Not yet," she answered, trying to sound more pleasant than she was feeling, then slumped deeper into the pillow, closed her eyes, and seemed to drift off though her breathing did not change. Harris was startled when a minute later she asked with eyes still closed, "Will you talk to me?"

"Sure. Of course. What do you want to talk about?"

"I guess the thing that I'm most concerned about is... is there an afterlife?" Her tone indicated the seriousness of her question. "It really consumes me now."

Suddenly Harris felt his neck and face get hot. He realized how on the spot he was, how important this had to be to her, and how ill-equipped he was to come up with meaningful words. And yet here they were… just the two of them. There was no one to pass this off.

He looked at her for a long second before beginning hesitantly, "Probably…maybe…I don't know."

She looked up at him, her eyes open, head tilted as if beckoning *tell me something, anything*.

He continued, this time with a more clear, resolute voice. "I've always felt that *yes* there's an afterlife… maybe not the heaven and hell that I learned about in Catholic school, or what the classic painters tried to portray…but something that doesn't resemble this world…and maybe, just maybe, that *something* is really good."

Miranda didn't respond or move her head, but Harris sensed she liked what he was saying, so he continued. As I've aged, I've fallen into the camp that also thought *so what if I'm wrong*? Will I somehow be embarrassed at my death to learn I've been duped, or have regrets that I could have lived differently?"

A tiny smile emerged on her face.

"I mean, if we've all been duped…those of us who fell for the heavenly afterlife notion, only to find out there is nothing…then there's also no regret, no embarrassment...because THERE'S NOTHING... JUST THIS BIG THOUGHTLESS VOID." He let his voice get more animated, dramatic with the last seven words.

"The notion of an afterlife probably caused me to live a certain way...more noble and virtuous," he added.

With her eyes locked on him now, Miranda said weakly, "Virtuous and noble strangely don't seem so important right now."

He studied her face, surprised at her last remark then asked, "If you had known for certain all along that there was no afterlife, would you have stolen money, treated people badly...had more sex partners?"

She let out a weak chuckle then offered, "I may have had more sex partners ...for a month or two."

He met this remark with a warm smile and said, "Yeah, I bet you had some choices, some possibilities that not everyone gets." He was quiet and so was she while she recalled some missed opportunities, two in particular.

When a new line of thinking came to him. he said, "I think it's very normal to want to know these things at the end, to be reassured. But trying to decipher all this now is going to be futile and frustrating, Miranda. No one knows. Most religions call it *faith*."

She remembered that Mondo said the same thing. Right then *faith* seemed like a semi-fancy word for a *belief* that had no scientific basis, and could never be proven either way. She tilted her head slightly as she looked at him and said kindly, "I don't want to decipher it, I just want *your* opinion. It matters to me."

He took her right hand in both of his and looked at her eyes more intently than he ever had. "Listen to me, and listen to me good." It was a line his dad had used on him once and Harris had waited all his life to use it. "My opinion is that there is an afterlife and there's a good chance that it's way better than this life. And if there is a better place, you are definitely going there."

He stopped, thinking that was enough. She'd probably let him know if she needed more though she seemed weaker, more tired than he'd ever seen her. Her eyes were closed now, but she moved her thumb a tiny bit over the bony knuckles of his hand. After a time, she opened her eyes and said meekly, "Thank you for your opinion."

"You're welcome," he replied.

"But I've been far from perfect. I know that now."

"Nobody is. That's not the expectation or requirement. You're going to heaven if there is a heaven."

He released her hand and took the glass with the straw to her mouth for a drink "Is there anything else you need?" he asked.

Without hesitation, she answered, "I need to not be afraid. Waves of fear have been hitting me broken by times of calm."

"I'm staying with you, and I'll take care of you no matter what."

"Thank you. That's good to know."

CHAPTER FORTY-FIVE

"Brian," the receptionist hollered into his office, "Diana, just left the parking lot." Brian jumped up from his desk. As he was heading out the double doors, the receptionist added, "She went right."

Brian jogged stiff-legged on the sidewalk along the busy street before catching up with Diana about a half a block down the main thoroughfare. When he got alongside her, he, near breathlessly said, "Hi, Diana. Where ya headed?"

"Oh hi," she replied cheerily. "Just takin' a walk. Keeping these million-dollar legs moving."

Brian gently touched her elbow and said, "How about we head back where you live, You're getting a bit far away."

Diana jerked her arm away and said, "No, I'm fine. I live right up here."

"Actually, you live back there," he said pointing in the direction they had both come from. "It's a busy street, and I need to get back to work. Will you walk with me?" He held out is arm in a herding manor to get her redirected.

"Leave me alone, damn it!" Her eyes widened and her fists clenched. For a moment Brian feared she might strike him. Brian pulled out a business card from his shirt pocket and showed Diana he was the General Manager at The Ridge, the place where she lived. She calmed down.

When they got back to The Ridge's main entrance, Diana thanked him for walking with her. "That was nice," she said. "What is your name?"

Brian called David and asked him to swing by when he could. Late that afternoon when Brian explained the incident to David, he added, "I never like delivering this message, but I think we've reached the point where it is no longer safe for your mother here." Brian explained how easily Diana could have wandered off without anyone noticing. David understood. It was the moment he knew was coming, the one he hated arriving. He already dreaded the next conversation he needed to have with Keshia.

Keshia had done a lot of thinking about this new dilemma in her and David's lives. Some of that thinking was in the middle of the night when she should have been doing something else. Ever since David had sprung the choice they would eventually have to make regarding Diana's next place of residence, she knew the script called for her to be the good wife and let Diana live with them. But she had been the good wife by letting David pursue and eventually find his mother. She knew back then that those search-and-find-steps might not play out well for David in different ways, but she didn't see it evolving this way. She had no idea David's pursuit of his mother would have this impact on her own life, and so quickly. In the quiet of her own thoughts, she had wondered how odd the empty-nesters house would feel once the boys headed off to school, and was more than willing to wade through that life phase with her husband. That quiet house adjustment, she hoped, would be punctuated by sex anywhere, anytime, a fantasy long pushed aside by the reality of raising kids. She had been the practical one in their marriage, and the family money manager. From a practical standpoint, she supposed to herself that adding an 82- year-old relative to their living arrangement was probably doable, it just flipped the script of this next phase of life for her family. From her money-managing perspective, there were some questions, but she sensed what needed to be done.

When David asked her for some time after dinner and led her to the family room sofa, she was folded-arms-across-her-chest ready. David explained his mother's latest excursion outside The Ridge and the subsequent conversation he'd had with Brian. She didn't wait for David to say that it was time to revisit their discussion regarding his mother's next residential address.

"Financially it's an easy decision," she said cutting him off. "$10,000 a month versus hiring someone for eight to ten hours a day, five days a week to watch over your mother. When we want or need to go out, we'll get a mother-sitter for that. You're right, the boys will be gone soon, so we'll have the space. What we don't know is what impact that will have on our quality of life and how long bringing your mother here will remain the better choice." She stopped suddenly and let uncertainty take over the room. Just as suddenly she began again. "I'm willing to try it, David…her living with us. I'm not thrilled about it, but it could work. I think it's the best option."

David sat in amazement watching, listening to his wife get to the bottom line faster than he could have believed was possible before saying, "Are you sure about this? This is a big decision and will have an impact on our lives. There's no way around it."

"I'm not sure about anything," she said tersely, "other than I won't be having middle-of-the-day sex in all the places I was imagining once the boys left."

A closed mouth, crooked smile came over David's face before saying, "Well maybe you can tell me about some of those imaginings sometime and maybe we can figure out ways to still make them happen."

"I won't," she said. "You'll have to imagine them for yourself."

"I will. I promise you I will," he said softly. "But getting back to the issue at hand before you rudely and nicely distracted me, from a very pragmatic standpoint, that seems like the place to start for me as well. We'll pay for her daycare, medications, and some food expenses out of her savings. It may well be less than what she's paying now to live at The Ridge. Clearly, this will be a lifestyle adjustment for us. It shouldn't be a financial burden as well."

Keshia unfolded her arms and said, “Thank you.”

“We’ll give it a try,” he added. “If it becomes too tough for either of us, we’ll move her into a memory care facility.”

Once they found a Tongan caregiver through a friend of a friend, they moved Diana to her new home. On the final drive away from The Ridge, Diana was sitting in the passenger seat and David asked her if she knew what was happening.

“I guess I’m moving,” she replied.

“That’s right,” he said. You’re coming to live with us. We thought it would be better for all of us. There’s a woman who cooks and cleans for us,” he added, fibbing a little, “that will keep you company when we’re at work.”

“Oh, I don’t need a lot of company.”

“I know, mom. I’m just letting you know that there will be someone around during the day that we’ve hired to do some things. If you want to take a walk, Lei can go with you.”

“Well okay. If you think it’s best.”

“I do mom.”

CHAPTER FORTY-SIX

Harris did what was asked, though he had no way of understanding it. When he mentioned Miranda's request to Rex, Rex was about to begin his motorized ride back to his apartment at the conclusion of lunch. Rex replied, "Sure I'll see her. I knew she'd come to her senses sooner or later. I just didn't expect she'd make you come and fetch me."

"She's dying, Rex," Harris said with no emotion.

Rex looked down at the handlebars without comment. After some time, he gazed up at Harris and said, "Are you sure"?

"She's under hospice care. She's hoping you'll come by at 3:00 this afternoon."

Rex knocked on the door and Harris let him in with a "Glad you could make it," and held the door open while Rex drove himself in.

Rex looked around. He was surprised to see Miranda propped up in the hospital bed in the living room and some furniture pushed out of the way at odd angles. He moved himself near the right foot of the bed and stared at her. After some awkward silence, Miranda looked at Harris and said, "Can you give us a few minutes?" When Harris didn't move, unsure what she meant, she added, "It'll be all right."

Finally understanding what was being asked, he responded, "Sure. Take your time. I'll be right outside."

After Harris shut the door softly, Miranda and Rex looked at each other. He still hadn't said anything. The decades of crass remarks that had floated into his brain and quickly out of his mouth were silenced by an inner warden who knew better right then. The shades were closed, with only minimal light entering the room from the window edges. A lamp was on in her bedroom that did just enough for where they were. Finally, she offered, "So this is what it comes to…me first."

"I'm sorry. I-I didn't know."

Her speaking cadence was slower, and the volume was less than what he was used to from her. His mind flitted to hearing a different voice from her on the phone less than four weeks earlier. It made little sense to him seeing her this way. "Those ugly cells were going to rear up sooner or later," she said, then she coughed lightly but uncomfortably, trying her best to sit up while doing so. When she was able, she said, "Can you get me some water?"

Rex noticed the half-filled glass on the tray table near her and moved himself to get it. He pushed the table out of the way, then held the glass up near her mouth. She took a short drink through the straw while thinking that this was the only act of kindness that she could ever recall Rex doing.

"Thank you," she said. She moved her arms feebly and adjusted the covers on herself. "I wanted to follow up on our phone conversation last month or whenever it was."

Rex scrunched up his face and ran his big right hand quickly over it while saying, "Now dagnammit, Miranda…it wasn't supposed to happen that way."

Her face kept a flat expression for some time before offering, "Well, it did…so maybe it was."

"You know I ain't gonna do nuthin'."

Her eyes narrowed and she soon responded though still speaking slowly, "I don't know how serious you were. It's your choice. I hope you don't. I also hope you know that people who commit suicide aren't sick or bad, they just want some peace."

He winced when she said *suicide*. It seemed like such a big word when she said it and he felt some shame for bringing it on, but remained quiet.

"I just wanted to say *goodbye* while I could," she continued. "We've had a complicated relationship, haven't we?"

He thought for a moment, then said, "It didn't seem complicated to me."

"Hmmm," she said, lacking the energy to make a case otherwise. "I also wanted to say I'm sorry for that thing I did to you the last time you were in here. That was a bit much."

He was quiet again, taken aback by her words and the moment. He had never been at a dying person's bedside. And he never expected to hear what she'd just said. "It wasn't," he said. "I had it coming."

He reached up from his seated scooter position and touched her left arm near her elbow. She didn't have more to say and neither did he. They looked at each other not unlike how lovers do. "Goodbye, Miranda."

"Goodbye, Rex."

He removed his hand from her, put his transportation in reverse, and backed up. Near her bathroom entrance he did a u-turn to get facing the door properly. Before he grabbed the doorknob to open it, he turned, smiled, and said with bravado, "See you on the other side."

She smiled back and said, "Maybe. But you might not be going where I'm going."

He laughed a real laugh, opened the door and maneuvered himself through it.

Several seconds later Harris came in. Her eyes were closed. He grabbed the empty glass near her and refilled it at the sink. He then went into the freezer and pulled out the bowl of ice chips. They were nearly frozen into a block. With a fork he broke some off. He took the water and chips to her bedside and waited, believing that she was asleep. Harris looked over at the light coming around the edges of the curtains and blinds. Without opening her eyes, she said, "Be nice to him, okay? He's just a mess like the rest of us."

"I'll do my best," he replied, "but his messiness is more irritating than the rest of ours."

She opened her eyes and reached for his hand. "Thank you."

"Rest now," he said. "Do you need a little something for the pain?"

"I'm okay. When's the nurse coming? I may have made a little mess myself."

"It might not be for a few more hours," and he went to grab one of the adult Depends.

She thought about saying *no, Mr. Archibald*, but did not.

As he wiped her, she looked to the side, seeing nothing, thinking everything.

After changing her, he adjusted the bed to where she felt most comfortable. She quickly drifted off, waking only when the hospice nurse came in a little after 6:00. The nurse drained nearly a pint of bright yellow fluid from her abdomen, checked her clean diaper, rolled Miranda onto her left side, applied ointment to her back and upper buttocks, and inquired about her pain level. When informed that it was 6 or 7 and that the last morphine dose had been given over six hours earlier, the nurse suggested another. Miranda did not fight it. "I think you're being more cautious with the morphine than you need to be," she said to them both, but mainly to Harris. "She needs to be comfortable. Every four hours is appropriate or any time the pain is above six. My sense of her is that she doesn't inflate her pain level."

Together the nurse and Harris checked the inventory of morphine on hand and made arrangements for a refill. "Ice chips are critical from now on. Swallowing may become more difficult. Someone should be with her at all times."

"I'll be here 24/7."

"Good, but when you take a shower or go to the bathroom, someone should sit with her. Maybe you can take a walk or time your showers when one of us is here."

"Okay."

"Also, her voice may get so parched you may not hear her call you in the middle of the night. Maybe you could hang a bell from the ceiling that was near her upper body that she could just hit to alert you."

"I'll do that."

While the nurse was still there, Harris got a Christmas ornament from The Ridge's holiday storage… some fake mistletoe with three little bells tied to its top. With several feet of string from the front desk and an eye screw, he hung the mistletoe and bells above her bed but within reach. As soon as Miranda awoke, he explained its use. They practiced with it before he turned in for the night, and then she used it for real twice during a fitful night of sleep for both of them.

Several more days passed in a similar manner. There were no other bursts of energy, but rather much sleeping, hand holding and arm stroking, simple requests, and light conversations. The bell ringing two or three times a night ensured a lack of quality sleep for Harris. Now continually exhausted, he never let on to Miranda what a grind it had become. He took to taking cat naps during the day on her love seat while she slept.

He lost track of which day of the week it was, and it didn't matter.

One afternoon while Miranda slept, Harris asked the nurse who had been there the most, "What is your sense? How close are we?"

The nurse glanced at Miranda then back at Harris. It's definitely days…not weeks. And it probably isn't that many."

"Really? That wouldn't even be two months since she found out," he said surprised.

"Well, it works that way sometimes," the nurse said.

Mondo came by later with his guitar. He played some soothing instrumentals while she slept. While she had someone with her, Harris took a quick shower then went to the main kitchen for more watermelon. When he returned, Miranda was awake, and Mondo was giving her ice chips.

"Father," Harris said calling Mondo that for the first time ever, "Miranda wants you to do the Anointing of the Sick. Is that something you can do now, or do you need special vestments or a bible?"

"I can do it now. It doesn't need anything special."

"It can wait," Miranda said looking at Harris.

"It might be best not to wait too long, don't you think?" Harris asked.

After the Anointing of the Sick, and after Father Armando had left, Miranda asked, "Mr. Archibald, could you get my toothbrush?" He did and she cleaned her teeth, rinsing using two glasses, one filled with clean water. When she finished, she asked, "Mr. Archibald, would you kiss me?"

He smiled, leaned forward, and kissed her. An innocent kiss that neither chose to rush. When she made a pleasant sound, he slowly raised up and the two of them looked at each other with sad affection. She slumped back onto her pillow and closed her eyes.

After many seconds she reopened her eyes, gazed at Harris, and said softly, "If that's the last one, I'm okay."

"You silly girl, you said something like that about a hug once."

"Ahh, I must be in the repeating stage of my life."

As the hospice nurse had predicted, those days of energy bursts by Miranda had given way to decline. She grew weaker, was never chatty, and never left her bed. When she did speak her voice was thinner but there was weight behind her words. She often lay there with her eyelids half open for long periods. Harris said little, fearful it would sound trite. Rather, he stroked her hair or her hand. Once, after staring at the door of her apartment for some time, and without preface, she said meekly with Harris at her side, "We wasted so much. There were years, decades, when anything was possible. We shuffled through our routines…being comfortable. Now nothing is possible."

She closed her eyes. Harris held her right hand with his, rubbing his thumb gently across her fingers. Reaching for his iPad with his left hand and deftly scrolling, he found the bookmarked *Clar de Lune*. He played it twice, not knowing if the end was near, but believing Miranda had sensed it was before asking for a kiss. It wasn't.

She rang the bell three times that night. He gave her morphine after the second bell at 2:58 AM. He stayed up after the third bell, though she went back to sleep. For the next day she mainly slept. He often put ice chips near her lips. Sometimes she would sense they were there and take them. Occasionally she groaned and tried to reposition herself, appearing very uncomfortable. He asked every half hour about her pain level. Most times she did not respond. Harris was inexperienced in all this, but he couldn't stop thinking that death was very close. When hospice was later arriving than expected the next day, he phoned the lead nurse unsure what to do. She'd ask when the last time morphine was given and again encouraged him to stay on a four-hour schedule. He assured her he had.

During the following night, as he lay there unable to sleep, Harris thought how different it would have been if she had proceeded with her original plan. He had little doubt that she would be gone by now. The scripted ending would have included just himself and Mondo at her side. The reading of her favorite part of *Plainsong* would have been sandwiched between her selections of recorded music and Mondo-Harris live tunes. They would have held her after the final medications had been taken and said some loving and kind things as she slipped off. Perhaps there would have been an opportunity to spoon with her while she drifted off if she would have been able to get onto her side. There would have been an order to it all, a sense of control and purpose that was missing now. How glorious it would have been, he thought, if she had drifted off during *Clar de Lune,* while spooning. But the reality now was an unscripted death. And that death had its own timeline, and those on its edges could only watch, wait and provide the dignity it deserved.

The following morning just after sunrise, her breathing changed. There were unnatural gaps between them. When the hospice nurse arrived shortly before 9:00 AM, Miranda was barely able to speak. While the nurse tended to her, Harris called Mondo. His friend, arrived with his guitar almost immediately. Before the nurse left, she whispered to Harris, "It's going to be soon."

Mondo played some soothing instrumental music, then asked if he could have a couple of minutes with Miranda. Harris reluctantly waited in the hallway.

Father took Miranda's hand and said, "You're a good woman. You've led a good life. You'll be with God when this is all over. I'll watch over Harris. He'll miss you, but in time he'll be fine." And then he blessed her.

Mondo brought Harris in and said, "If you have anything to say, it should be soon."

Harris said, "I'll get my guitar."

Together they strummed and tuned their strings. Then they began "*I knew a man Bojangles and he danced for you…*"

They sang it sweetly, watching her breathing get shallow and slower. When they finished the song, her breathing stayed that way. There were 30 to 45 second gaps between breaths, gasping each time she resumed. Twice she tried to sit up, barely getting her head off the pillow, while reaching out in front of her with her right arm and making indecipherable noises. After the second time, Harris took her hand, bent close to her and whispered something in her ear that even Mondo, a few feet away, could not hear.

As he straightened up, her breathing stopped again. They waited. When it did not restart after a minute or so, Father put a hand on her shoulder, and said clearly, "Have a good journey, Miranda."

Harris looked at him quizzically until Mondo nodded his head rapidly three times and moved his right hand in circles while prompting Harris to join him.

Mondo said again, "Have good journey."

Harris added, "Have a great journey, Miranda."

Together they continued their chant, with each interspersing, "We'll see you soon."

The two men fell silent. They stood there on either side of her bed, not knowing what to do next. Harris stared at her for a couple of minutes, foolishly wondering if she would take another breath, barely breathing himself. When she didn't, the permanence of death hit him. Death was real. It was absolute. They had seen her death approaching, but now that it had arrived, it seemed more significant than he had expected, certainly much different than deaths portrayed in the movies and books. There was a finality that Harris had never known.

Eventually Harris sat back on the sofa and wept. It was a strange cry. Not loud, but jagged dry-sounding sobs. The sound that came from his mouth was understated for a man of his size, but there was no mistaking his grief.

Mondo sat near his friend until Harris had finished. The men remained there for some time without moving or making a sound until Mondo rose and went to the refrigerator. Upon opening it, he was pleased to see some beers that Harris had brought from his place. Though it was still early in the day, he grabbed two and brought them to where they had been sitting. He opened them and gave one to Harris. Mondo sat and raised his up a little and said, "I told her she was a good person. I meant it."

Harris nodded in agreement, then added, "That was a first for me…the first time I've ever seen someone die."

"I've only seen a couple…no one I was really close to," Mondo replied.

Miranda had yearned for intimacy with Harris, and had orchestrated it from the onset of their special friendship. As he sat in sadness, Harris realized that Miranda had invited him and Mondo into the most intimate chapter of her life, the last one. "It seems like such a privilege, something so intimate and private, to be invited into the final portion of a person's life," Harris said, trying his best to put a fine point on the experience.

Mondo remained quiet, being the perfect friend for the moment. He wanted Harris to get out whatever he needed. After some time, Harris concluded with, "I told her that I was grateful for our time together, that she should go when she was ready, but I needed her to know I loved her before she did. As I was saying it, I knew it wasn't enough."

"Maybe it was. Maybe it was all she needed because she passed right after that."

Harris didn't really buy it, but said, "Maybe so," before taking another sip.

The two men finished their beers before Harris abruptly stood up, announced his intentions, and went to the front desk to ask for Brian. When Arquelle, the receptionist, said that Brian was at a doctor's appointment, Harris said, "Miranda passed. A few minutes ago. I'm hoping you or Brian know what to do next."

"Miranda was on hospice, right?" asked Arquelle. "I think you're supposed to notify them now."

"That's right. Thanks," replied Harris.

Harris headed back to Miranda's apartment, along the way recalling the intake meeting with hospice where Miranda had stated cremation was her preference, and had to select a mortuary. It was towards the end of that meeting, he now recalled, the case manager had told Harris he needed to notify them whenever Miranda passed.

After he made the call to hospice and they told him they would be there within 30 minutes, Harris rejoined Mondo in sitting near her. Harris was surprised to see how much color had already left Miranda's face and hands. He also noticed how her fingertips under her unpainted fingernails were turning purple. Her mouth was open, her eyes mostly closed. He wondered silently if they should try to adjust either, but decided against it. He felt the finality of it all once again...long before hospice arrived…and long before they established the official time of death and then called the mortuary.

CHAPTER FORTY-SEVEN

"Good morning, mom. How'd you sleep?" David asked.

"Pretty good, I think," Diana replied.

It was Saturday, and most weekend days the three of them, including Keshia, ate breakfast together. This morning David had made Salzburg eggs with toast, and a half an orange for each of them. Salzburg eggs were simply soft-boiled eggs that he and Keshia had developed a fondness for on their honeymoon to Austria. They were never simply soft-boiled eggs thereafter.

"This is very good. You're spoiling me," Diana added.

"We like spoiling you, mom," Keshia said. "You are a very easy guest to have in our house." That was the truth and it had surprised both David and Keshia. Yes, they had a new person living with them, but Lei, the weekday caregiver, proved to be a respite and beneficial in other ways. Lei not only watched over Diana while walking, bathing, and grooming her, but also did some laundry and usually put together a dinner when Diana napped. David's and Keshia's careers had not been impacted. The cost of the caretaker was less than what Diana had spent at The Ridge.

Not surprisingly, there were little issues that surfaced from David's mother's short-term memory loss.

"Mom, I think you've worn that blouse three or four days in a row," David said hinting a change was in order.

"I just put it on this morning." Diana responded with incredulity.

"I know you put it on this morning. You didn't sleep in it. But I'm pretty certain I've seen you wearing it almost every day this week."

"I don't think so," Diana responded.

"Mom, how about we go to your room after breakfast and pick out something nice to get your son off your back," said Keshia knowing full well that David wouldn't mind her playing the good cop. It was a routine they had refined in the eight months that Diana had lived with them.

They knew there would probably be bigger issues coming up, but this arrangement was fine for now. Diana was being cared for, she was not demanding of anything, seemed very content, and was appreciative of the things Keshia and David did for her.

For David, this had been a strange journey. What started as an innocent yearning to find his mother had morphed rather quickly to this living situation. He was good with it. He shuddered whenever his mind drifted to how things might be playing out for his mother had he not surfaced for her when he did. He was also so grateful for his wife. How did this fall into *for better or for worse?* She had been cautiously resistant at first, rightfully so in his estimation, but had adapted so nobly.

For Keshia, she witnessed the joy it brought to her husband to have his mother around. But it was much more than that. There had always been a little hole in David ever since Keshia met him. That void got filled when he searched for and found his birth mother. Of course, Keshia hoped this arrangement would stay this trouble-free, but sensed that she and David would figure out next steps when the need arose. Their boys would be coming home soon from their first year of college, and that would add complexity and chaos for which their 19-year-old sons were specialists.

Having moved Diana from The Ridge just before Miranda's quick decline, David, Keshia and Diana had been oblivious to those developments and of her passing. At this point in time, all three were content, and they chose to relish these comfortable moments and not make any return visits to The Ridge. Mondo had called David twice the first few months to check on how they were all doing, but had not done so recently.

While they had fallen into a routine that even their sons adjusted to in the summer prior to their sophomore year, there was one thing Keshia and David became aware of quickly that every caregiving offspring or sibling experiences…the little voice inside their heads that incessantly cycled *what's next?...when's it going to happen?…how bad is it going to be?…it could be this, this, or this.*

It would not be until nearly two years later when things did get messy for the couple. Incontinence and Diana's growing irritability about having to do most anything, then arguing that she'd already done it, began wearing thin. It was, however, a middle-of-the-night cooking whim when Diana left the gas range on for hours that tipped things, and prompted David to revisit the memory care facilities. Sundowning, delusions, and middle-of-the-night exit-seeking that woke them all to the home security alarm were the final large nudges that necessitated a move.

After they moved her, David and Keshia discovered that the very anxious, little voice in their heads did not go away. *What's next?...what if she gets skin sores from wetting her Depends?...what if she needs to hospitalized? ...With her lack of cognition, we'd need to be there 24/7.*

Diana's decline was steady. Alzheimer's had racked her memory as well as her ability to converse. She had her fallback phrases...*It is what it is* and *Isn't it a lovely day*... and especially nice to hear *This is a nice place,* but Diana was always happy to see David and Keshia, remembering their faces more than their names. It was, however, pancreatic cancer that brought her back to David and Keshia's home for her final twelve days under hospice care.

CHAPTER FORTY-EIGHT

"The knight can go up two and over one, or up one and over two," said Setesh while explaining the basic moves of chess for the third time.

"So, the queen can do that too?" asked Rex.

"No, the queen can go as far as she wants vertically, horizontally, or diagonally," answered Setesh, "but she can't do the L-shaped move of a knight."

"Well, I could'a swore you said the queen could do everything, that she was the best and most powerful. Hell, now you're telling me she can't even do what the little knight can do."

"She is powerful, my friend. You do not want to lose her. You must protect the queen at all costs."

"This is the gol-damnedest game I ever heard of."

The two men had begun spending more time with each other shortly after Miranda's death. Setesh had eaten two meals a day with Rex for years, and had observed a change, a sullenness in Rex near her passing. He didn't know if they were related because the two men did not talk of such things. Setesh had also noticed multiple attempts by Harris to engage with Rex, but there seemed little interest on Rex's part.

One warm spring morning, Setesh saw Rex out on the patio in the part sun, part shade sitting on his scooter just looking at the trees. He rolled his wheelchair near Rex and the two men talked about the weather and the emerging foliage. When those topics ran its course, Setesh said, "There seems to be a lot happening with immigration right now in the news."

With that, Rex's energy changed. "It's about damned time we took control of our borders. I'm glad we finally have a President who's willing to do something about keeping the illegals out."

"But there are families in cages. Some are being separated with no process to get them back together."

"Oh boo-hoo. Are we supposed to put them up in a Marriott?"

Setesh sat looking up at the trees before answering. "You know, I tried watching your channel in the evening a few times after dinner, but I can't take more than seven minutes of those guys. I bet you have the same trouble watching my channel."

"You got that right."

"What if you watch your channel tonight and I watch mine. If you want, we can meet here at the same time tomorrow and tell each other what our channels said."

"You're not going to convince me, you know that?" Rex warned.

"I know that. I won't even try. We'll just tell what each of us heard from our channels, okay?"

"Don't even try to indoctrinate me with your liberal bullshit. I'm warning you."

"It's a deal," replied Setesh.

And so that is how their friendship began. Three or four mornings a week when the weather was nice, the men sat in the part sun, part shade, sharing what each had heard on their tv station of preference. They were each often surprised to hear certain topics or newsworthy items had been on one channel but not the other. After several days of these conversations, Rex noted, "Your channel never focuses on the good our President is doing, It's always negative and critical. That why it's fake news."

Setesh pondered for a moment, then said, "It is not fake, my friend. I grant you that they focus on the negative, but there is a lot to be concerned about with this administration."

"Well, I think you all are being indoctrinated, showing only one side of the story."

Again, Setesh was not quick to respond, but finally said, "Your station ignores the things that our President says and does that are ignorant, foolish, and divide us as a country or jeopardize our relationships with our allies. Instead, they focus on the homeless problem in some Democratic-led state."

"Yeah, well are you telling me the homeless situation is not a problem? Is it the President's fault that most of the homeless are in Democratic cities?"

"Not showing anything negative about this President and his administration is worse than fake," replied Setesh. "It is propaganda…the kind they have in North Korea and Russia."

"Now hold on, See-tesh. Dagnummit, I told you not to try to convince me of your socialist-commie stuff."

"You brought it up. You were critical of my station, I simply responded, my friend."

In an attempt to wrap up the disagreement and ease the tension that had surfaced between the two men, Setesh said, "That is why we are so divided as a country, we watch very different channels."

"I think you might be right on that one, See-tesh," Rex replied, getting in the last word on the subject.

The two men would never convince each other of which was worse…withholding positive stories and commentary, or never mentioning anything that was negative or controversial.

When the morning weather was not to their liking, the men were driven indoors. It was then that Setesh suggested chess, playing on the board that was always set up in the common area and never used except by him. After teaching the basic moves to Rex, he focused on the opening game tactics, the first five or ten moves… how the knights, bishops and rooks could work together to gain an advantage, why it was important to never waste a move---to have it be part of series of moves to apply pressure, and why it was important not to give up the lowly pawns too freely. "They seem unimportant, but can be critical toward the end."

That was the extent of the strategy that Rex was willing to absorb, deflecting more with "yeah, yeah, yeah…let's just play." He was energized by what he knew, the complexity of the game, and was certain that with his logic, he could navigate ways to beat Setesh. Little did Rex know that Setesh understood many different strategies for the middle and end games, and that if Setesh didn't let his mind wander, Rex had exactly zero chance of winning. Ever.

Setesh was also fully cognizant that he would lose his chess companion if Rex never won. Setesh realized he had to be the best of character actors to make it seem like he was trying…to not let his pacing, language, or mannerisms change. He believed that Rex was perceptive, more so than most others at The Ridge understood. Rex won close to a third of their games, sometimes twice in a row. They continued playing until one day they didn't.

The new Rex-Setesh friendship was not lost on Harris. He had kept his promise to Miranda, but he and Rex were never going to be comfortable around each other. He was glad that Setesh had figured out how to make it work with Rex. He was pleased that both men seemed more content, more engaged with life.

He, on the other hand, had floundered, as could be expected after Miranda. After her passing, Harris remained tired for weeks and spent far too much time alone. He also drank too much and gained weight. He didn't shave for days at a time, looking every bit the caricature of a person in mourning.

Mondo was patient with him at first, trying to spend time with his friend. But suggestions of beers and ballgames, guitars, or grabbing a meal out were usually dismissed, and it wore on Mondo. He loved his friend. He knew Harris needed time and space to dig himself out. So, he gave his friend both of those, never completely abandoning him, never being far away.

Eventually Harris, too, tired of the isolation. He became embarrassed by the image of himself in the mirror, seeing himself fatten and age. He remembered the talk Mondo gave to the residents on liminal space. He knew he was between his life before, which was a relationship with Miranda that was hard to characterize or define, and whatever his life would become once this funk ended…if it ever did. In due time, it was the experience of witnessing Miranda's death, the permanence of it, which motivated him to live. The magnitude of fully experiencing her death, her final intimate gift to him to help him realize his own mortality, proved to be the necessary nudge from the couch.

Like Miranda, Harris felt no inclination to travel frantically to the places he'd missed, but he knew he didn't want to waste any of his remaining days either. Initially, he took to walking off property, through the neighborhoods, just to get away. The modest change in scenery served him well. Then he took to hiking the trails of nearby Mt. Diablo, Tilden Park, and Sunol Regional Park. His days and his attitude were better whenever he spent hours away from The Ridge.

He made a conscious decision to do things that brought him joy, and that included being kind to others. He never ate alone, asked more questions of his meal-mates, and was freer with compliments. He often walked with others at The Ridge who used a cane or a walker. He began to feel love, respect, appreciation and esteem come back to him because of these simple changes.

When bold enough to strike up simple conversations with people on the trails and in the parks, he sensed the wariness of families and especially females of the lone male. While wishing it were different, he respected that as an element of the times and didn't press it. He began using his iPhone for photographing scenes of interest in those parks. Initially it was the landscape, then birds, then how the sun played through the foliage. In the evenings he'd review the photographs, discarding many, but making folders for the keepers.

More than a year after Miranda's death, he turned to observing the people in those parks and photographing them when they didn't notice him doing so. He captured people hiking by themselves, in pairs, in groups. He shot people sitting alone, sleeping, eating or playing. He thought he could tell which people were happy or at least content, and those that were troubled and hoping the park, that day, could help them.

For that latter group, he had been a full-fledged member. The parks had helped him. He held hope and said a silent prayer each time he encountered someone he believed was another member of the group needing a mental or emotional boost.

He knew he would never get over Miranda and that it was senseless to seek a replacement. Their time together had been brief, but it awoke in him unimagined possibilities of human connection, and simple love. They had never had sex, not real sex anyhow. But like sex, especially good sex, having had what they had was both a blessing and a curse. There was a large void in his life, one that could not be filled. That made him sad, likely clinically depressed for much of that first year. Would it have been simpler if he had never met her? Certainly. But his life would have been less if he had not. He understood that, and any thoughts of wishing he had never met her were quickly dismissed.

Fourteen months after Miranda's passing, Rex died of a heart attack in his bathroom. He squeezed the pendant around his neck when he realized what was happening. When the Ridge staff arrived and found him on the floor, they called 911 and performed the life saving techniques they had been trained in until the paramedics arrived. They removed his body at 10:30 PM that night. A memorial service was held on site the following week spearheaded by Brian and Father Armando. Most residents attended as well as Rex's only daughter Lauren. She spoke and said how much her father loved The Ridge, and based upon the turnout for the memorial, she realized how much her daddy was loved back. Setesh spoke of the unlikely friendship the two had forged, how they were so different, but that he would miss his friend. He mentioned that Rex had been a considerable presence wherever he went and that there would be a large void at The Ridge in his absence. "Rex was passionate about his beliefs. He engaged in life as much as he could. His comments kept us all thinking. I am grateful for that, and am blessed I was able to call him my friend." Several of the residents attending nodded in agreement.

Shortly after Rex's death, Setesh began teaching chess to Mondo who, in turn, rekindled Harris' interest in the game. The three men played chess often. Both Mondo and Harris were keen on learning middle game and end game strategies. End game tactics particularly intrigued Harris, recalling and adding to what he once knew. "When there are few pieces left," Setesh warned, "it can be difficult to get to checkmate. If you have more pawns or more rooks, you can make it happen, but you have to know certain things, my friend. On the other hand, if you are behind, and play the correct moves, you can extend the game and might pull out a draw."

Harris listened with interest and was an eager student. Setesh enjoyed the esteem of being the knowledgeable one. Mondo soaked up the information too, but was more appreciative of the companionship.

"Knowing what you are doing at the end is as important as the opening or middle," coached Setesh. "We must be good 'til the end. And remember, the pawns can tip the game late, so respect them as much as your other pieces."

The men played multiple times a week. As with Rex, Setesh went easy on his latest competitors initially, but it wasn't long before Harris could beat him when Setesh was trying. Harris became more successful when he heeded his new friend's advice about pawns. When an extra pawn or two worked with an aggressive king late in the game, the game often turned his way.

The three men enjoyed the game and the time with each other. For Harris, it was an especially meaningful return to the game of his youth. He was surprised knowing he could play it better than before. He enjoyed all aspects of the game…the thinking and strategy it required, the ebbs and flows, the length of time a game took…he even respected the ending… how the loser, when realizing he had been checkmated, gently turned his King onto its side, resigning with dignity.

Besides learning chess, Mondo also began giving liminal space talks to other senior living communities in the area. The Diocese of Oakland heard about it and the bishop called him in to understand more fully what Mondo was up to. When Father explained, the bishop tried to dissuade him, saying that it was out of scope from what priests did. Catholic priests needed to focus on the gospel, Father was reminded. "Plus," the bishop said, "Father Armando, you are retired. You should be enjoying life."

"I am retired, and I am enjoying it. Speaking gives me esteem and is part of my enjoyment. I also know my message provides comfort to many of those who hear me."

The bishop knew he could not reel Father Armando completely in and so, without fully blessing liminal space, gave in. It was a short while later that, Father Armando signed on with a speaker's bureau and was paid $300-750 each time he delivered any of the three versions of the talk he had refined. Mondo also continued with his tuck-in service on a selective basis, never losing his virginity despite some flirtatious suggestions from three tuck-in ladies over the next few years.

Harris found a firm that, for $1100, helped him self-publish a collection of his photographs. Every 16 or 18 months, he published a new volume. Copies could be found in The Ridge common area. At night, at bedtime, he often read aloud to himself a few pages of *Plainsong*, then listened to *Clar de Lune* or *Mr. Bojangles* on his iPad.

The three men ate dinner together every night at 5:30 at a four-top. They had an open seat for anyone who wanted to join them. Often it was a new resident who was led over by the staff. Sometimes it was a long-time resident who wanted to try some different company. No one was ever yelled at for sitting in the wrong seat. All were treated to warm and welcoming fellowship.

While Setesh didn't say much at mealtime, when he did it was usually about news of the world or a political development at home. It was likely to be something that could be found on one channel but not the other, and generally insightful. Mondo updated the men on a recent liminal space talk or where the next one was scheduled. Harris kept everyone informed about the latest Warrior or 49er trade or injury. The men enjoyed their meals together. Harris even found himself occasionally moving his food around his plate with his fork to keep pace with Setesh and Mondo lest he finish 12 minutes before them.

One evening as the three men ate, an instrumental version of *Mr. Bojangles* began playing as part of The Ridge's recorded background music. Within a few notes Mondo and Harris looked wistfully at each other. Setesh noticed this and, while recalling that the men had played the song together at the talent show, thought he understood what the men were feeling. He did not. The men finished their meal in silence before bidding each other a pleasant evening and heading to their apartments.

Harris' and Father Armando's money lasted, as did Setesh's. The three men remained friends and lived out their days at The Ridge until the end.

ACKNOWLEDGEMENTS

Pawns, Queens, Kings…The Endgame is **almost** entirely a work of fiction. It is true there is no single character that mirrors anyone I know. It is equally true, however, that it is a stitched array of personalities, events, and sayings that have hit my life directly or skirted its edges.

While this is also not a story about my father, Robert Brynjulson, and his eight-year struggle with aging and the impacts of dementia after my mother's death in 2014, as his only child and unofficial caregiver who interacted with my dad every day, I did glean many general ideas and specific incidents from his decline and different living arrangements. In the early days of my dad's first senior community, he did have the unfortunate experience of taking the 'wrong' seat at a table and being shouted and cursed at by the late arriving wannabe 'king'.

Also at that facility was a woman who wore three of four hats at a time, *Spoiled Rotten* often getting top billing. Paula was her first name but she migrated to a memory care facility before I knew I would 'borrow' her signature attire to weave into Diana's character. I never knew her last name, therefore cannot give her the appropriate credit.

Over my dad's last five years, he lived in three different senior communities, the first as an independent resident, the second needing some services, and the third requiring full memory care. Along the way the 60-40 women to men ratio played out in somewhat predictable ways for both women and my dad, who remained handsome and mobile until his early 90's.

During my several-year observations of the super seniors on my visits to see my dad, which were interrupted by periodic Covid quarantines, I saw some who retreated and resigned to the darker corners of life. Most, however, sought out some versions of esteem, significance, purpose, and physical or emotional human connection. All the main characters in *Pawns, Queens, Kings…The Endgame* are looking for some of these things from life, from each other. A couple of the characters simply need to make their money last but gain other things along the way.

I'm grateful to my friend, Marianne Brucker, who had a late in life surprise half-brother, a result of a DNA search and her mother's life-long secret. Thank you for giving me permission to weave that thread into Diana's character, Mar.

Thank you also to Bill Grady, Shirley Dourgarian, Ron Schaefer, Joanne John, Michelle Roberts, Catherine Brynjulson, and Drs. Sara and Keith Hurvitz. Their topic-specific knowledge and insights contributed to a more realistic story line.

More than twenty-five years ago, I heard the cornerstone idea for this novel on the local news… some male students at a nearby university had started a tuck-in service for $.25. It apparently made them quite popular until the administration squashed it. I hope their popularity somehow continued. Shortly thereafter I wanted to write a novel using the tuck-ins as an element of the plot. The initial concept I envisioned then was more of a *Revenge of the Nerds* spinoff for unathletic, lesser popular college males (not unlike myself), to change their social standing on campus. That writing project never got legs. However, decades later, tuck-ins seemed a natural fit when I decided to write a story about a senior living community.

It's been said that aging is not for the feint of heart and that the Golden Years are not always golden. The characters I've chosen reveal some of the complexities of getting old, not only for the seniors themselves but for the closely tied family members. Getting the phone calls anytime day or night that your senior loved one is being taken to the ER, or is experiencing extreme sundowning, has hit a waiter, or has behaved inappropriately with a person of the opposite sex and that the police were needed, are just a few of the real examples of phone calls a family member might get concerning their senior. Keshia and David wondered *what's next?...when is that next phone call coming?...how bad is it going to be?* This story is also about the thousands of loved ones who are dealing with phone calls like that today or simply waiting, wondering, and worrying when they'll get the next one.

It is important to mention more fully my friend, Joan, to whom this book is dedicated. Joan had her own Death with Dignity planned out. In great physical decline, Joan knew she would end her life on her own terms when it came time. She was at peace with the notion, had a role model who had chosen a similar ending, and was very open about it. When I knew that I wanted to weave Death with Dignity into this story, I asked Joan if I could interview her about it and her thought process in February 2020, immediately before the Covid outbreak.

Joan was comfortable and honest with me. When I asked what would tip it, what would make her select a date, she explained she still enjoyed a steady stream of visitors, social media gave her pleasure and purpose, as did her art work. She would schedule a date when the sum of those things no longer outweighed the physical misery she was going through.

A few weeks later, Joan fell out of bed, but was able to call the paramedics. She hoped and expected that they would simply place her back in bed, but fearing a broken hip (it was), the paramedics took her to the nearest emergency room. Due to complications of the broken hip and no hospital visitors permitted during those early days of Covid, Joan died alone in the hospital. She had planned a different ending and deserved one.

Many other aspects of this story are taken from real life, but not all. Harris' story about dodging airplanes at San Francisco International Airport in the Fall of 1971 is true. I did it with Joe and Terry, two high school buddies, who met me at the Tender Trap bar before the two times we dodged airplanes. Every word of Harris' story to Miranda is accurate, including hiding in the discarded cement slabs at the edge of the Bay. I'd like to think we would have exercised good judgement and not done it a third time, especially after our close encounter with airport security and the realization that what we were doing was horribly stupid and reckless, not only for ourselves but for the pilots and passengers. The reality was, however, that we had not exercised good judgement at all…ever. Plus, the plane-dodging experience was extremely stimulating. I was relieved when D. B. Cooper did his thing, airport security tightened including new razor-wire fencing, and we never considered another late-night excursion to the SFO north-south runway.

And lastly, thank you to my wife, Michele Brynjulson, for putting up with the messiness of floating workspaces around the house, and especially for her multiple reviews of my manuscript. Her edits and thoughts about poor transitions, sentences that didn't make sense, along with general beliefs about scenes needing to disappear or be rewritten made *Pawns, Queens, Kings…The Endgame* better.